USA TODAY BESTSELLING AUTHOR
DALE MAYER

Ice Pick in the Ivy

Lovely Lethal Gardens 9

ICE PICK IN THE IVY: LOVELY LETHAL GARDENS, BOOK 9
Beverly Dale Mayer
Valley Publishing Ltd.

Copyright © 2020

ISBN-13: 978-1-773362-68-7
Print Edition

Books in This Series:

About This Book

A new cozy mystery series from *USA Today* best-selling author Dale Mayer. Follow gardener and amateur sleuth Doreen Montgomery—and her amusing and mostly lovable cat, dog, and parrot—as they catch murderers and solve crimes in lovely Kelowna, British Columbia.

Riches to rags. ... Chaos never calms. ... Time fades memories. ... Or at least most of them!
Who knew two small maker's marks could lead to such chaos? Doreen has been enjoying a few well-earned days of peace and quiet after solving her last mystery. But all good things must come to an end. Like when Thaddeus, her independently minded African gray parrot, digs up two rectangular metal pieces from the path along the creek. Then Doreen is sent down another rabbit hole of the past: connecting the dots from a long-defunct tool repair company and a young girl who disappeared at the same time.

Corporal Mack Moreau doesn't think these events are connected. He doesn't believe the spate of recent deaths is suspiciously tied in either. Mack wants Doreen to focus on the materials and the cost analysis to replace her backyard deck and to leave the detecting to him. But how can she, when she knows so much more is going on than Mack believes?

Heart attacks, unfair wills, and a missing ice pick are all related. She just needs to understand how ...

Chapter 1

Friday Noon ...

THREE DAYS. ALL Doreen had wanted was three days of peace and quiet. At least that was what she'd thought she wanted. But by noon on day two, she was bored out of her mind. She had pulled one of her café table chairs off the veranda and onto her little deck, where she could bathe in the sun with a cup of coffee in her hand, but her foot kept tapping the floorboards.

Finally she jumped up. "This is ridiculous," she announced to Mugs, who was sprawled out on the deck in the sunshine beside her. "We have to get some work done. Either that or I'll go stir-crazy." She bounded off the deck steps, wondering where her full-blown energy had come from. Yesterday she'd been dragging her sorry butt around the kitchen, trying hard to put all the random thoughts in her head into the right places. But now? Well, now she was full of energy and ready to go.

She grabbed the shovel and headed to the backyard to start on the next section of garden bed. She kept looking back at the markers still in her lawn to show where the expanded deck was supposed to go. She hadn't done anything further because, of course, it would not be just her working on this project; it also required Mack. Was a project this size doable on a weekend or several weekends?

Today was Friday, and normally she would be gardening at Millicent's, but Millicent had again asked Doreen to come tomorrow, on a Saturday instead. After weeks of working on Mack's mother's yard, Millicent's garden was looking pretty good. So, unless Mack and his mom had anything extra they needed Doreen to do, it would probably take about an hour tops of weekly weeding to keep that garden in perfect shape now. And she didn't really want to drop her gardening income, but she also didn't feel good about taking money for two hours' work if she was only putting in one.

With her first kick on the shovel into her backyard, she could feel that same satisfaction rolling through her. She loved working on her own land. She loved working on this place. She looked back at Mugs to see he hadn't moved from the sunny spot on the deck. "You're just being lazy."

Mugs opened his eyes, but he didn't budge. She spied Goliath sprawled on the grass behind her, his tail twitching.

"Well, at least you're here beside me," she said. She bent down, lifted a clump of weeds, gave it a good shake, tossed it off to one side, creating a new pile, and kept working as she headed down the right side of her property. Then she stopped when she realized she had seen no recent sign of Thaddeus.

She turned and looked around. "Thaddeus? Thaddeus, where are you?"

Doreen heard a flutter of wings, and Thaddeus muttered, "Thaddeus is here. Thaddeus is here."

She spun around again and found him waddling toward her from the creek. "You know you're not supposed to go to the creek on your own," she scolded. "Not with it rising like it has been."

He just squawked and gave a full-winged feathered ruffle. She laughed. "Like you care what I say."

Looking closer then, she caught a glint of something in front of him on the ground.

"What did you find?" She stabbed her shovel into the dirt and headed toward him. But, instead of being cooperative, he picked up the small object and bounced backward.

"No, no, Thaddeus. We're not making a game out of this."

But Thaddeus wasn't listening; he was too enthralled with whatever he'd found.

She glared at him, knowing the more she chased, the more he would back up or fly away.

Goliath joined her, studying Thaddeus with great interest.

"And you're not allowed to go after him either," she snapped at Goliath. He just gave her a slow-eyed look, as if to say, *Seriously?*

At that, Thaddeus stopped and stared at both of them.

"Thaddeus, come here," Doreen said, and she crouched in front of him. Thaddeus backed away. Goliath crouched down low, as if to pounce. She put a hand on top of Goliath's back and neck and said, "We don't do that to friends."

He made a weird chittering sound, arguing with her.

She tapped him gently on the nose. "Goliath, behave yourself."

Thaddeus hopped forward, as if willing to give her whatever was in his beak. It was metal and small. She didn't understand, but it looked like a label.

"That's cool, Thaddeus," she said, as she held out a

hand.

He looked at her, cocked his head to the side, and then dropped it.

She snatched it up before he could change his mind. She looked at it, noting the little markings—it was like a nameplate or label for something. "I don't have a clue what it means, but thank you."

She popped it into her pocket, got back up, and returned to her digging. Only Thaddeus wasn't happy with that. He squawked at her, "Thaddeus. Thaddeus."

"What's the matter, Thaddeus?"

He hopped away a few steps. She frowned, dug the shovel deep into the ground once more to prop it up there, and took another few steps toward him. He ran back toward the creek. "Oh, that's not good," she said. "Please tell me that you didn't find any more bodies."

He just gave her that gimlet eye and kept on going.

She walked around to the path, where the creek flowed, loving the trickling sounds. She asked, "So what were you looking at?" She noted how quiet Goliath and Mugs were as they joined her. That was never good.

Thaddeus hopped farther, like he wanted her to follow. With her heart sinking, she walked toward the little bridge, where he hopped across the wooden slats. "Thaddeus, be careful. We never fixed that side."

He called back, "Thaddeus is fine. Thaddeus is fine."

She laughed, and, with Goliath and finally Mugs's attention, she carefully made her way across the bridge. "We'll have to get Mack to give us a hand with this," she said. "I know it's city property, but surely they wouldn't mind if we fix the broken boards." Since she was the one who had gone through the wood recently, she would at least like to stop

4

herself from falling through a second time. On the other side of the creek, Thaddeus headed toward the lake.

"Thaddeus, that's not good," she said. "I don't want to take a walk right now."

But he continued on farther in the direction of the lake, and then he finally stopped.

"You worry me, Thaddeus, when you wander off this far all by yourself. Something could have happened to you out here."

"Thaddeus is here. Thaddeus is here."

"But *Thaddeus* should only be here if I am with him. Meaning, you." She came up behind him and saw a second glint, spied another little nameplate. She frowned, bent down, picked it up, and studied it. Mugs and Goliath neared to take a look too. She then pulled the former one from her pocket and said, "Weird. They are the same." One was slightly bigger though.

Thaddeus hopped onto her foot. She reached down, placed her palm out so he could hop on, then rose and let him glide up to her shoulder. "I'm so glad you weren't hurt on your scavenging hunt all alone." Once he had settled there, he crooned gently and rubbed his beak against her cheek. "Thank you for these shiny gifts," she murmured, chuckling as she gently stroked his feathers.

She studied the nameplates curiously. "What are these, and what the devil are we to do with them?"

Of course she knew. Likely they had something to do with a new case—whether she was ready or not.

Only she spoke too soon.

As she headed back, Thaddeus securely on her shoulder, she turned at the bridge to make sure Mugs and Goliath were following along. Mugs ran past her and jostled her gently. It had been a slight contact, but it was enough. Her foot hooked the edge of the weakened and weathered board, and down she went. Her leg slid inside the woodwork, even as she went over the edge into the rising creek. "*Ack,*" she cried out, arms flailing, as she fell halfway into the water, hanging over the side of her little bridge, her ankle and calf screaming in pain.

"*Squawk,*" Thaddeus cried out, as he tumbled off her shoulder to land on the wood beside her—only to add insult to injury by calling out, "Body in the river. Body in the river."

Carefully righting herself, she gingerly unhooked her injured and bleeding ankle and sat on the edge of the bridge to catch her breath and to assess the damage. She splashed some creek water on her wound, and the bleeding was already contained. *This will be swollen in the morning,* she thought.

"*Woof, woof,*" Mugs barked beside her, staring up at her with his huge sad eyes.

"I'm okay, Mugs, honest. It was a stupid fall. I'll be fine."

"*Woof,*" he said, then shook his head, his great big floppy ears flying out on both sides.

She sighed and smiled at him. "It was just a light tumble. It's not your fault."

Goliath snorted—or was that a sneeze?—beside her. She reassured all three of them. "I'm fine. I'll get up and show you."

In a moment of bravado, she hopped to her feet and cried out in agony. Shuddering at what a moment of weight on her sore ankle had brought her in pain, she stood flamingo style on her good leg. Biting her lip, she attempted to take a small step with her injured leg, only to wince and to stop to breathe deeply for a long moment. The house was right there—but had never seemed so far away.

Yet her options were limited.

Mugs woofed at her again. She smiled down at him. "I'm fine. I'll get there. But, if you could find a big stick, that would make my life much easier."

He raced away at the word *stick*, and she watched as Mugs grabbed a small one, more for his size than for her, from the back garden. She groaned. "That's not quite what I meant."

Her phone rang.

Grateful it hadn't ended up in the river with the rest of her, she tried to dry her hand quickly on her pants and then pulled it free of her pocket. It was Mack.

As soon as she answered, he snapped, "Where are you?"

Immediately her back bristled at his tone. "Why are you so suspicious?" she demanded.

"You didn't answer immediately."

Thaddeus flew up to her shoulder and leaned over her phone, shrieking, "Body in the river. Body in the river."

Silence. "Please tell me that bird is joking," he roared.

"He is, … well, sort of." Darn. She still couldn't tell a lie. Not convincingly.

"*Sort of?*" he asked in an ominous tone. "What's going on, Doreen? What are you up to?"

She gasped in outrage. "Nothing is going on—" and accidentally put her weight on her bad foot. And immediately cried out in pain.

"Doreen, what the …"

"I'm fine. I'm fine," she said, trying to breathe normally. "You just caught me at a bad time."

7

"What do you mean, *a bad time?*"

"I might have just fallen through that little bridge across the creek."

"*Might have?*" He took a long, slow breath. "What does *might have* mean?"

"Okay, so I did," she said crossly, brushing her wet hair off her face. Standing on one leg was starting to hurt too. And she still had a long way to go to get home. "I don't suppose you have any crutches, do you?"

"*Crutches?*" His tone turned immediately businesslike and asked, "Where exactly are you?"

"On the bridge," she said in surprise. "Didn't I just say that?" She shook her head. "You're getting as bad as Nan now."

He said something that made her straighten and glare into her phone. "That's not required."

He snorted. "With you, sweetheart, it sometimes is. Stay where you are. I'm almost there."

"No—"

But he'd hung up on her—again.

Chapter 2

Monday Late Afternoon ...

"I'M FINE," SHE snapped for the umpteenth time, as Mack walked around the house three days later. "Stop coddling me."

He met her glare with a grin. "Who knew you'd be such a difficult patient?"

She sniffed. "I'm not a patient. I'm just resting."

"Whatever makes you feel better."

She should be grateful, but it was hard to when she was still in pain, but what she really missed was her independence. Nan and Mack had been taking turns watching over her, like a child. Yes, that was nice, but ... she was grouchy. Even she had to admit it.

Mack had brought down her mattresses and had put them on the floor in the living room so she could avoid the stairs. Which was good since she didn't have a couch down here anymore. He loaded her up with all the pillows in the house too so she could comfortably sit up.

"You're the one who fell off the bridge," he said, whistling.

"I did not fall," she muttered, but, not willing to blame

Mugs, she guessed she should admit it was her fault.

"Just a few more days. Then you can resume a normal life." He gave her a slow smile. "You'll be back to normal, ready to terrorize everyone, on Thursday. That's not long to wait."

Still he was right; a couple more days wasn't too bad. Particularly as he'd been looking after her. Now that the pain had eased, she knew it wouldn't be long before she could bear her full weight. She didn't let him see, but she had managed to get to the bathroom more easily today. "Ha, you're enjoying this. Hopefully you're making good use of me being off work and catching up on yours," she warned. "You know I'm just raring to go, right?"

"That's good," he said smoothly. "In the meantime, you've got a TV, books, and time to rest—like *really* rest right now. So take advantage of it," he urged. "You've been attacked so many times in recent weeks, let your body catch up."

She subsided on her bed. Her ankle felt better—especially when propped up on pillows—but, in some ways, Mack was right. She just didn't want him to know that. "Fine. As instructed, I'll give it until Thursday, but after that ..."

He grinned. "After that you'll be meddling in my affairs again. Got it."

"*Ftppp.*" She made a face as he turned and walked back into the kitchen. But he hadn't said anything that Nan hadn't repeated time and time again these last few days. And the doctor. *Sigh.* He'd told her not to go back to work for a full week and to stay off her leg completely, if she wanted it to heal properly. At the time she'd wondered if Mack had coerced the doctor into saying that, but her research for sprains online had showed a similar time frame.

She groaned. "I'm bored."

"No, you're not," he called out from the kitchen. "You could find something to keep you occupied on your laptop with no problem."

"But I don't have a case to work on," she complained.

He poked his head around the corner, gave her a fat smile, and said, "I know."

"I could work on the Bob Small stuff," she said in a considering tone. "It's not like I can do much else, but I could start researching that case—or rather cases. As in many cases really. He was a serial killer, after all. Still at large."

"Too bad you can't get to that basket of clippings by yourself anytime soon, and no way will I pull it down for you," he said in a bright cheerful voice. "That's hardly resting if you're sleuthing."

Her irritation at being bedridden melted as soon as she heard him say *sleuthing*. It was almost a validation of what she did. And anything was better than *meddling*.

"Dinner is ready," he called out. "Do you want to eat there or make your way to the kitchen?"

"Kitchen please." She grabbed the crutches Nan had gotten her from somewhere, and, no, she'd not asked where, and made her way to the kitchen. Doreen stopped and sniffed the aroma and cried out, "Spaghetti!"

"Absolutely. Now sit down and get that leg up," he ordered. "At least this way you'll have enough leftovers until you're cleared to walk again."

She beamed and immediately obeyed. Anything for spaghetti. "I really appreciate the leftovers."

He walked over, bearing a heaping plate of spaghetti and, oh joy, … meatballs as well. "Oh my," she whispered softly, staring at the plate in rapture.

"You know how they say the way to a man's heart is through his stomach? Now I don't know that for sure about all men, but it's definitely the way to your heart."

She nodded but didn't waste time talking. She forked up part of a meatball and some noodles dripping with sauce and took her first bite and closed her eyes.

There was an odd silence. She opened her eyes to find him staring at her. That was a new look on his face, but the look in his gaze was universal.

He dropped his focus to his own plate, breaking the moment.

But it would be a long time before she forgot the heat in his eyes.

Chapter 3

Thursday Morning ...

YES, FINALLY FREEDOM called. She woke up bright and early, knowing today was the day. She'd promised Nan and Mack she'd behave and stay off her ankle until today. And she didn't know what her problem was, but she couldn't break a promise once made.

But today was Thursday, and she could walk on her ankle. She noted only a slight stiffness to the movement, but, other than that, it felt great. But she'd go easy. No running or long walks for a few days. She'd ease into those.

She got dressed and went into the kitchen. She'd have to ask Mack to move her mattress back upstairs when he came by next. She fed her animals, which made them all very happy. With her first cup of coffee she stepped out onto the deck and walked to the water's edge, absolutely loving the fresh air and the soothing sounds of the water, her trio glad to be outside as well. It was a beautiful sunny morning and an absolutely gorgeous day. She looked at how her little creek had turned more into a river here as it neared the lake itself, and the river was quite a bit higher than she had expected. Also a lot faster moving now.

She studied the little bridge and frowned. Mack must have fixed it because the broken boards were gone. All of them it seemed. The bridge had brand-new flooring. She smiled. He must have done that this week, while taking care of her. She wondered how he managed that without making any noise. She'd have to ask him later. And thank him.

She turned slowly and made her way carefully back to the café table on her veranda, testing her ankle. *All good*, she thought. Then she sat down, only to wince as something poked her hip. She reached inside her pocket to find the metal pieces Thaddeus had found before her tumble into the water.

She'd forgotten about them. After Mack had helped get her home, she'd quickly changed out of her wet clothes and Mack had done laundry for her. She'd been living in dresses all week. Until this morning ...

At least the metal pieces were clean now.

With her coffee gone, she walked back inside, refilled her mug, then came out and picked up her shovel. She'd missed her garden all week too. No one came to weed her beds. And she had Millicent's to do tomorrow too, if she was up to it. Which she already planned to do. After weeding one bed, she checked the discharge from the sump pump hoses that lay stretched across her yard, but no water came from them. With that reassurance, she returned to her gardening. She studied the two little tags once more and then shoved them back into her pocket. Just as she went to pick up the shovel again, her phone rang. "Good morning, Nan."

"My, don't you sound better," Nan said. "Are you out-side?"

"I feel better too. And, yes, I'm out working in the gar-den."

14

"Well, that's much safer than catching robbers and murderers," Nan said. "How about tea?"

"Sure. As much as I'm enjoying being outside, I'm always good for an excuse to leave the work and visit you."

Nan laughed. "I think you're a workaholic. But why don't you come down? One of the residents here dropped off a huge basket of veggies. I'd love to share."

"Perfect. I'll walk down now. My ankle could use a short walk to loosen it up."

"I'll put on the teakettle."

Nan hung up, and Doreen looked down at the two animals at her feet, with a side glance at Thaddeus, still on her shoulder. "What do you think? Shall we go for a walk to Nan's?"

She quickly locked up her house even as Mugs barked and raced back down to the creek, heading to the path that would take him around the corner. Goliath sauntered along beside her, as if to say, *Well, I don't have anything better to do.* Thaddeus was happy for any chance to visit. "Visit Nan. Visit Nan."

Smiling, Doreen walked back down beside the creek, loving the way the water gushed beside her. The bank was still several feet above, even though the water overflowed the rocks. It was just beautiful. She looked back to where the old ratty fence had been at the creek side of her property, wondering again what it would take to put a bench there. She didn't have any real lawn chairs or outdoor furniture, something to withstand the sun and the bad weather alike, but it would be nice to have something close to the creek, where she could sit and have her coffee. At least sit long enough to relax and to take a few moments off. Something was just so delightful about the sunlight bouncing off the water as it ran beside her.

She walked along the creek, turned the corner, and headed toward Rosemoor. With Nan living there since she'd handed over her house to Doreen, Doreen came to visit on a regular basis. So much had happened in the couple months that she'd lived in Kelowna, BC. Not just all the cold cases she'd been involved with but also selling the antiques, emptying the house. Yet it would still be months and months before everything was sold, and the transactions completed, and she had a check in her hand from Christie's.

Before the auction house could sell it all, some of the furniture had to be refinished. Some of the paintings needed a heavy professional cleaning. Everything was getting spruced up and ready for photographs for the catalogs, but Scott had warned her it might take longer than the three months—at the earliest—that he'd originally thought. As long as she was doing okay, that three months was fine; four months was even fine.

But, if it went too much longer, she wasn't sure. So far though, everything had come up roses, and she was seriously happy with the way things had worked out. Her house was basically empty. She had reorganized the last few pieces of furniture left. She had an old bed to get rid of in the spare bedroom. Thinking of that, she brought out her phone and jotted down a note to contact Mack about a dump run. As she walked forward, Mugs barked. Huffing, he picked up his pace and ran, and she looked up to see Nan, standing at the edge of her little patio, waiting for her and the animals.

Chapter 4

Thursday, Just Before Noon ...

DOREEN LIFTED HER hand in greeting and smiled as she pocketed her phone again. Nan waved as she bent down to greet Mugs, who'd raced up to see her. Goliath sauntered closer, not quite as eager or open about his affection, and yet his love for Nan was still there for everyone to see. It did Doreen's heart good to see how much the animals loved Nan. And Doreen thought it probably did Nan a lot of good too. Who was she kidding? These animals did Doreen a lot of good as well. Nothing like knowing you were loved. Not to mention the fact that Nan's and Doreen's relationship was unbelievably wonderful now too. They'd been separated a lot over the years, mostly as Doreen grew up with her mom and then throughout Doreen's disaster of a marriage.

She walked along the flagstones, stepping over the little lip to her grandmother's patio, before bending to give the beautiful woman a hug.

"It's so lovely to see you," Nan said gently.

"Lovely to see you too," Doreen said with a smile.

"How is the latest injury?"

Doreen shrugged. "It's fine. I've got a bruise still. In truth, I keep forgetting about it until I poke it somehow."

"Maybe, but you've got to make sure you look after yourself," Nan scolded.

"I will," Doreen promised. She sat down at the little table as Nan gently fussed over Thaddeus, who had hopped off Doreen's shoulder and walked across the table to greet Nan. He appeared fascinated by the treats awaiting the humans on the table.

"You said vegetables," Doreen said with a chuckle, as she eyed a plate of cookies. "And those cookies are monstrous."

"That way, when you only have one," Nan said, "you're actually getting something. You don't need more than one."

"So you're trying to trick your eyes. Is that the main idea?"

"Maybe, but when you only get one cookie, and it's small, it's depressing."

"Making them the size of four cookies defeats the purpose because, for whatever reason you were told to only have one, this will hardly be the correct answer."

"*Psshaw*," Nan said with a wave of her hand. "What do those dieticians know anyway?" She picked up a cookie and handed it to Doreen. "Now, you enjoy yours."

While Nan poured their tea, Doreen accepted the large cookie and stared at it in fascination. "How does it even stay in this shape?" she asked. "This thing's got to be five inches across."

"If you can't eat it all, you can take it home," Nan said.

"I thought we were splitting it." Doreen raised her horrified gaze to Nan.

"No," Nan said with a smile. "I've got my own cookie." She pointed just to the other side of the cut flowers—at another big cookie, just the same as Doreen's.

Doreen chuckled. "You are incorrigible," she said in a lightly scolding voice.

Nan grinned. "We're conspirators in crime. And that's the way it should be at my age—a cookie is a cookie."

"Well, not if it's the equivalent of five cookies," Doreen said, eyeing the monster in front of her. The trouble was, she was looking at it with absolute joy. "I really want this cookie, but I'm hoping halfway through that I'll get full."

Nan laughed. "But you know what it's like when you have a cookie. Once you start, you have to eat the whole thing."

"No, you already told me that I could take it home, if I couldn't finish it," Doreen said, "so that's what I'll do."

Nan chuckled. "We'll see how you do."

At that, Thaddeus walked closer and lowered his head to her cookie. "I'm pretty darn sure you're not allowed to have chocolate," she said. But a piece of walnut stuck out one side. She gently broke it off and gave it to him.

He attacked it with great pleasure.

"This is a really bad habit," she scolded Thaddeus.

Thaddeus eyed her cookie as she lifted it to her lips. "That's all you get," she snapped. Thaddeus ruffled up the feathers around his neck and said, "Thaddeus is here. Thaddeus is here."

"Be good," she said, "or you'll go down on the patio with the others."

As a response, he squatted down, so he was basically sitting with his tail feathers dripping off the edge of the table. She laughed, looked over at Nan, and said, "We've created monsters between us."

Nan laughed. "And I love every one of them." She added

a little milk to both their teacups and said, "Have you recovered from that last case yet?"

"I asked for three days of peace and quiet," Doreen said with a chuckle. "And somehow, ended up with almost a week after falling off that dratted bridge. So yes, I'd say I'd recovered. In fact I felt so good this morning, I started digging in the backyard garden again."

"I wish you hadn't," Nan said. "You needed time to let that ankle heal."

"I would have stopped if there'd been any pain and there wasn't. I think the ankle is fine now." She dug into her pocket and brought out the two little metal plates and placed them on the table. "Besides I have a new puzzle. The day I fell, Thaddeus brought me these. I had them in my pocket but only found them after they went through the wash and I put these pants on today."

Nan picked them up and looked at them in surprise. "Oh my, I know somebody who did this."

"Did what?"

"Those numbers are a date," she said, "and that's a name."

"What is that name? Kelowna something or other?" Doreen asked. "I figured it was a company."

"Well, it kind of is. But not really. He tried to make a go of repairing and sharpening tools and stuff like that. He had these little metal plates made up out of tin, and he stamped them with his mark and dates. Interesting that Thaddeus found them." She raised her gaze. "Where did he find them?"

"He brought one to me, so I don't know where he got that one. Then he took me to a spot where the second one was. I presume it was close to the first one, on the opposite

20

side of the creek, almost down to the lake."

"Interesting." Nan replaced the two little metal plates in front of Doreen. "Something's rattling around in my brain, but I can't remember what it is."

Doreen nodded and kept working on her cookie and her tea. She had hoped seeing the pieces would nudge Nan's brain to fire in the right direction, but sometimes Nan's memory wasn't so good. After a moment, Doreen asked, "How have you been this morning?"

Nan smiled. "Like you, *bored*. All that excitement with your last cold case was awesome, but it's time for you to get a new one."

Doreen groaned. "I don't think so," she said. "I'm pretty sure Mack figures I've caused him enough trouble."

"What you've done is solve multiple murders. And that needed to happen. Who knew we had so many criminals in this town?"

"Who knew?" Doreen repeated with a nod. "You said I should come to *quiet sleepy Kelowna and relax and retire in this peaceful town*. And yet here I am in the middle of complete chaos."

Nan chuckled. "I'm not apologizing. I'm too delighted to have you close."

Doreen laughed. "Good, because really I might have been totally bored without all these cases. They've kept me … I would say, they've kept me out of trouble, but they've had the opposite effect instead. I've been in trouble with each one of them, but they have kept me busy."

"And you've had so much going on," Nan said, "with the house alone."

Doreen laughed. "Scott said they have to fix a few of the furniture pieces, and the paintings needed to be professionally cleaned."

Nan nodded, as if she expected that. "They obviously want to show the furniture and the artwork in the best light. You won't get the best price when they auction your things unless they are in such a pristine condition."

"I never considered that," Doreen said, "but it does mean the money could be delayed."

"It's always delayed," Nan said, reaching across and patting the back of Doreen's hand. "Whenever they say three months, just automatically double it."

Doreen groaned. "I was afraid of that."

"Are you okay for money?"

Doreen shrugged. "I will be. I mean, I've been thinking of using some of the money I have to take care of repairs, like redoing the deck out back. But I don't want to spend that money yet, if I don't know when I have more coming in."

"Good point," Nan said. "You should still have some money in that bowl, or did you take it to the bank?"

"No, I didn't get it to the bank yet. Some of it I should keep at the house. I still have the cash you gave me last time. I've done pretty well so far. I had a few groceries to buy, plus a few bills to be paid, and it felt good to get them paid too."

"It does, doesn't it?" Nan said. "You'd think some of the residents here would have helped you out as a thank-you."

"Most people don't know if they should thank me or ask me to leave town again," Doreen said candidly. "I've stirred up quite the hornet's nest."

"Particularly with Darren."

"I know. Between his grandpa getting into his own mischief here at Rosemoor, so the administrator calls Darren directly, and being a local cop under Mack's direction, I guess Darren gets twice the trouble when I solve a cold case.

And that's still an ongoing process."

"Maybe," Nan said, "but I'm sure everybody will be much happier knowing all these murderers have been caught, and all these poor victims have come to light, so the families can get the truth of the matter, then can mourn and hopefully move on."

"I can't imagine," Doreen said, "because mourning the death of a loved one taken too early would be terrible."

"I hear you," Nan said. "And losing someone is very difficult as it is, even when old age takes them. But the bottom line is, you're doing a wonderful job, and all these people thank you."

"No, I'm not sure they do, and I certainly get an awful lot of odd looks as I move around town."

"Those odd looks," Nan said, "could just as easily be because you're walking around with all the animals."

"Well, that's true enough," Doreen said. "Particularly after this last case, I've completely changed my perception on being homeless."

"No," Nan said. "Your perception was never off."

"Anyway"—Doreen thought about the fact that she was here now—"you know I wouldn't change my life at this point, don't you?" She gently grasped her grandmother's hand. "I'm so delighted to finally have time to be with you."

Nan's fingers squeezed hers tight. "And you brought joy to this old woman's heart. The fact that you bring me immeasurable amounts of excitement and something else to think about other than growing old is just an added bonus." The two women smiled at each other.

"What about the gardener here? Well, the current one. Granted, it's hard to tell Fred apart from Dennis because they are both grumpy and because they both hate me and my animals."

"But," Nan interrupted, "Fred has a limp. You can tell them apart that way."

"Doesn't seem to make a difference otherwise. So, is Fred *still* cranky over your flagstones, so the animals and I have a shortcut to you?"

"Oh, is he ever," Nan said with a chuckle. "He brought it up at our last tenant meeting."

"Wow," Doreen said. "He must really have strong feelings about them to still be angry after all this time."

"He does. He doesn't want you to have access to me at all."

"I wonder why?" Doreen asked. "Sounds like he has something to hide."

Nan's eyebrows shot up. "Oh my," she said. "Wouldn't that be interesting?" Then she stopped and picked up the little metal plates. "You know something? He's related to this guy."

"What guy?" Doreen asked.

"The man who made these," Nan said, looking up at her with a frown. "I just said that. Are you having trouble with your memory, dear?"

Doreen slowly sank back. "Nan, you were thinking you couldn't remember who made these."

"And then I told you who made them," she said, holding one up. "It's the gardener's brother."

Doreen stared at her grandmother. It wasn't the first time she'd wondered at Nan's strange switches from one memory to another. "What about him?"

"Just this," Nan said. "Remember, dear? Your memory? I just told you. He made these."

"But what are they?"

Nan patted her on the hand. "Oh, dear," she said. "Remember? They're labels."

Doreen tamped down her growing impatience. "Labels for what?" she asked gently.

"Tools, of course."

"Tools?" She looked down at the little metal stamped items and said, "Really?"

"Yes, really." Nan chuckled. "They take pride in their work." Just then she looked up and caught sight of the gardener, glaring at them, and she hopped to her feet and called him over.

He looked at her in surprise, then looked left, then looked right, but not seeing anybody else she could possibly be talking to, he crossed the grass to reach her.

Doreen stared at him with barely concealed resentment. *How come it was okay for him to walk on the grass but not for me?*

But then Nan held up one of the little metal plates, asking, "Isn't this your brother, Frank's, work?"

Fred looked at it, turned it over, and said, "It looks like it. Yeah, why?" And he turned his suspicious gaze on Doreen.

She gave him a bland smile back.

"No reason," Nan said.

He looked at the second label, turned it over, nodded, and said, "I think they are Frank's work. But they're not normally loose like this." He looked at Doreen. "I suppose you found them." The accusation in his tone was quite clear.

Mugs stood, not liking Fred's tone of voice, and he barked. Doreen reached a hand down but accidentally hit the table. The teacups bounced and the tea sloshed. Thaddeus half flew to the edge of the table and tried to peck away to get his metal pieces back again.

The gardener backed up and said, "Dirty animals." He tossed the two metal pieces at Nan. "Keep them. Frank has lots." And, with a final glare, he left.

Nan sat down, trying to calm Thaddeus. She gave him one of the metal plates, which he immediately brought back to Doreen.

"Oh, dear, he feels very strongly about that, doesn't he?" Nan said. She looked at the gardener, who raced away. "And so does he, apparently."

Doreen watched as the gardener retreated. His footsteps were faster than necessary, as if he couldn't wait to get away from them. But she didn't think it had anything to do with her "dirty" animals.

Chapter 5

Thursday Noon ...

D OREEN REACHED FOR one of the metal tags. "Other
numbers are on here too."

"Sure," Nan said, "he used to keep a ledger of the tools
he sold."

"What kind of tools did he make?"

"Technically the wooden handles to the otherwise metal
tools. It wasn't much of a business, but he was really proud
of these, and they were attached to various hammers and
sledgehammers and things."

"Huh, so he made just the handles?"

"Don't forget, dear. Back then it wasn't like you could
turn around and get a handle from China on any given day."

"Any idea how old these are?"

"Oh my," Nan said. She pressed her fingers to her lips to
hide her smile and stared at Doreen.

Doreen glared at her. "Now what?"

"Remember that memory of yours? These are dates,
honey."

Doreen stared down at the numbers on the tin piece and
then groaned. "Mine is much harder to read. I didn't see

that. Okay, but they're what? Twenty years old then?"

"Sure, and, yes, you could have bought stock plastic or wooden replacement handles back then, but he was trying for a small business where he could custom make stuff like that."

"Interesting. So Frank used to repair tools as well as make handles?"

"Yes, that's correct," Nan said. "Now, the name of his business was something funny. I can't remember for sure. A weird name, like, Kelowna Tool Repair or something."

Doreen thought privately nothing was funny about that. It said where to find the business and what the business was all about, so it wasn't a bad commercial name. "I might be able to look it up."

"Oh, do that," Nan said with a handclap and a bright smile. "Maybe we'll find something exciting behind it all."

"Maybe," Doreen said cautiously, "but I don't know what that could be."

"Maybe not. On your way home, maybe walk on the far side of the creek, and see if you can come up with anything else around the same spot."

"I can't go home on that side now. I need to stay on my side of the creek to avoid the rising water."

"Of course, the water level is quite a bit higher now, isn't it?"

"It is, but still no water is running out of the sump pump hoses."

"Perfect," Nan said. "The ground water hasn't soaked that far from the creek, so it's not putting the basement in any danger."

Every time she heard "water, basement, and danger," it frayed Doreen's nerves, and her blood ran cold. The last thing she wanted to consider was her basement flooding. But the basement flooding now versus the basement flooding when full of very expensive antiques were completely different stories. That Nan had kept those antiques down there all those years when they could have been destroyed still gave Doreen nightmares.

"Let me not forget the vegetables," Nan said. She hopped up and raced into her little suite. She returned a moment later with a large wicker basket and placed it on the table. "Now tell me. Is there anything here you would like? Other than these zucchinis?" she asked, and she pulled out zucchini after zucchini after zucchini.

"They're all zucchini?" Doreen asked.

"Yes. These came from the grocery store," Nan said. "Somebody bought too many and brought them in."

"Right, because it's not that time of year for these to be ready in our local gardens yet."

"Nope, not yet. End of July or August. Greenhouses of course would be earlier." Then Nan pulled a few more items from the basket. "But here we have tomatoes and early salad greens."

"Early salad greens I can definitely use," Doreen said. "I'll take one zucchini, but I can't use four or five."

"Are you sure, dear?"

"I'm sure," she said. "One stir-fry is more than I can handle."

"I suppose I could make zucchini bread," Nan said with a smile. "When I have them done, you can come down and have a slice or two."

"That sounds like the best way to make use of these," Doreen said. "I do love your zucchini bread."

Then Nan brought out some white onions, green onions, tomatoes, and radishes. "The tomatoes aren't mine," she said, "but somehow they ended up in this basket." She stared at the basket as if completely confused on that part.

Doreen smiled. "I'll be happy to take the other vegetables."

With that, Nan walked back into her little suite and brought out a paper bag in which she carefully packaged some of the vegetables for Doreen. "You should probably go home and research Frank's company," Nan said in a low tone.

"Why is that?" Doreen asked, as she finished her tea and the last bite of her cookie. She stared down at her empty plate in disbelief. "I can't believe I ate that whole cookie."

"I warned you," Nan said. "They're deadly."

"They're more than deadly," Doreen said. "Each one is huge."

"But there's nothing like a cookie. When you're having it with something like a cup of tea, it's even more special."

"Maybe."

"It'll be fine," Nan said with a chuckle. "Besides, here's the fresh greens to go home with you, so you'll be eating a nice healthy salad later in the day."

As Doreen looked down in the paper bag, she noted there were a lot of greens. As in three full days of salads. That was something she was really grateful to have. "That'll save on my budget a little bit," she said with a laugh. She looked at the zucchini, wondering if she should take a second small one, because, after all, it was free food. If she could find a way to cook it, with Mack's help, then maybe it would be a nice supplement.

On that note, Nan slipped a little one into the paper bag and said, "Here, and I'll make zucchini bread from the rest."

"Now that would be lovely," Doreen said. "Nothing's like your zucchini bread. Thank you for all this." She leaned over, kissed Nan gently on the cheek, and then called the animals to her. At the last moment, she picked up the two little silver metal tags and put them in her pocket. "And I'll see what I can find with some research."

Nan nodded, while reaching down to say goodbye to the animals. "I'll ask around too."

"Just remember," Doreen said. "No mystery is here."

"Of course not," Nan said with a big smile. But it was too big a smile.

"Do you know something I don't know?"

"I don't know," Nan said in confusion. "Do I?"

Doreen groaned. "Is there a mystery surrounding your gardener and his brother?"

"Well, their parents disappeared from one day to the next," Nan said. "So that's a mystery."

"It doesn't have to be a mystery. When did they 'disappear'?"

"About fifteen*ish* years ago," Nan said, as she tapped her chin. "I think it must have been at least fifteen years ago."

"Interesting. So a few years after these particular metal pieces were made."

Nan brightened. "Yes. So maybe you should check into that. Maybe the brothers murdered their parents," she said with relish.

Doreen worried about her grandmother somehow tying one incident to another, when the two might have been five years apart. Granted, each involved the same family. Doreen sighed. Now she knew how Mack felt when she posited some of her theories to him. "Or maybe the parents died naturally in a cancer clinic, and the brothers just didn't share any of their troubles because they're not the kind of people who wear their hearts on their sleeves."

"It's possible," Nan said with disappointment. "I don't remember too much about it. I don't even know if it was such a mystery back then. I just know the parents were here one day and gone the next. Everyone thought they'd upped and gone back east, as in East Coast, without telling anyone."

"That's what happens with old age and death," Doreen said drily.

"Their sister disappeared too," Nan said, as she stared off in the distance where the gardener had gone.

Doreen frowned. "All three at the same time?" That didn't bode well.

Nan nodded, still staring off into the landscape.

Doreen made a mental note to clarify these dates with Mack. "What happened to her?"

"I don't know," she said. "She had Down syndrome. She was a lovely girl though. Beautifully happy and always smiling, such a great help to have around."

"You knew the whole family?"

"I did, indeed. Used to see them a fair bit because we belonged to the same gardening club, and sometimes we would go on long nature walks together with the rest of the group. There were always tea times and, you know, various little social activities. They were a lovely couple and devoted to their family."

"Just the two boys and the sister?"

Nan nodded. "And not one of them had any kids."

"Oh, too bad," Doreen said. "It's sad when the family line is about to run out."

"It is, indeed," Nan said, with a meaningful look in

Doreen's direction.

She rolled her eyes as she stepped onto the first of the flagstones. "Don't even go in that direction with me, Nan."

"Mack would make lovely little babies with you," Nan called after her.

That didn't even deserve an answer. Not in public, for sure.

When she and her animals got to the other side of the lawn, Doreen turned and waved goodbye and walked toward the creek. She didn't even want to think about Mack and making little babies. That was not a path guaranteed to get her in the right frame of mind. Mack had a brother, that she knew of—an attorney checking into her own divorce attorney for her lack of ethics. Yet Doreen was an only child, raised by her mother. So Doreen wasn't used to being around many males as she grew up.

She and Mack got along well enough, but they were not even close to having that kind of relationship to be thinking about *babies*. At least she didn't think so. In the back of her mind this little voice said, *But you could be, down the road. You know he's interested.* At the same time it was so not what she needed to hear from her grandmother. Especially with Nan practically yelling it from Rosemoor, where the residents were deeply engrossed in hearing all the latest rumors.

Doreen shook her head and then thought more about a set of parents and their daughter all going missing at the same time. But the trouble was, even though Nan had said it was *at the same time*, it could have been over several years. It was possible the sister died of natural causes. It was a sad fact that a lot of people with Down syndrome didn't have the same life expectancy as their parents did. She could have had other health issues too. Maybe she passed first. Doreen would have to look it up when she got home.

Her fingers played with the little metal plates as she headed home. She had no way to get across the creek to the same spot where she'd found the second one—or rather, where Thaddeus had found the second label. She reached up and gently stroked Thaddeus under the chin. "We're not going back there to take another look."

He gave a loud squawk in her ear. It was loud enough that she had to twist her head to the side as she listened to him. "Okay, fine," she said. "Let's go take a quick glance."

Moving carefully, with Mugs racing ahead and Goliath right on his tail, Doreen and Thaddeus made their way across the creek at the narrowest and safest point from this end, wondering if she could do that again anytime soon. The water flowed with serious force. On the far side of the creek she carefully headed to where the second little piece had been. It took some backtracking and, after a while, she finally found the spot. Thaddeus's footprints were all around the area. She used her sandal to kick away some of the sand and a few of the smaller rocks. The ivy served as ground cover and was tangled all around the area. She pulled several long strands out of the way. "If these came off tools," she said, "what would they be doing here?"

She kicked away a few more rocks, and, sure enough, she found some wood sticking up. She bent down for a closer look. "Aha!"

She popped her head up, finding her bearings. They were almost at the mouth of the river. This whole side of the river could be turned into a walkway to the lake, only maybe twenty-five feet ahead of her. It was possible the river was wider back then too, sometime after these particular plates had been crafted some twenty years ago. Yet tossing the nameplates here could have happened one day after the labels had been created, or yesterday.

Doreen sighed, wishing she had a more finite time frame for when these tags had been discarded back here.

She used her fingers to dig out the handle. This wooden handle was bigger than the one, say, on her gardening spade. Which gave her a clue that this could be a much longer and sturdier tool. Mugs realized she was on the hunt and came to her side, his big sniffer moving up and down, sending sand flying everywhere with each snort. Then he started to dig, his big square paws churning out the dirt. But also a lot of rock was here.

She helped him out by moving a bunch of rocks as he dug a decent-size hole. Still she saw no end to the tool. *To be buried by so much soil and rocks and sand—courtesy of the flowing river activity—not to mention the well-established ivy growth here, all must mean this tool's been here for years and years. Maybe a decade? Unless, of course, somebody purposely buried it here like this.*

When she could finally grab the handle with both hands, she tugged it hard, and more dirt and rock shifted. But it was still stuck. She eventually coaxed it from its deep hole and lifted it up, as she studied the odd-looking thing in her hand. "Wow," she said, "what is this?"

She noted a place on the handle where the plate should have been. It was ever-so-slightly indented and had little pinholes, as if the metal had been nailed right into that place. She laid it off to the side and said, "You'd think there would be two of them, since I have two tags."

She kept searching but found no sign of a second handle, at least not with her small and limited ability to move the ground and dig by hand. She'd have to return with a shovel to make better headway, as this area had become very overgrown with time.

She spied the partial lake view from where she stood. On the opposite side of the river were private properties. Million-dollar homes went from there all the way around the lakeshore. She walked forward, leaving the tool on the ground. Another twenty-five feet and, of course, the lake just opened out in front of her. "I wonder how popular this area was way back when, twenty years ago?" she muttered. "Or if these tools and tags were tossed when the parents disappeared, possibly fifteen years ago?"

She turned to look at her animals, but they weren't leaving the tool alone. She smiled, walked back over, and picked it up, surprised at the hefty weight, and turned toward her home and her little bridge.

When she crossed the bridge, smiling at Mack's handiwork to make the bridge safe and sturdy again, and came back into her yard, she felt a certain relief. She placed the tool on her little café table on the back veranda and walked inside her house. She still was amazed at the empty rattling sound as she made her way through the residence. She had minimal furniture, most of it now gone to Christie's for the inevitable auction. And something was just so joyous about this emptiness. She walked around and opened up all the windows to let the breeze fly through the house. Curtains lifted, but so did a layer of dust, and she loved that. She wished the wind could go right from one side of the house to the other and take all the dust with it. Too bad that couldn't happen.

Chapter 6

Thursday Midafternoon …

WHEN DOREEN'S PHONE rang again, she looked at it and sighed. "Hi, Mack."

"Please tell me that you're not in any trouble," he said by way of a hello.

"What kind of trouble could I be in?"

"Somebody saw the gardener running away from you and Nan at the patio. Shouldn't you be at home resting your ankle?"

"Darren again?" she asked, rolling her eyes. Another cop who worked with Mack and whose grandfather lived at Rosemoor. "And I am home. I just walked to Nan's and back. A short walk to ease my ankle into the movements."

"Well, Darren didn't see it, but his grandfather did. Just make sure you don't overdo it."

"I didn't see him anywhere." She chose to ignore the rest of his comment.

"It's quite possible he was inside Nan's apartment," Mack said delicately.

Doreen froze and then a sigh escaped. "Jeez, that meant he heard everything we talked about. Why didn't Nan tell me he was there?" she asked. "I nibbled on a cookie outside on the patio for at least an hour. I hate to think he was sitting inside waiting for her."

"I think he was trying to visit with her but didn't want to disturb you two."

"That's just sad," she said. "He'd have been more than welcome to join us."

"Maybe he just wanted to get away from the nurses. According to Darren, they're on his case about his diet."

"Ha. He was probably stealing a cookie then from Nan," she said. "They were huge and totally stuffed with chocolate chips."

"It sounds wonderful. You didn't bring a spare one home, did you?" Mack asked hopefully.

"I meant to bring half of that one home," Doreen said regretfully, "but I ate the entire thing while I sat there talking with Nan."

"So the gardener ..."

"Well, he left us, but it had nothing to do with me or the animals this time," she said. "Well, not directly. Thaddeus found these two little metal plates with dates and names on them, but the names and dates are hard to read. I took them with me when I went to have tea. I asked Nan, and she remembered something about the gardener's brother, Frank, having a tool repair shop or some such thing and put these little tags on his creations."

"Interesting."

But she could tell Mack had already tuned out of their conversation. She smiled. "How are you doing?"

"I'm doing okay," he said. "I was just checking in to make sure you were good. Have you recovered?"

"Almost," she said. "Last week I was begging for three

days of peace and quiet, but today I found myself bored out of my mind."

"You could try living with boredom," he said. "It's good for the soul."

"No, it's not," she said, laughing. "I got out and started digging in my backyard, when Thaddeus brought me the first one of those little plate things."

"They could be nothing," he said.

"Well," she said, her voice turning suddenly cheerful as she walked out of her kitchen, "I did find a tool. On the way back from Nan's, we returned to where we'd found one plate. Out of the weeds and ivy that had taken over the area, I dug up something with a long handle, down near the mouth of the river."

"Interesting. What kind of tool?"

"I'm not exactly sure. A sharp point at one end and more of a shovel blade at the other."

"Huh."

She could almost hear the frown in his voice. "It's not like Nan's old hoe, but yet it is somehow similar. But way heavier."

"Somebody probably just left it behind."

"That's what I thought. Now I'm about to put on a pot of coffee and get back outside and start some more digging."

"Any more thoughts on the deck?"

"Yes, but I don't think I can do anything about it anytime soon," she said regretfully. "Scott said they're having to do some repairs on some of the furniture, plus the overall cleaning, and then the paintings needed a bit more in-depth cleaning as well, so it'll delay them going into the pre-auction catalog. That'll delay sales, which will delay me getting any money."

"Huh," Mack said. "I suggest we sit down, take a look at how much of the deck materials we might scrounge from other people, and, once we get enough of the parts and pieces, we can start your deck renovation."

She liked the idea of that. "Do you think we can get any of these pieces and parts?"

"That's why I'm bringing it up," he said, "because one of the guys here said he had a bunch of cinder blocks he doesn't need."

"And he's willing to sell them?"

"Possibly," Mack said, "but I've helped him out a couple times at his place, so we might just grab them for free."

Her face lit up. "Free?"

"That's why I wanted to go over that plan of yours, to see just how many we needed."

"I think I noted at least twenty." Doreen walked over to the little corner of the kitchen where she had all her papers on that. She pulled out the pad of paper and said, "Yes, we've got twenty down here."

"He's got twelve," Mack said.

"That would help a lot. We'd only need to get eight more."

"I think I've got two around my place. I don't know for sure. I thought I saw them a couple months back. Mom might have some too."

"Wow. If we had those, we could get them in the ground and leveled off, ready for the next step, right?"

"Exactly. I'll stop by after work and take a look at that plan of yours to make sure we have the right amount."

"Sure," Doreen said, "or maybe go to your house and your mom's first and see how many you have."

"They're not very expensive, but, when you have to buy

twenty, it can add up."

"Any penny we can save is a huge help. By the way, Nan also sent me home with some vegetables. Honestly I didn't have any clue what a zucchini looked like before she gave them to me."

"Do you like zucchini?"

"I'm not sure I've ever had it," she confessed. "Except in bread. I took one, and then Nan tucked in a second little one and also a bunch of lettuce and some green onions and tomatoes."

"Perfect," Mack said. "You can use all that, can't you?"

"At least the salad stuff I can, yes. I can't remember what we planned to do for our next cooking-lesson meal together."

"I don't think we decided. Check what you've got in the freezer."

"I will. Do you want to come for dinner tonight then?" She walked to her freezer and pulled out what looked like a pack of meat. "I think it's pork chops," she said. "They're frozen though."

"Too bad you don't have a barbecue. We could do barbecued pork chops and zucchini strips."

"Can you barbecue those things?" She walked to the paper bag and pulled out the zucchini. "It's long and skinny. Do you bake it whole?"

He chuckled. "You can make thick slices, oil them, and put them on the grill. Or you can slice them and sauté them. All kinds of stuff you can do with zucchini."

"I have a few mushrooms in the fridge too," she said.

"Take out the pork chops to thaw, and we can have those for dinner. At least this way I can make sure you're not involved in any new cases. Remember. You're supposed to be recuperating, not getting into more trouble." And, with that, he hung up.

She laughed. "Look at that," she said to the others. "Mack is worried about us."

Mugs woofed, and she noted he stood beside his empty food dish. "It is past lunchtime, isn't it, buddy? I'm the one who ate a cookie, not you, and, from the looks of it, you are hungry."

She fed him and then gave Goliath a little more dry food in his dish. Next, she brought out a few seeds to put down for Thaddeus. After that, it was time to feed herself. She returned to the fridge and opened it up. Some bread and cheese were left, and she now had fresh lettuce and tomato, so her belated lunch sounded like a sandwich for her. And she was totally okay with that. As far as she was concerned, a sandwich was a basic necessity of life. It didn't mean other people agreed with her, but, hey, that was okay.

She made a sandwich and then sat down at the veranda table outside. The deck was too tiny for the café table, which was why she was desperate to build a proper one. She had the plans sitting beside her as she ate. Of course, she didn't have enough information or DIY knowledge to figure anything out. She would have to wait for Mack to see what they needed, but, if they had twelve, maybe fourteen, cement blocks already, that was a great start.

She thought maybe she could get all the materials for the deck out of the money she'd sold the car parts for, but she was pretty sure that wouldn't leave her enough to make it through the next few months while she awaited the Christie's money. Sure, Mack would pay her a little bit for working in his mom's garden, but it wasn't enough to keep her in food. Nan had been extremely generous as well, but Doreen couldn't spend that money on a deck renovation and not have enough to pay her utility bills, plus food for her and her animals, over the next three to four months.

Speaking of which, she walked back inside with her empty plate and removed the rest of the vegetables from the bag. As she upended the bag, something small fell out.

Chapter 7

Thursday Midafternoon ...

DOREEN PICKED UP the item and groaned. "Nan, really?"

Nan was the sweetest woman alive, and Doreen hoped she was okay for money, but she kept putting things like this into Doreen's pocket, and, instead of giving it to Doreen herself, Nan had put it in the veggie bag. It was, indeed, a roll of money. Doreen slipped off the elastic band around it and found two hundred and fifty dollars. She stared at the bounty in front of her in amazement. "Nan, I can live off of this for three weeks or more, if I have to."

She unrolled them and put them underneath a book to stretch the bills out. Then she picked up her purse and took a look. She still had over four hundred in cash there, and she had just recently taken out the other five hundred she'd been carrying in her purse and added it to the bowl of money. She wouldn't need much to get through a few months, but she didn't have any way of planning for the unknowns that could pop up. And to take all her cash-on-hand money—all $2,150 approximately—and put it into something like a deck seemed extravagant. And stupid.

She was hoping maybe the books would have sold by now. She got five hundred for a couple chairs Scott had sold for her, and she had that money too. Matter of fact, she brought out her laptop and checked her bank account. She was doing okay, but it depended on if they could get any more donations toward her deck addition. That was where the real trick would be.

She really wanted that bigger deck. And she didn't want to wait until next year. As it was, June was upon them. Doreen wanted to enjoy her new deck addition this summer. However, she may have to just wait for the next one instead.

She closed out of her bank account and searched for Kelowna Tool Repair. It took about thirty seconds, but none of the search hits were recent. The trouble was, there wasn't any website, although she did find a notice in an old newspaper article about how the physical shop was closing down. She sighed at that and realized it would mean a trip to the library to get more information. Apparently the business had shut down almost fourteen years ago. She wrote that down and then the name Frank Darbunkle. She laughed at that surname.

"Who goes through life with the name Darbunkle?" But then that would mean it was the gardener's name too. Fred and Frank Darbunkle. She shook her head. "I can't imagine."

She found no mention of a sister. She would definitely have to make a trip to the library after all. But, as she looked up, she noted her coffee had been sitting there, already brewed and waiting for her, and she'd gotten so involved in the Darbunkles that she'd missed pouring herself a cup while it was fresh and hot.

She did so now and brought the two little pieces of metal back over and checked into how they'd been used and why they'd been used. It took a bit of research, but she found it was a common practice for people who made tools to put a metal plate on them, usually with two nails to hold it in place, and that matched up with what she'd seen on these. She looked at various tools online, trying to figure out what the tool was she had on her back veranda. It was pretty dusty and covered in dirt, but, underneath that layer, it seemed to be stained and rusted. Still it was fascinating. It was heavy too.

She figured Mack would know but maybe not. It was old and used. Speaking of *used*, she remembered she had another source of money potentially. She picked up the phone and phoned the consignment store. As soon as Wendy answered, she said, "Wendy, this is Doreen."

"Hi, Doreen. How are you doing?" Wendy said in a bright, cheerful voice.

"I'm doing fine. I was just wondering how we were doing for time and money?"

"Ah," Wendy said. "Most of your stuff is moving. Obviously not all of it because you did bring me a lot, and more was left recently too."

"I know," Doreen said. "And I understand it hasn't been ninety days yet. I was just wondering if I could look forward to any money at that time."

Wendy chuckled. "Last we talked, I told you how we already had several hundred in sales, but I can tell you that it's way more than that now. But, of course, it's not all coming in ninety days though."

Doreen tried to work her mind through that. "So, it's ninety days after the sale, is that correct?"

"Yes. Ninety days after the month ends that the sale was

made in," she corrected. So that means, I will pay you for the first pieces sold in, say, roughly two months or so. And then there'll be more every month after that. The first payment could be small, remember that."

"Perfect. I don't suppose …" and then she let her voice trail away. How small was small?

"You want me to find out how much I owe you already?"

"Sure. Would you mind?" Doreen asked. "I'd really appreciate it."

"No, let me take a look," Wendy said, silent for only a couple moments as she checked. "You've done very well. I owe you over two thousand dollars to date."

Doreen gasped in joy. "Seriously?"

"Yeah, seriously, but remember. You won't get it all at once. The first batch isn't bad though. There's over six hundred dollars, but you won't receive it for another roughly seven weeks."

"Fine," Doreen said, writing notes. "That at least helps. I'll see the money coming then."

"Exactly, so you'll get your first payment in another seven weeks and then another in eleven weeks and then the balance in fifteen weeks roughly. Of course that's just on the clothes you have turned in so far that have sold. And payment is always at the end of the month. And you can come down on the last day—or the first day of the next month is better for me."

"Right," Doreen said, understanding. "I suppose if I was early, you can just maybe take a moment and write a check for me?"

Wendy laughed. "Possibly. Do you have any more clothes to bring down?"

"I think there are some," Doreen said. "I just haven't had a chance to go through it all."

"Considering that you're doing as well as you are, why don't you go through the rest of it, and then you'll hopefully get money continuously, after your initial payment in two months, for the following three or four months."

"Perfect," Doreen said after thanking Wendy, and she hung up. "That would be possibly when I'll get money from Scott too. That'll be a big month for me."

On that note, she went back out to the garage for some bags she had haphazardly put to the side to go to the charity. She loaded those into her car, so she could drop them off on her next trip to town.

But she still had stuff in her closets to sort, both in the master bedroom closet and maybe some *undecideds* in the spare bedroom closet. With a cup of coffee beside her, she decided she'd rather try on clothes and make more money reselling them than returning to work in her garden. So she slipped on and off the next four or five outfits and didn't like any of them. She tried on another couple. One shirt was fine and a pair of pants too, but the other items weren't for her. Several elegant dresses she had put off making a decision on, but they didn't feel right, not on the hanger and not on her body.

Another load all ready for consignment, she packed it up in a bag, set it off to the side, and dove through more clothes. By the time she was done for the day on this part of the project, she had another nine pieces for herself and fifteen to go to Wendy. She packed them up and decided that was enough. It was already after four in the afternoon. She took the two bags down and parked them in front of the car and then thought no, she'd better put them right in the car. She stuffed them in, grabbed her keys and Mugs, and headed straight to Wendy's, by way of Goodwill first.

When she walked into the consignment store, Wendy laughed. "I didn't mean you had to bring stuff down now," she said.

Doreen shrugged. "I figured I should go through some more stuff while I was thinking about it, so here's two more bags full." She handed them over, and Wendy sorted through them.

"They're beautiful," she said. "Are you sure you want to part with them?"

"I tried them on," Doreen said, "and either they didn't fit properly or I didn't like the way they looked on me."

"Somebody else will love them."

With that, Doreen smiled and headed toward the exit. She stopped and said, "I don't remember how long you've been here. Do you remember a Kelowna Tool Repair?"

Wendy frowned. "I think so," she said, "but I can't remember for sure. I think my parents used to go there."

"Interesting," Doreen said.

"Is something wrong?" Wendy asked, looking up at her. "Another case to follow?"

"Oh, no, no. I just found some little metal plates from tool handles that got my interest."

"Oh, I've seen those. Yeah, he put them on his tools."

"Frank, wasn't it?"

"Yep. Frank Darbunkle."

"Right, it's the last name that caught my interest," Doreen said with a smile. "And they had a sister, didn't they?"

"Frank and Fred, and, yes, I can't remember the girl's name. That was …" Wendy stared off into the distance.

"Lovely little girl."

"If you come up with a name, let me know."

"Henrietta," Wendy announced triumphantly, as Doreen reached for the front door.

"Henrietta, okay, that's great. Do you know the parents' names?"

Wendy shook her head. "No, I don't remember them."

"Perfect, thanks." With a wave of her fingers, Doreen led Mugs back out to her car. Knowing Mack would be arriving soon to cook dinner, teaching her how to do it herself, hopefully, she drove back home and got out just in time to see Mack pull up behind her.

"Where have you been?" Mack asked lightly.

"Just delivering yet more clothing to Wendy's," she said. "Plus a quick stop at Goodwill."

"Are you done yet?"

"I am, and yet I'm not. I kept back a bunch. Remember? Thinking maybe I would want them for myself?"

Mack nodded. "I remember that, and are you keeping those?"

"I went through those, and I'm keeping about one-quarter of the clothes, and the rest went to Wendy—who is doing a good job of selling them for me, by the way."

"You're doing well."

"Very well. So far I'll get a couple thousand dollars from Wendy eventually."

At that, Mack's eyebrows shot up. "That almost pays for a deck."

"I know," Doreen said. "It will be distributed piecemeal though, like the first bit coming in a couple months and a bit each month thereafter, until I'm all paid up. Then I'll probably go through all the clothes that are still here once again, before I can hopefully call it quits on that front."

Mack led the way into the kitchen. "I stopped at Mom's, and she has six of those cinder blocks, and, no, she doesn't want them."

"I can work them off," Doreen offered.

He shrugged. "They're sitting in the garden shed, in the way. With twelve from a guy I work with and six from my mom, we have eighteen. Plus I have two more."

"That's all twenty," Doreen said triumphantly. She grabbed the notepad she had. "We have twenty of them written down."

"Right. It works perfectly." Mack reached for the pen and put a big checkmark beside that entry.

"But we still have to get them."

"We do. It is better to have them all here." He looked around and then stepped out onto the small deck. "Maybe we should stack materials alongside the house there," he said, motioning between her place and Richard's.

"That's a good idea. And, if we fill that area, it should kill off the weeds too."

Mack nodded. "It won't hurt. And you've got a decent-size overhang here, and, with Richard's house right beside you, it'll keep these materials stashed there all pretty-well dry from the weather."

Doreen got really excited. "How do we get the stuff from your friend though?"

"I'll have to pick those up with my truck to get them all in one load," he said with a laugh. "Your car could take a couple, but it won't take many at a time."

As they walked back inside, Mack stopped, looked at the tool on her veranda table and asked, "What are you doing with an ice pick?"

Chapter 8

Thursday Late Afternoon ...

D OREEN LOOKED AT the tool and then at Mack. "A what?"

He lifted it up and held it in his hand. "This is an ice pick for ice fishing. It's an old-fashioned one, sturdier than the newer versions."

"Seriously?"

He nodded. "We have ice fishing here."

"I never even thought about ice fishing." As a matter of fact, she couldn't think of anything worse. Why would you sit on the middle of a frozen lake with a hole in it to coax fish out?

"It's very popular," Mack said, "at least it was when the lake froze over all the time, but it hasn't frozen over for quite a few years."

"I found this tool at the mouth of the river."

He frowned at that. "Not many people would fish at the mouth of a river because the ice will never be as solid as it is farther down. But there have been years ..." He tilted his head, thinking about it. "Honestly, if we talked to a couple old-timers, I'm sure we'd find some tales of years where they went ice fishing at the mouth."

"Maybe," Doreen said, studying the ice pick. "Didn't I say an ice pick could be next?"

He glared at her. "Nothing is suspicious about this."

She pulled out the two little silver plates she had and held them up. "This is the one Thaddeus found, and this is the one I found when I went back to the place Thaddeus showed me."

Mack shook his head at that. "Most people don't listen when a bird wants to show them a place."

"I've learned to listen. My animals have my well-being at heart."

"Not to mention they're as curious and as crazy as you are." He picked up a tag and placed it into the notch on the pick, and it sank in beautifully. "Of course you can't guarantee this is the same piece."

Doreen held up the other tag, but it was bigger.

"So that one won't fit this ice pick," he said.

"Maybe it went with an even bigger tool? Another ice pick or something bigger? Is there a long-handled ax for ice work?"

"Potentially. You have to gauge the hatchet size with its respective handle, so it doesn't damage the integrity of the wood."

Doreen nodded as if she knew what he was talking about, but, for her, it was just a tool. "All that is rust on the head, right?"

Mack nodded, his gaze narrowing as he studied it. "Was it along the riverbank or up on the high part?"

"Where the riprap wall and the loose rocks meet the property fence."

He frowned. "That riprap is often boosted, depending

on the flooding. But, at that section, I'm not sure any work's been done in a long time."

"So then our ice pick could have been buried here on purpose like a year ago or Mother Nature could have buried it even as far back as twenty years ago."

"Exactly." He laid the ice pick down again and handed her the little metal piece. "Hang on to this."

Doreen did as he asked and then said, "Is there any reason why?"

"Well," he said, "like you, I've learned to trust your animals."

She gazed at him in delight. "So, do you think the ice pick was involved in a murder?"

Immediately his hands came up. "Whoa. How did you jump from this little loose tag to our ice pick here being a murder weapon?"

She wrinkled her face up at him. "Mostly because I'm involved," she admitted.

Mack laughed. "Just because you keep tripping into this stuff," he said, "does not mean every tool you see—even as you thought or joked about it being an ice pick next—is a murder weapon."

"Of course not," Doreen said with a smile. "You know my imagination runs away with me."

"You'll have to watch that. And, besides, I'm certain this guy sold hundreds of tools."

"Sure, but then why would these two tags and this tool be back there near the lake?"

"It wouldn't necessarily have anything to do with the actual maker," he said. "It could have been left behind by one of his customers. Remember that."

But Doreen didn't want to let it go. "Maybe it's because

I don't like the gardener," she announced.

He looked at her in surprise and chuckled. "If we looked at all the people you didn't like, we'd have nothing but issues with people."

"What do you mean, *issues?*" she protested. "I get along with everyone."

He gave her a droll look. "Except for all the people you put behind bars."

"If they hadn't been murderers or thieves or God-only-knows-what-other-kind-of-lowlife, I wouldn't have had to, now would I?"

Mack wrapped an arm around her shoulders and led her back into the kitchen. "How come you had coffee this afternoon and left half a pot?"

"I don't know. I just forgot about it."

"What were you researching?" His guess had been a little too accurate. She glared at him. He put his hands on his hips and tapped the floor.

"Okay, fine," she said. "I was researching the Carboncles."

"Darbunkles," he corrected.

She snickered. "Can you imagine if that was your name?"

"I don't imagine I'd like it," he said, "but, the fact of the matter is, it's their name."

"According to Nan, their parents disappeared, and so did their sister," she said triumphantly.

Mack stopped, looked at her, and said, "Seriously?"

"Nan said so, but Nan says lots of things."

"She is quite a character," Mack said sympathetically. "And I do understand sometimes that she gets forgetful."

"You think?" Doreen said with an eye roll. She watched

as Mack poured the cold coffee into a pitcher. "What are you doing?"

He just smiled and put the pitcher in the fridge. And then he proceeded to put on a fresh pot of coffee.

"You're chilling the coffee?"

"Yes, and, when it's cold, you just pour yourself a glass and add ice, and you have an iced coffee."

She stared at him in delight. "Oh my, I used to get fancy iced coffees at the coffee shop all the time. Are you telling me that they served me leftover coffee and charged me a fortune for it?"

Mack laughed. "Probably not, but you can do it just as easily this way and doctor it up as you like it—with cream and sugar and flavorings. I see the pork chops are here but not quite thawed." He poked the top of one, and his finger indented it slightly. "But almost."

"Yes," Doreen said, and then she turned back to him and asked, "What do you know about the Darbunkles?"

"Not much. Don't remember any time they've been brought in on a crime."

"Of course not. Speaking of crime, how is Steve?"

"Steve is Steve," he said. "Complaining madly."

"Of course he is," she said with a nod. "He did murder all those people. At least he can't be much of a character reference when defending Penny anymore."

Mack looked at her for a long moment. "That's really bothering you, isn't it?"

"Steve said Penny denied attacking me, and it would be my word against hers. *She* was an upstanding local citizen, and everybody trusted her, whereas I was nothing but an interfering interloper." She hated that her voice dropped sadly at the end, but honestly it was a little depressing.

"You don't worry about Penny," Mack said. "Remember? I was there."

"Sure, but people will say you're my friend, and you can't be trusted."

At that, his gaze narrowed. "I can tell you, for one thing, that's not what people will say."

Doreen frowned. "Are you saying you are not my friend?" she demanded.

He groaned. "Of course I'm your friend, but that's not what people will say."

"People are people," she said with a wave of her hand, dismissing his argument. "You know perfectly well they'll say anything they want to you to get out of trouble."

Mack laughed. "And I'm telling you that you'll be fine."

"At least Steve is in jail with Penny," she said with relish. "So they're both in trouble now."

"They are, indeed."

"And what about Crystal and that whole kidnapping mess?" she asked.

"It's too early to tell. It's been turned over to the prosecutors, and it's up to them to figure out what they'll do. And remember. A lot of other missing-children cases are potentially involved around Crystal's disappearance."

"Surely the brothers couldn't have taken them *all* down to Mexico," she said.

"That's what we're still trying to figure out, but every time we get something completed and off our desk, another case drops on the pile."

"You mean, every time you try to solve one problem, I come along with another one."

"In this case, you did a great job," he said. "Crystal is home. She's been accepted to university. She'll be just fine."

"At least she was loved on both sides of the border," Doreen said. "It's got to make it a lot easier for her to understand."

"Exactly," Mack said with a big smile. He spied the zucchinis and said, "Now, if only we had a grill."

"If only we had a deck big enough for the grill," Doreen said.

"I'll ask around the division if anybody has any leftover decking stuff. I know a couple buddies built new decks recently. Even if we can get a little bit, it'll help."

"It will. It will help a lot." And, with that, Doreen watched as Mack took the packaging off the pork chops and put them in the microwave to defrost and then sliced the zucchinis to pop into a skillet. He reached into the fridge for the mushrooms and the fresh green onions, and, before she knew it, he had the veggies in a pan ready to sauté together. "That already looks wonderful," she admitted, hearing her stomach screaming. "I had a sandwich a while back, but it seems like that was now hours ago because I see this food, and I want to eat now."

"An appetite would be good," he said, "not to mention the fact that, when you're resting and recovering like you have been, you need food to rebuild."

"Says you," she said. "I find resting means I'm either not hungry or I'm really hungry."

"Exactly, and you should be trying to regain your strength and healing. You were attacked again. I'm not impressed with that."

Doreen smiled at him. "Of course not because, once again, you were trying to save me, and, once again, I was in trouble before you had a chance to even get there."

"I sure wish you would just stay out of trouble," Mack

muttered. When the microwave beeped, he sliced off the outside fat on the pork chops, added some spices, and while she watched, turned on the heat underneath a second skillet with a bit of the pork fat and fried the meat.

"That looks absolutely delicious." Doreen studied the veggies and frowned. "I guess I should have accepted more zucchinis, huh?"

"Does she have more?"

"She had lots when I was there, but who knows now?" She shrugged and added, "We have some greens here. Do you want me to make a salad?"

Mack nodded. "That would be good."

Doreen washed the lettuce and tomatoes and sliced them up together to make a salad. By the time Mack was done with the pork chops and veggies, she had the salad ready and the outside table set. "Seriously hungry here," she said impatiently, as she studied the crispy golden tops of the chops.

"I get that," Mack said, laughing.

"Wow. I don't know how it happens, but, every time you cook, it's like I haven't eaten in weeks." She rubbed her hands together as she eyed the food on the plate.

He sat down beside her, smiled, and said, "It's okay. You can eat, you know?"

She grinned. "I can, but it's been a few days since I had a home-cooked meal." She picked up her knife and sliced into the pork. It was tender and moist and so flavorful that she sagged back as she chewed with her eyes closed.

"That face," he said with a shake of his head.

"Don't bother me," she said. "This is a Zen moment."

Chapter 9

Thursday Dinnertime ...

M ACK BURST OUT laughing. "You really are funny."
"How can I be funny?" Doreen muttered. "This
is too delicious." She smiled as she attacked the rest of her
meal. She had barely laid down her fork when the phone
rang. It was Nan. "Hi, Nan," she said cheerfully.

"Henrietta," she said.

"Yes, Henrietta is Fred and Frank's sister. What about
her?"

"There were rumors about her and her life. Not nice
ones. But I don't know in what way." And she hung up.

Doreen set her cell phone on the table. "Nan says Frank
and Fred Darbunkle's sister, Henrietta, had some not-nice
rumors about her life."

Mack groaned. "You need to just leave it alone," he said.

"Do you know anything about that case?"

"No," he said, "I really don't."

"Okay," she said, "because Nan had mentioned something earlier about it, and I just don't want murderers to go
free."

"And they won't," Mack said. "But, if they murdered

anybody, we don't have any bodies."

"Do me a favor," Doreen said. "When you go back to the office tomorrow, just make sure the Darbunkle seniors and the sister are not missing, okay?"

"How do you expect me to find that out?"

"I want you to confirm you don't have anything important in a file on them."

He sighed, then shrugged and said, "I'll see what I can do."

"Otherwise," Doreen said, "I'll have an awful lot of obituaries to go through."

Mack laughed. "It's almost worth it to think how busy that'll keep you. I won't have to worry about you for at least a week."

"Unless I get lucky," she said craftily. "And I come up with something elsewhere that's interesting."

Mack shook his head. "What about the files from the journalist? Did you even look in there?"

Doreen bounced to her feet and bolted inside. "I forgot." She returned a few moments later with her laptop. "I did tell you how I indexed them, right?"

"Indexed?" he asked cautiously, as he stacked their empty dishes.

"I wrote down all the names of everybody we have a Solomon file on. Then scanned in the summary notes from the journalist's own handwriting." She brought up her file. "Do you know how to spell *Darbunkle*?"

He gave her the correct spelling of Darbunkle, and she typed that into her document and searched for it. Almost immediately it came up. "Oh my," she said. "There is a file."

"Seriously?"

Doreen nodded. "I'll get the box." She headed back inside, but this time Mack was right there with her. They pulled the boxes down until she found the right one. Mack lifted it up and put it on the kitchen table, and they searched through it. Her hand found the Darbunkle file first, but he snatched it from her so he was the one holding it. She glared at him. "That's my file."

He gave her the sweetest of smiles. "You can pour us some coffee," he said.

Doreen glanced at the pot and saw enough was left for a cup for each of them. She finished cleaning up and poured the coffee as she waited impatiently, while Mack flipped through the file.

"Interesting," he said.

"What's interesting? I remember typing notes about it, but I didn't have any connection to it at the time, so it was just words on paper."

"That's the problem with some cases. They become just words. You really must have a personal connection, and then they come alive."

"What kind of connection exists here?"

"Information on the family. The parents went bankrupt a couple times. Never very good at business, but the couple themselves were married for a good forty-plus years. Then they disappeared." At that, he stopped and frowned. "Wait. Rumor had it they moved to the East Coast. That was … maybe a tad more than fifteen years ago. But then Solomon found where the sons filed a missing persons' report—but in the other district where the parents had moved to—again about fifteen years ago. After the legal waiting period, the sons filed for a certificate of death. Yeah, so just seven or so years ago the house could have been legally in the sons' names. … I will cross-reference this by checking our records in the morning. But, if the two police districts weren't communicating, we won't have all the related documents."

"It could still be a missing persons' case, right?"

"Hopefully, if the journalist has a file on them, the corresponding police jurisdiction will too."

"But only if somebody reported them missing, correct?"

Mack nodded.

"So then, how would this journalist know about them being missing if there wasn't a police file?"

"Don't get ahead of yourself. I can check tomorrow if our district or the other one has a missing persons' file."

"Unless anything else is in here in Solomon's file." Doreen already was at her laptop, going over the notes she'd scanned in. "Okay, I found what you just read off. Still so suspicious. One day to the next, just gone. Sons reported it, but nobody ever saw their parents again. After seven years the parents were declared dead, and the sons inherited everything." She whistled at that. "That's always suspicious. Whenever money's involved, and people disappear, as far as I'm concerned, they're already guilty."

"Hey," Mack said, "no jumping to conclusions. Besides, I don't know that the Darbunkles had much in the way of money because of those bankruptcies."

Doreen nodded. "I get that. Did you see any mention of Henrietta in there?"

Mack read through the Solomon file and shook his head. "Not in the journalist's notes, nothing. According to this file, she's not missing."

"So maybe Nan was wrong."

Mack closed the file. "Did you scan this one in?"

She nodded.

"Can you email it to me, please?" he asked.

Doreen brought it up, attached it to an email, and sent it to him. "Done. Do you think Nan is wrong?"

"The question really is," he said, "if Henrietta's not missing, where the hell is she?"

Chapter 10

Thursday Evening ...

DOREEN HAD TO admit that was one of the things she liked about Mack. He didn't dismiss what she said. He tried to downplay it a lot of times to keep her on track and tried to stop her from jumping to conclusions, but, when something potentially was there, he didn't knock her sideways, laugh at her, or mock her. Something her ex would have done in a heartbeat. But then Mack was nothing like her ex. She watched as he got up to leave. "Did you ever hear from your brother?" she asked out of the blue.

He looked at her and nodded. "I was wondering how to bring it up."

"Bring what up?" she asked.

"Him and the whole lawyer issue," he said. And then he gave her a gammoned grin. "I know exactly how you feel about lawyers."

"I feel the same way about my ex," she said with spirit, and she gave him a lopsided smile. "But that doesn't change the fact we've put something into motion. What does your brother have to say?"

"He wants to meet with you," Mack said.

Her eyebrows shot up. "So, you won't be the middleman anymore?"

"Well, we both figured it's probably better if I stayed as a middleman," he admitted, "but he wanted to bring you up to speed on what he's doing."

"That's fine," she said, "just not anytime soon."

Mack chuckled. "What's the point of doing this if it won't be anytime soon?"

Doreen shot him a look. "It's just, as soon as you do it, it becomes part of something I have to deal with."

"And right now you have enough to deal with?" He studied her carefully. "If you do feel that way, it's time for you to back off from these cold cases."

Immediately she got defensive. "That's not what I meant. I'm just trying to figure out how to make enough money to do this deck and then ..." She waved her hand. "I don't know what I'm saying. The bottom line is, I'd rather do anything but talk to your brother about my ex."

"That's honest, at least," Mack said. "Let me talk to him and see what time frame he's looking at."

Doreen smiled. "I haven't thanked you for linking me up. For your brother doing this pro bono. I know I don't appear to be very grateful, and he is just investigating, but he certainly wouldn't even be doing that much if it weren't for you."

Mack was already at the front door but turned to look at her. "What brought this on?"

She frowned. "Can't I show appreciation?" But she had to admit to feeling a little uncomfortable. She wasn't sure what brought that on either.

"Appreciation," he said, "is always good."

"I thought so too," she said and then laughed.

Mack looked down to see Mugs had dropped himself on top of his shoes.

"I think he's got a message for you."

"What? That I can't leave?" Mack said in a dry tone. "I don't think that's quite what Mugs's owner wants."

She had to admit it was really nice to have him around. "I was going to ask if you could move my bed back upstairs and we were supposed to go over the plans for the deck."

"Ah, the first I can do right now. As for the second," he said grunting slightly as it picked up the mattress, sheet still on, and started up the stairs, "I took a look at the list and remembered what we were talking about, and I do have a couple guys I'll ask."

"Right," she said trailing behind him with the bedding and pillows. "How many days do you think something like this deck expansion would take?"

He dropped the mattress on the box spring and shifted it into the right position. Then he stepped back, caught his breath and added, "For a professional, probably a weekend. For me, who isn't a professional, maybe a couple weekends, maybe longer."

"Plus it involves your days off," Doreen said as she quickly made up the bed so it was ready for the night, "which is hardly fair."

"Maybe not," he said, "but maybe, as punishment, you'll have to help me and not go off on these wild goose chases and stop tracking down killers."

They walked down the stairs to the front door. She opened it to let him out. As he walked out she chuckled. "Meaning, as long as I'm out there, moving cement blocks or whatever, I can't get into trouble, right?"

That little slip of his lips twitched, and he nodded. "Exactly." He headed out to his truck with a wave of his hand. "Are you coming to Mom's tomorrow?"

"I thought I'd go around ten in the morning."

Mack nodded. "Sounds good. I'll remember to bring some money and drop it off on the weekend."

"Perfect." She leaned against the doorjamb and watched as he drove away. It was getting to be a habit, the two of them. A nice habit. She didn't have any aspirations to make it more, at least not at this point, but no way did she want to lose what she had either. But the fact of the matter was, onto more tangible concepts, they had already scrounged up some pieces she needed for her deck addition, and that made her very happy. And his truck would haul the stuff here, and she wouldn't have to pay for gas or delivery, at least for these pieces.

Feeling much better, Doreen called Mugs back inside and closed the front door. She'd hardly done anything all day, but somehow she was tired. She figured she was still recovering. She had dealt with a lot of cold cases and had suffered several attacks lately, and maybe it was time to chill for a few days.

But then that would mean Mack was right—again.

As she walked back into the kitchen to make herself a cup of chamomile tea to maybe take upstairs to her room, she caught sight of her open laptop. She went to shut it down but found a couple articles still open on her screen that she had missed. Once she saw a mention of Henrietta, Doreen sat down to read them. She leaned forward to read the rest of the article. Apparently the little girl had gone to school and not come home—before her parents went missing. There'd been a neighborhood search, everybody stepping up to find her, and she was found, so a happy ending that time. Then what happened to her after her parents went missing? She shouldn't have just up and disappeared a second time with no one looking for her.

Doreen sat back and wondered. *Was it because she was deemed as less than perfect? Or did she go missing again soon afterward, this time with her parents? Or did the brothers relocate her once her parents went missing, and so it became no news as she just went to live with someone else?* All these thoughts ran through her head. She confirmed in this online article the date that Henrietta went missing from school—just before both parents went missing.

"And that's very weird too," she muttered. She wrote down both dates and then printed out the article. As she was printing it off, she noticed Henrietta had been fourteen. Hardly a little girl—a young blossoming teen. Yet she might have been fourteen in physical age, but, with Down syndrome, she may have acted much younger in age.

And that brought more ugly thoughts to her mind. With the article printed off, she checked the other articles but nothing interesting was there. She shut down her laptop and walked out onto her veranda to take another look at the ice-fishing pick. The fact that she had brought up an *ice pick* as a joke to Mack just made her laugh, but the fact that it was something dangerous and murderous looking was a whole different issue. She had the little metal tags still sitting inside on the kitchen windowsill, and she wondered why she found two labels but only one tool. Surely a second ice pick or another tool went along with the second label.

She wanted to do more research, but it was kinda late to get started on something like that, which usually took her down the rabbit hole for hours. But, her curiosity piqued, she decided it wasn't yet *that* late. She brought her laptop and her cup of chamomile tea with her to sit outside. She began by researching images of ice-fishing picks to see if it truly was one. Even though Mack had said so, she didn't want to take his word at face value. But, as she studied the images, she realized he was correct. Next question was, did Kelowna Tool Repair produce ice-fishing picks. And, lo and behold, she happened to stumble on an old article, potentially a webpage. She wasn't exactly sure what this was.

"Oh," she muttered to herself, "this is a blog on old tools." And it wasn't so much that this was an old tool, but she stopped and stared because right in front of her was an image of a little tiny tag, the same as the ones Thaddeus had found. It seemed the two maker's marks belonged to a set of custom-ordered ice pick tools created by Frank.

Doreen laughed in delight. "Well, look at that." She wrote down more notes because she would have to return to the library to get additional information, if she could. She checked her watch and found it was only eight p.m. The library didn't close until nine. Should she leave it for tomorrow? But she knew it would run around in her head, and she'd struggle with sleeping now if she didn't deal with it before bed. She decided she would dash off to the library first. She stopped, stared down at her mug of tea, and sighed.

"Leave it until morning, Doreen," she said. "Leave it until morning." But then, come morning, she had to do the gardening at Millicent's. Warring with herself, she let the potential cold case win out. She brought her laptop and tea inside, got her keys, and dashed to the library. She hated the fact she couldn't bring Mugs with her. She couldn't even bring her tea with her. But libraries were like that, where no food or drink was allowed. And no dogs.

Once inside, the librarian watched her suspiciously.

Doreen gave her a bright sunny smile. "Just need to find a new book," she said cheerfully.

"We close in an hour. Remember that," the librarian said.

Doreen thought librarians must have a specific mold— gray hair with a bun on top, stiff backs, and *that* look. The look just nailed it. Like a *What are you up to and don't you dare touch my books* type of a look.

She headed for the microfiche files and researched the parents and the sons and Henrietta and the family in general. She found a couple things she saved in an email to herself, but she couldn't take the time to read them because the library wouldn't be open that long. When she sensed somebody breathing down her neck, she turned to find the librarian. Doreen raised her eyebrows, shuffled so she was a little farther away from her, and asked, "Is there a problem?"

The librarian sniffed. "Maybe," she said. "Maybe."

At that, Doreen frowned. "And what is the problem?"

"I don't want you hounding that poor family."

"What poor family?" Doreen asked in exasperation. "The Darbunkles?"

The librarian gave a louder snort. "No, definitely not them. I meant the Hyacinths."

"The flower?" Doreen asked in confusion.

The librarian glared at her. "Harlowe and Hilly Hyacinth. Henrietta was their daughter."

Doreen stopped. "Henrietta, who was raised by the Darbunkles, was actually Harlowe and Hilly Hyacinth's daughter?" It was a bit of a tongue twister getting out all those *H*s.

The librarian nodded. "Yes."

"Why would that be?"

"The poor couple couldn't handle having a Down's child," the librarian said starkly. "And you can't judge them for that."

Sensing something behind the librarian's abrupt, almost critical manner, Doreen said, "I'm not here to judge anyone. Did they give her up for adoption?"

The librarian shrugged. "There was an informal deal between them, but afterward Hilly wanted to move."

"Okay," Doreen said. "Any idea how far away they moved?"

The librarian shook her head. "No idea. They just didn't want to be around. They were overwrought with guilt, but they also couldn't handle seeing their daughter, so they left in order to make it easier on them all."

"How old was Henrietta when this happened?" Doreen asked, her heart sinking to think of a poor girl ripped away from her parents to live with somebody else and then still see her parents around town. She imagined it would be easier for everybody if her birth family did leave—maybe the little girl would forget faster.

"I think she was young," the librarian said, crossing her arms, her fingers tapping a tempo on her opposite arm. "Maybe three—four, five. I don't remember."

With the names all written down, Doreen said, "Thank you." Then she asked, "Any idea where she is now?"

The librarian looked at her in surprise. "She moved back east."

"Back east?" Doreen questioned.

"Yes, with her adoptive parents." And then she shook her head. "Are you making something out of nothing again?"

Doreen slowly released her pent-up breath. "Who knows?" she said lightly. She logged off the computer, knowing it was already ten to nine. She picked up her stuff and her notepad and said, "Thanks for the information."

The librarian stalked her all the way to the front door. It gave Doreen a bit of a creepy feeling. "Were you related to the families?" she asked lightly, as she turned to open the door.

The librarian shook her head. "But back then the town was much smaller, and everybody looked out for each other."

"Right," Doreen said. She deliberately didn't say what was on her mind, which, considering the number of really old cold cases covering the last twenty or so years that she'd solved over the past many weeks, not a whole lot was supporting the librarian's philosophy. Sounded much more like the town was all about themselves, *not* about helping each other. But, of course, there were always the outliers, and probably a much stronger core who did look after each other.

She gave the librarian a brief smile and said, "Good night." She let the door fall closed behind her and heard the *snick* of the lock as the librarian secured the door for the night.

Back at her vehicle, Doreen hopped in, realizing she hadn't picked up a library book. She wouldn't have minded something new to read. But it wasn't to be. She headed out of the parking lot. With that creepy feeling still with her, she turned toward the window while stopped at the intersection, and looked behind her.

The librarian remained at the door, staring at her.

Chapter 11

Friday Morning ...

FRIDAY MORNING DAWNED bright and clear. Doreen loved mornings, at least normally. Still a little restless after an uneasy night following the librarian's strange behavior, Doreen hopped up, got dressed in her gardening clothes, and went downstairs to get herself something to eat. It would have to be a sandwich because she really didn't want eggs this morning. She ended up making toast with cheese and then more toast with peanut butter.

By the time the animals were fed, and she'd had her fill of coffee, she needed to head over to Mack's mom's place. With her gloves in one hand and a thermos of ice water in the other, she led her crew to Millicent's garden. As she walked into the backyard, she saw Millicent sitting on the veranda. She waved. Doreen smiled and called out, "Good morning."

"Good morning," Millicent said. "Don't you look all bright and chipper and ready to go to work."

Doreen laughed. "We've done such a good job in here, it's just basically maintaining our progress now."

"Isn't that the truth." Millicent looked like she hadn't

had the best night.

As Doreen gathered the wheelbarrow and the compost bins, she asked the older lady, "Not a good night?"

Millicent gave her the briefest of smiles. "Memories," she said. "Tough ones."

Doreen's face thinned. "I hear you there," she said. "Definitely not the easiest things to deal with."

"They get worse as you age," Millicent said. She sat there while Doreen worked. It was all Doreen could do to hold back the questions, and then finally she wiped her brow and asked, "Do you know anything about Henrietta Hyacinth?"

"Oh, Hilly and Harlowe's daughter, yes. That was pretty sad."

"What was sad?" Doreen asked.

"They really couldn't handle it. Their religion was something that didn't allow them to have anything other than a perfectly normal child. And Henrietta was an absolute sweetheart, but obviously she wasn't what they had expected."

"What's religion got to do with it?" Doreen asked.

"They felt God would give them perfect children," Millicent said.

"Maybe God gave them what they needed," Doreen said quietly. "Sounds like Henrietta was a dream child."

"She was the bubbliest, happiest little girl you could ever meet," Millicent said with a smile.

"Did you know the Hyacinth family well?"

"They had a little produce store around the corner here, so I used to go all the time."

Doreen sat back on her haunches. "I didn't know they ran their own business."

"The Hyacinths did until they left. They tried to sell it

but couldn't," she said, "so they just ended up closing it. I believe they moved to Penticton so as not to be so close."

"Penticton? Doesn't it follow downriver, south from Kelowna? I thought it was just about an hour's drive from here?"

Millicent nodded.

"So the birth family remained easily within visiting distance. It's not like they moved across the continent or to a new country. Being so close geographically, I would think they'd want to remain close to their daughter," Doreen said, frowning.

"It was too much pain for them to handle. And I think guilt too. And then possibly remorse."

"And those are all very heavy emotions," Doreen said, as she attacked a set of weeds with particular vengeance.

"Exactly."

"And Henrietta's move to the Darbunkles?" Doreen asked. "How did that work?"

"The family opened their arms to her," Millicent said. "I think Henrietta was doing very well there."

"*Hmmm*, Nan thought something might have been off about the situation."

"Not that I know of. I think everything was fine."

"Until?"

Millicent just looked at her in surprise. "Well, until they moved to the East Coast, of course."

Doreen nodded. "I understand she went missing one time, and the whole town turned out to look for her."

"Yes, we did and it was great when we found her."

"Interesting," Doreen said. "I remember reading something about that."

At that, Millicent laughed. "Oh my, you really do have

79

the bug, don't you?"

"Bug?"

"Curiosity."

"I have to admit, yes," Doreen said with a smile. Mugs barked several times and rolled over onto his back, as if they'd been talking too much, and he hadn't had anywhere near enough attention. She sat her butt on the grass and gave him a moment of just belly scratches. Almost immediately Thaddeus walked over and head-butted her hand.

Millicent laughed. "They're just like children, aren't they?" she said in wonder.

"Yes," Doreen said. "You give one too much attention, and the others all have to be given the same amount." As soon as she could, she got back to work, and, before long, she was done with the weeding. It had only taken forty-five minutes. She grabbed the edger and trimmed up the grass alongside the concrete. It always gave a nice crisp look to the grassy edge.

"I do love it when you do that," Millicent said with a happy sigh. "It all looks so beautiful."

"In another couple weeks, we'll have to come in and clip down some of these early bushes."

"I like to leave them until at least the end of August," Millicent said.

"Good enough," Doreen said cheerfully. "Let's go take a look at the front then." With Millicent moving slowly at her side, they walked out to the front yard, and Goliath led the way this time. He seemed to like Millicent's shrubbery as much as their own as he immediately went into the box-woods to stalk something.

"Goliath," she warned. "We don't go after birds or anything else that's alive."

He just shot her an odd look from underneath the leaves, as if to say, *Who, me?*

She turned that glare on him. "Yes, you."

"What about all those antiques, dear? Did you ever get them all sold?"

Doreen explained the little she knew, with Millicent nodding wisely. "I imagine it'll be months and months yet."

"I'm afraid it will be," Doreen said, "but it is a fascinating thing to have an empty house."

"Is it totally empty?"

"No, not really. I have two pot chairs in the living room, and I have an old bed I've got to get rid of, and I have a bed for myself. Or rather I have the mattresses but no frame."

Millicent smiled. "You'll have a lot of fun refurnishing."

"Maybe," Doreen said. "It hasn't been an issue yet. Honestly, I'm outside so much of the time that it doesn't seem to really matter where I sit in the house. When I'm inside, I'm usually at the kitchen table."

"That'll change as we get closer to winter," Millicent said. "I spend a lot of time in front of my fireplace."

"That sounds lovely," Doreen said. "I don't have one." She'd love to have a gas one, but that would take more money than she had at the moment.

"It'll all work out. I'm sure it'll be great."

"I'm not upset about it," Doreen said. "It's been a long time since I've had an opportunity to do any decorating on my own. It will be fun."

"Set yourself a budget," Millicent said. "Break it down by rooms. Obviously, your living room and bedroom should have the higher part of the budget. Then, whatever it is you want to do, scrounge the second-hand stores. Take your time. Figure out exactly what you want, and don't settle for anything less."

Such vehemence was behind Millicent's tone that Doreen looked at her. "Have you done that a lot?"

"Yes," she said. "When my husband was alive, we had very different opinions on furniture, and what I wanted versus what he wanted were opposites. I always gave in. Since you don't have anybody you have to give in to, I highly suggest you wait and get exactly what you want."

"That's very good advice," Doreen said. "I don't know how long it'll take though, to get something I can afford, because money is tight."

"But, once you get the antiques sold, you'll be fine."

"Quite true, but it still will be months down the road before I see any money from that."

"Mack said something about a deck you wanted to build? And you wanted some cement blocks?" Millicent turned around and led the way to her shed. She opened it up, and Doreen cried out in delight.

"That's exactly what I was looking for," she said. "I was hoping to get enough blocks to build a real deck. I have just this little dinky strip that goes alongside my house."

"No, you need to have a deck where you can actually sit," Millicent said. "And Mack is really good at that stuff. I'm sure he won't mind helping."

"He's offered, but I don't want to take advantage."

"Oh, my dear, take advantage. You should because it's definitely in Mack's nature to help, but he can't help if he's not aware of what's needed."

"There's helping, and then there's being taken advantage of," Doreen argued.

Millicent laughed. "I bet he can't wait to dive into a project like that."

"Well, I hope so," Doreen admitted. She looked around and then casually asked, "Do you know anything about the Kelowna Tool Repair shop?"

"Frank's old place?" Millicent asked.

That was the thing about Kelowna—everybody knew everybody. "I found an ice pick at the mouth of the river and a couple little metal tags that look like they fit onto them."

"Oh, yes, he did that for all the tools he made. He won an award for a set, something like two ice picks or an ice pick and a hatchet. It was just a local thing, but he was proud as punch."

"That sounds interesting. I found just the two little tags but only one weapon ... or one tool," Doreen corrected.

"The other one will be around," Millicent said. "They were always together."

"But they're tools," Doreen said with a laugh. "You don't always need to take both when you go somewhere."

"I believe he ended up selling the award-winning pieces to Ed Burns."

"Did Frank make the metal parts or just the wood?"

"I think he just made the handles," Millicent said. "The metal parts were forged, but I don't know if he had them specially made, or maybe he dabbled in it himself." She gave a shrug. "Who's to say with guys like that?"

"*Guys like that?*" Doreen pounced on the wording, but she didn't want to let Millicent know she was investigating something.

"Just the kind of guys who, you know, thought a lot about what they did," Millicent said.

"The tools must have been nice."

"I did see the set he won the award for. It looked fine. I mean, I didn't think anything was special about it." Then she looked at Doreen and gave her a conspirator's grin. "It's not like I would be out ice fishing. Frank was a big fan of the sport, but, back then, the lake used to freeze over much more so than now."

"That's an interesting thing," Doreen said. "I can't imagine wanting to sit out in the cold to kill some poor fish who is just equally trying to survive in the cold."

Millicent laughed. "I do like the way you look at life."

Doreen smiled as the older lady chuckled. Doreen busily pulled weeds to make sure she gave value for the money she would get for these couple hours, but, at the same time, Millicent was a great source of information. "Interesting how the ice pick ended up at the mouth of the river."

"I know a lot of guys used to go ice fishing, but they wouldn't fish from the mouth of the river because that's often where the ice is thinnest. Yet they used to camp along the sides and have barbecues and stuff like that."

"Oh," Doreen said. "I guess that makes sense."

"Odd that you found it though," Millicent said suddenly.

"Why is that?" Doreen said.

"Because of the cases you solve."

"Surely it was just a coincidence."

Millicent chuckled. "Mack doesn't believe in coincidences," she said. "He says there's a reason specifically why something happens."

"That's possible, but I don't know of any crime, so I don't think it's necessarily connected to an existing cold case."

"Speaking of cold cases, what about that Penny? What's happening to her?"

"I don't know," Doreen said. "Maybe you should ask

Mack that."

"He doesn't like it when I get involved in his cases."

Doreen laughed out loud. "Well, he *really* doesn't like it when I get involved in his cases," she said with a big grin.

"I think he's actually tickled pink," Millicent said. "He said you have a fresh way of looking at things. And look at how much good you've done each time."

"I don't know how much good it is," Doreen said. "I have certainly shaken things up a little though."

"And that's good. Not everybody wants to be stuck in the mud."

"No, but all these people involved in the murders and kidnappings, I'm pretty darn sure they would just as soon I disappeared."

"The victims and their families are the ones who need you to keep doing this," she said seriously, all the laughter falling away from her voice. "Some of these families have suffered a very long time. They certainly don't need to be traumatized more, but, at the same time, by you solving these cases, they get a chance to find closure and hopefully to move on."

"That's how I was hoping people would look at it," Doreen said. "I don't want to be considered a nosy busybody for nothing."

"You keep doing just what you're doing," Millicent said. "Honestly, you're doing a public service. They should reward you."

"I don't know about that," Doreen said. "Speaking of which, Mack said you're okay if I take those cement blocks. Is that true?"

"Oh, my dear, I'd be glad to get rid of them. They're in my way."

"Perfect," Doreen said, "and apparently Mack knows somebody else who has a bunch he wants to get rid of. I think we have enough for the base of my new deck addition."

"Keep asking around," Millicent said as she turned slowly. "I'll head in now, but you keep asking if people have any spare stuff. It's the way we used to do things around here. If you didn't need something, you handed it on to somebody who did."

Doreen smiled, loving that thought, as she watched the older lady go into her house. Doreen was just about done here. She put away what she had pulled out, then whistled for her animals. "Come on, guys. Time to go home."

Chapter 12

Friday Midmorning ...

ONCE BACK HOME, Doreen's mind rolled around with the new information she had gotten from Millicent. Just so much went on with these people. Why would everybody assume the Darbunkle parents had moved back east, and yet the brothers had filed a request that they be declared legally dead? Had that just been the story they told everybody at first to explain their parents' absence? And then it was easy for them to say they passed on later—or went missing later? It would only make sense to somebody in a position to see the legal documents. And that then meant a journalist might have taken an interest in the matter. She hadn't heard anything from Nan recently about Solomon. He was in hospice care. Had he passed away? She sent Nan a text, asking her about him.

Nan responded, **Nope, still hanging on.** And then a **Why?**

No reason, Doreen typed and put her phone down, hoping Nan would let it go. But, of course, Nan was almost as curious as Doreen was, and, when Nan got a hint of something, Nan wouldn't let it go. Doreen was kind of surprised when Nan didn't pressure her more on this topic.

Once inside, Doreen put on coffee and took a look in her fridge. "We'll have to go shopping again," she stated to anyone in the room who cared. Considering the animals all had lots of pet food, she doubted any of them did care.

Mugs, however, shoved his nose into the fridge. Doreen backed him up and said, "Nothing's in there for you."

He barked once, then wagged his tail.

She shook her head. "Seriously, nothing's in here for you." She tried to discourage him by shutting the door to the fridge. But Mugs let out a howl then.

"What's gotten into you, Mugs?" she asked, noting he wasn't stopping his tirade anytime soon.

She opened the refrigerator door again to show him proof of how little was in there. But, when Mugs raced forward, he wouldn't relent until he nosed his way onto a lower shelf. She watched him closely, wondering what he was after. When he retreated from the fridge, he seemed to smile at her, telling her, *I told you so*, then dropped something at her feet.

A twig. From outside. Doreen shook her head, then had to laugh. "I don't remember you playing with a stick outside. And I certainly don't remember you bringing it inside. And how did you get it into my fridge without me noticing?"

Mugs barked, did his little happy dance.

"Yep. You got one over on me, Mugs." Still shaking her head, she reviewed the inside of her fridge again.

They'd eaten all the pork chops the previous night. She had a little cheese left, which Mugs would love also, but she would save that for a sandwich for her. She had more salad greens. After all the work she'd done this morning, she should have something more substantial. She had no cooked veggies or leftovers, and that was just plain sad. As far as she was concerned, Mack should cook five times as much, and then she'd warm it up throughout the week. She didn't know if he'd go for that. Maybe it was harder to cook larger quantities.

As soon as she had her first cup poured from her freshly made coffee, Doreen walked over to her laptop and looked for the various locations where the Darbunkle family had lived here in town. She figured they had to move with each bankruptcy, right? Yet she found only one address. With that information tucked into the back of her mind, she brought up Google and checked for that location. A residence. Wouldn't be an easy walk from Doreen's house; matter of fact, it would have been more of a full afternoon's stretch to get down there. "Too far to walk." Her ankle was back to normal but she didn't want to push that.

Mugs barked at that last word.

She smiled. Better that she drive partway, and then she could walk the rest of the way. She wondered how Fred and Frank would feel about that. Then she looked up the location, where Frank's old shop must have been, and it was about four blocks away from the Darbunkle home.

Mugs barked at her side, jumped up, and put his heavy paws on her legs. She looked down at them and frowned. "We just came home from a walk. Surely you're okay?" But at her repetition of the word "walk," he woofed and started to dance. She groaned. "We don't want to go that far though." Thaddeus, who'd been sleeping on a little window ledge, walked over in front of her to stand on her keyboard and cried, "Thaddeus is here. Thaddeus is here."

She stared at him. "Right, you didn't get to go with me and Mugs earlier, I suppose, is what you'll say. So we all have to go." She looked around for Goliath only to find him underneath her chair, looking up at her. "Fine, road trip it is then, but not until I eat."

At that, she walked back to her nearly empty fridge and sighed. "If I take you all, it means I can't go grocery shopping," she said, "because I can't leave you guys in the vehicle while I go into the store."

But the animals just stared back at her; they didn't give a darn. Such was her life.

She made a tomato sandwich and then added cheese on the side and the fruit she still had left. She could do this research trip with her crew, but then she'd have to come home, lock the animals inside, and go back out to shop for groceries. She didn't have much left for dinner.

As soon as she was done cleaning up after her lunch, she rinsed out her mug, filled up her travel mug with more coffee, and, with the animals in tow, headed to the garage and her car.

With everybody loaded up, she said, "We're only going for a little trip, and that's all."

Mugs, in the front seat, just woofed at her. Goliath, sitting along the back of the headrest behind her shoulder, dug his claws in. Thaddeus, however, was sitting on the gearshift. She looked down at it and sighed. "Thaddeus, you need to move."

He hopped up onto the shoulder brace of the passenger seat and stared at her.

"Fine. Let's go."

As soon as she started going backward, Goliath appeared to not like his perch and jumped down and into the back seat.

She winced as his claws grazed her skin. "You could

learn to move without using your claws," she snapped at him.

He just glared at her, his tail twitching, as if to say it wasn't his fault.

As soon as she headed in the direction she was looking for, she checked the traffic, but it appeared to be calm. It was a Friday morning, and she expected a lot more traffic. But, so far, most of the world had forgotten Kelowna existed. She was happy about that. She knew it got busier in the summertime with the tourists, but, for whatever reason, today was a calmer day.

She should make an attempt to check the beaches too. So far, all she'd done was work on cold cases. She knew very little about the city. Hadn't had a chance to play the tourist herself. As it was now her city, she really did want to get to know the ins and outs of it. As she drove, she realized it led her past Rosemoor. Mugs sat up and barked, his tail wagging. And when they went on past, he looked at her in horror. She smiled and said, "Maybe we'll stop on our way back home."

He woofed several times more, but she kept going. It made sense that the brothers would live close by, with one working as a gardener for Rosemoor. At least Fred didn't have to travel far to go to work.

As Doreen came up to the correct neighborhood, she drove slower. The area was middle-class, nice but older homes. All fairly small, with one or two stories, not the huge monstrosities she saw everywhere else. Small houses and yet the properties themselves appeared to be slightly larger than normal.

She kept heading toward the downtown area just behind the lakefront. She studied the houses as she drove and finally came up to the one she was looking for. At that, she parked on the opposite side of the street against the traffic and studied the house for a long moment. She took several photos, not sure what she was supposed to do with them. Just because these people had disappeared didn't mean anything had happened to them. Or that it happened here. And neither did it mean that just because the brothers inherited the house that they still owned it—or maybe owned it but rented it out to someone else.

If it had been her, she might have wanted to dispose of it quickly. Particularly if she was involved in something nasty to have achieved possession of it. If there was evidence to hide, then it made sense to hang on to the property. If sold, anyone could poke around and find what the brothers didn't want to be found. But then, not everybody looked at it that way. After all, look at Steve's case, and the several bodies found buried on his property.

She looked at this property and wondered. The Darbunkle parents had supposedly disappeared out of the blue. Everybody thought they'd gone back east. Yet the brothers had reported them missing soon afterward. Did the brothers know more than they were letting on?

She frowned at that, but, just then, the front door opened, and the gardener from Rosemoor walked out. He headed to the front of his garden, looked at the roses, lifted a set of clippers off the lawn, and clipped the bushes.

She found that very suspicious too because roses were supposed to be clipped at a different time of year, *not* when they were just about to come into bloom.

She knew a lot about gardening, but she wasn't a pro about every individual plant, so his actions made her stop and consider. If he was taking off some of the blooms, it would leave more life force to go to the emerging blooms. He went through and did just one rosebush, cleaned up his mess, and put all the trimmings into the compost bins that would be picked up during the week. Kelowna had a recycling and compost system where they alternated weeks when each was picked up. She herself had made good use of the compost bins. She didn't cook enough or eat enough to make good use of the recycling yet. Hopefully she would one day.

As she watched, he turned his back on her.

Had he seen her? He had no reason to know her vehicle from anybody else's, but he certainly had a reason to know her. And to dislike her, he did. And, of course, if he noted any of her animals in the vehicle with her, then he'd know for sure who she was. With that thought, she started the engine, pulled forward, and parked down the block, while she continued to watch him. He kept on trimming the roses, completely unconcerned.

Feeling a sigh of relief, she went to the cul-de-sac, turned around, and drove slowly back. As she came up to the house again, he picked up his clippings, dumped them into the compost bin, and then walked around to the back of the house. She studied the front of the home for a long moment, then kept going. She hadn't learned anything.

"Maybe the brothers live there together," she said to Mugs.

He looked at her but didn't answer.

"You'd think one of them would have had a relationship that led to marriage, then gotten their own house and raised a family," she muttered. But then again, maybe they were sharing the residence. Life could get lonely, she imagined.

As she drove on, she searched for where the repair shop

used to be. It took her several tries to come up on the right side of it, but, when she did, she could see it was attached to a garage and a mechanic's shop, but that was a separate building on its own. It was currently a knife-sharpening business. She wondered just how much business they got, but the idea of having smooth, sharp knives was a joy she hadn't experienced for a long time.

One of the things her ex-husband had hated was dull knives. She was totally okay with that to a certain extent, if she didn't have to pay any money, but, if she could get sharp knives, then she would be in heaven. Now she understood more about the beauty and utility of sharp knives as she tried to follow Mack's cooking instructions.

She pulled up in front of the business and hopped out with Mugs. She left the other two in the car, even though they howled at her. She walked up to the knife shop window, looking for prices. The door opened, and a man stepped out. He looked at her in surprise. She smiled and said, "I was just checking out your prices."

He nodded and put his hands on his hips in the open doorway. "It's not too much. If you brought all your kitchen knives in, it probably wouldn't take me twenty minutes to give them a good cleanup."

"How much would that cost?" she asked hesitantly.

He grinned and said, "Fifty bucks?"

She thought about it and then nodded. "That's not too bad. Depends on how many knives I have."

"Best sharpening business in town," he said, pulling a rag from his back pocket.

She looked past him to the mechanic's side of the lot. "Do you own both businesses?"

He nodded. "I sure do. I bought this building a long

time ago."

"So you own the building, you don't just lease the space?"

"Yep. My daddy said never to pay rent to anybody if you didn't have to."

She smiled. "It sounds like your daddy was a good businessman."

"Better than I am, that's for sure," he said, "but I'm getting there."

"I'm sure you are," she said. "This store used to be a tool repair shop, didn't it?"

"A long time ago. Frank leased it for maybe a year, a year and a half, from my dad. Frank did some good work. Won a couple awards locally. Seemed to be quite the character."

"I heard about that. I was perusing some old papers and saw something about him winning an award."

"Yeah, but he didn't have a head for business."

"I guess, in a small town like Kelowna, it's hard to keep a specialized business like that opened."

"If he'd work steady, it wouldn't have been too bad. But, between you and me, he was a bit on the lazy side. Of course Kelowna was a lot smaller back then too."

She nodded in understanding. "And that's death if you have your own business."

"It so is," he said, laughing. "Most people don't realize it. They don't see how much work it is before they get started, and then, when they're involved, they don't want to do what's required to keep it going."

"It's funny because I found one of his tools with a little metal plate on it," she said, "and I was just wondering if there was any record of who bought it, so I could return it to the owner."

"I don't know," he said. "Frank's still around though. You could always ask him."

She nodded and smiled. "If I could ever find him," she said jokingly.

"Him and his brother have a place around the corner," he said. "They inherited it a while back, I think. I'm not exactly sure."

"Maybe," she said, "but, if his brother's the one I know of, he won't like me talking to Frank."

"Frank's usually not too bad, but his brother's a bit argumentative," the guy said with a nod.

"You think?" she said, chuckling.

Mugs was doing a good job of quietly sniffing the front of the building.

"I was figuring out how to return the tool to the rightful owner," she said, "but, if there's no other way than talking to Fred or Frank, that may not work out so well. Thank you for your time."

She headed toward her car, but he said, "Wait. They left behind a bunch of crap."

She turned ever-so-slowly. "So, did you take over directly from his shop?"

She realized he'd gone back inside the store. Thinking it over, the guy had said his pa owned this place. So, even if this guy wasn't ready to run the business yet, his dad had made sure he had people leasing the property, like Frank. She scampered to the doorway and stood. It had a big glass double door facing the mechanic's shop as well as the front door she came through and a door in the back.

"Yeah, a bunch of ledgers and stuff. Let me see if I've still got it because I might have thrown it out."

"If you wouldn't mind," she said anxiously, "I'd really

appreciate it."

But he'd already disappeared into the back. She studied the knives he had with interest. Her ex-husband had been quite a collector. He had all kinds. But most weren't for kitchen use. The chefs had their own sets, as they were just as particular as her ex. Of course she never got her hands on anything but a steak knife, and that was only if she could persuade her ex that she should be allowed to cut her own steak.

In some circles he socialized in, the steak came already presliced in perfect little mouth-size portions, so she could eat delicately without having to strain her wrist. She never quite understood that. Just because you were wealthy didn't make you as weak as a child, but apparently people had very strange attitudes as to what was proper.

She waited in the doorway, not sure who this person was, but he seemed as friendly as could be, and it was nice to meet people willing to go the extra distance. Honestly, she'd met some really nice people in Kelowna.

She waited, studying everything inside, her nose liking the smell of the oil from next door but not too sure about the other odd smells. She could see a car up on the left hoist through the double glass doors. Presumably having a door like that meant he could come and go between the two buildings as needed, like, if he was working on a vehicle and then to help a knife-sharpening customer. Or maybe it was his way of having that aisle of small purchase items as you headed toward the cashiers. She used to call it *the trap* because they used to weave you back and forth in those items, just to taunt you. Maybe *the gauntlet* was a better term, but stores used it to guide you toward all these gift items and candies and things you could pick up on a whim at the last moment.

It was really two businesses under the same roof and run by the same person.

He walked back inside the front room with a plastic bag that looked like it had seen better days. Grease was on the outside, and she didn't know what the other smears were. He handed it to her and said, "This is all there was. I found it the other day when I was reorganizing up there, and I meant to take it to the dump, but if you think it's of any use ..."

"Perfect," she said. She reached out, took the bag from him, and smiled. "I'll go through it and see if I can locate the owner of the tool I found. This is much appreciated."

He gave her a wave. As she walked back to her car, he called out, "Remember now. Fifty bucks. Bring your kitchen knives in."

"Thanks," she said. "I'll remember that." She stowed the bag and its contents in the back seat area of the car, on the floorboard, grateful she had a plastic liner there to keep whatever was on the surface of the bag off her carpets. Once inside, she drove straight home. She couldn't stop the excitement in her gut. It could be absolute garbage in that bag, but it didn't feel like that. Her gut was screaming at her.

Mugs sat on the seat beside her, leaning forward, almost like he had on a racing helmet and was going at max speed.

She just laughed. "You look great."

He woofed, urging her on to get home faster. And she did get home in record time. She didn't understand why it always seemed to take so long to get somewhere, and then the way home was so much faster. Still, when she pulled into the driveway and up into the garage, she laughed with joy. She closed the big garage door and brought the animals out of the vehicle with her and headed into the kitchen. She still had her travel coffee mug and poured that into a ceramic cup, rinsed out her big travel mug, and took the bag and the mug of still-hot coffee outside onto the back veranda.

She set her mug on the little café table, picked up the bag, and slowly tilted it so everything tipped onto the table. There were indeed ledgers. Two. She pulled those out, flipped through them to see they included sales but a bunch of other numbers too. She set them off to the side and went through that bunch of loose paperwork. These appeared to be individual bills of sale. She noted a couple little receipt books too; she frowned when she saw they were only half filled out.

"So, obviously this was just a little hobby business—or he had no head for business or both," she said because surely this wouldn't work for an accountant long-term.

Her ex-husband's accountants had these massive ledgers and online Excel documents and various income statements. In fact, there was no end to that kind of stuff. She saw them often in her ex's hands. But, of course, she'd been deemed as not brainiac enough to understand anything, so not only was paperwork left around because she couldn't possibly understand it but she wasn't given any to read or to try to understand, much less asked for her advice. And she admitted she didn't have any accounting training or business acumen; yet now she was finding out how she was very good at some things—like solving cold cases.

Chapter 13

Friday Late Morning ...

FORCIBLY PUSHING ASIDE the reminder of her ex-husband—or he would be legally her ex-husband, just not soon enough though—Doreen stacked up the financial papers until she had a big thick good inch-and-a-half stack and slowly read through them. Some were advertisements Frank had created to bring in business; others were entrance sheets for competitions. Some were bills of sale, and others were design sketches. She went through them slowly, one by one, but didn't find anything terribly useful. With the original bag in the garbage now because of the icky stuff on the outside, she grabbed a large binder clip, put it around the loose papers, and then sat back down with the ledgers.

As she picked up the first one, only the starting three pages were full of entries. "Not much of a business then, was it?" she said to herself.

But, of course, she had that second ledger book too. Maybe he'd gone through dozens of ledgers, but just these remained. She pulled that one out and checked, and, sure enough, it was full. But that was deceptive, as this ledger was obviously missing pages, like half of them; the other half had been ripped out—as evidenced by the short torn edges still within the binding. She sat with that second one, went through it line by line, finding dates, some names, and corresponding numbers.

Fascinated, she read through as she got to hammer handles, ax handles, digging forks, pitchforks, and … ice picks.

She studied the ice pick entries for a long moment, then hopped up, grabbed her metal tags, and came back outside with them. As she compared the numbers on the two little metal pieces she had with those listed in the ledger, she didn't find a match. So she went farther into the ledger, looking for more entries of ice picks. There weren't any in that ledger, but, in the other ledger, she saw the first page listed one. She checked it and found it was exactly the same number as on one of her tags. Excitement rippled through her as she realized she'd found it.

The price seemed astronomical to her, especially considering this was made and paid for some twenty years ago. The ledger confirmed seventy-four dollars for the handle of an ice pick. She shook her head at that. Maybe other merchandise had been involved with the ice pick that she didn't know about.

The name beside it was indecipherable. She frowned as she tapped the sheet. "I can barely read that." With her pen, she made a faint little notation so she could find it again because so many one-line entries were on the page. Still, that was only one of her metal tags identified. What was the other one from? She really needed to know that. She went down the number column and checked for her second tag ID number against everything in that ledger but couldn't find it.

Groaning, she headed back to the other ledger, the deceptively "full" one and started on the last page. She went back through every one of the numbered entries, checking for the right number. She found her match around the middle of the book, and the notation was "ice pick." She stared at it, frowning. How had she missed it in the first place? *Ice pick* had been handwritten at a tilted angle, and her gaze had flicked right over it.

So her tags belonged to two ice picks. She went back, took another look, and realized they were one matched set by reading the small footnote, designating one of two and then later two of two.

So, was this then his ledger of products he made, or was it sales, she wondered. Why would there be one entry in one ledger and one in the other? Or maybe he made one first and would get to the other one later but just hadn't made it that far. And the two notations were months apart, but twenty years ago, matching the dates on the tags for each tool. She liked that idea of entering each handle as he finished it, particularly if he wasn't the fastest worker.

However, looking closer at these two messy handwritten entries, she found a line was drawn to the margins, from those original creation dates, updating them both to August three, some eighteen years ago. And the seller's name was written in different-colored ink from the ink of the original entries.

Makes sense. Frank created these twenty years ago for himself to enter into a contest, probably leaving the customer name blank in the ledgers. Then Frank won his award nineteen years ago, per that online article, but sold the award-winning set it seems some eighteen years ago.

She studied the name on the second entry and presumed it was the same name as on the other ledger. So both pieces went to the same guy. She took several photographs of the ledger entries, wondering how she could decipher the handwriting or the name. Nan might know. It wasn't late but maybe an inconvenient time for Nan. Doreen picked up her phone and called her grandmother anyway.

"Hello," Nan cried gaily. "I just won at lawn bowling."

Doreen laughed. "Did you win fair and square, or did you cheat?"

Nan laughed. "I didn't win at the game itself," she said, "but I did win in the betting pools."

"Ah, well, that makes more sense," Doreen said with a smile.

"Are you coming down?" Nan asked. "I made zucchini bread this morning. I was just thinking now would be a perfect time to slice some."

"That sounds divine," Doreen said warmly. "I was looking at my fridge, figuring out what I would make for dinner."

"If you come and have enough zucchini bread, you won't have to eat dinner."

"That makes logical sense to me too," Doreen said, laughing. She turned to the animals and said, "I'll come down right now then."

"Perfect. I'll put on the tea and warm up the bread, so don't delay because I'm hungry. Watching that bowling match wore me out."

"Like I said, I'm on the way." Doreen ended the call. She called the animals to her. Once they realized they were going out in the backyard, they raced off ahead of her. So she picked up her pace and raced across the yard, heading toward the creek. She loved hitting the creek on a daily basis because the water always changed—the levels rose and fell, according to the whims of Mother Nature. Logically she knew it had to do with the snowfall melting up in the mountains and how fast it trickled down, plus the surrounding weather had an impact too. She'd learned a ton about water levels since she'd arrived here. Even the cold cases themselves had demanded she research and learn about these local weather events. It truly was a fascinating field.

The water still looked to be at a reasonable level—not scary high. She wondered if the fact they were in more of a drought season would have an effect on how high it rose. It hadn't been much of a winter either. So the snowpack, although sitting at about 80 percent of normal, wasn't racing down toward her. Still no water came out of her sump-pump hoses either, which she'd take as a great sign.

Skipping along with the ledgers under her arm and the animals beside her, Doreen nearly ran down toward Nan's place, needing an outlet for all her pent-up energy. It made no sense because truly she'd been gardening today, and then had gone out for the drive. Now she was onto a whole new mystery, and she had to admit that was the best part of the day. Of course this was more of a curiosity, not a murder mystery. At least not yet.

Laughing at herself and her animals, she came tearing around the corner of the last residential privacy fence, almost hitting a small vehicle trying to park for a walk on the river.

She called out, "Sorry," as she waved and dashed past, heading toward Rosemoor Manor. The thought of fresh zucchini bread spurred her on like nothing else. She'd had a sandwich, but it wasn't as good as homemade fresh bread. As she got to the stepping stones, she saw the gardener. He glared at her.

She called out, "Hi there, Fred. How's Frank doing?"

The glare on his face turned to puzzlement. She gave

him a friendly wave and dashed across the flagstones before he had a chance to remember she was the one who insisted on visiting Nan with her animals and had to cut through the grass to do that.

Once she was on the little patio, she felt like she was in Nan's corner of the world, and Nan would tolerate no one hurting her family—feathered, furred, or otherwise. At her arrival, Nan came out with a plate of freshly sliced zucchini bread that Doreen could see was still warm. She hugged her grandmother and exclaimed, "I could smell it around the corner."

Nan beamed. "I'm so glad to hear that because I still have more zucchini. I'm hoping you'll take a bunch of this home. I did promise you a full loaf. And I made three."

"I can't imagine I wouldn't want to." Doreen's mouth watered as she gazed on the thick slabs in front of her, while Nan darted inside.

"And here's the tea," Nan said, as she came out a second time with the pot in her hand. She also had something in her other hand. As Doreen watched, Nan gave each of the three animals a little treat.

Doreen chuckled. "You are spoiling them. You know that?"

"Better to spoil them while they're still around," Nan said, "because you can't change things that have already happened, and one day these three pets of yours will all disappear, just like I will."

For whatever reason, the way she worded it struck a harsh chord in Doreen. She stared at Nan. "Please don't let that be anytime soon," she cried out. "I'm not ready for that."

Nan looked at her with understanding. "Bless you, dear.

I'm not planning on it," she said, "but you know we keep losing residents here. For example, Ruby—who I just had tea with yesterday—she woke up dead this morning."

"*Woke up dead?*" Doreen asked delicately.

"It's what I call it, as in, she went to bed, happy as a lark last night, and never woke up this morning."

"It's not a bad way to state it," Doreen said. "It just sounded odd."

"At my age, I get to be odd," Nan said, chuckling, "because either it's that or I might as well be dead. If we follow all the conformity, we'd be doing nothing but giving in to everybody else's expectations. Don't ever do that—be you. Find the inner you that's special and just let that part of you shine."

Doreen grinned. "I do love to hear you talk like that," she said.

"Well then, you're the only one," Nan said as she settled into her chair. She lifted her plate and reached for a big slab of zucchini bread. "Now, I'll enjoy this. That lawn bowling today took a lot out of me."

"How many times have you played?"

"Oh, dozens," she said with an airy wave of her hand. "Yesterday Ruby did too. Well, Ruby'll be pushing up grass in a few days."

Doreen didn't know what to say. Nan was definitely in an odd mood, but then losing a friend, just one of many in a place like this, was a good enough reason. Doreen stayed quiet, offering as much silent support as she could as she tucked into the zucchini bread. At her first bite, she moaned. "Did you melt butter over this as soon as it came out?"

"Of course I did and again when reheating it," Nan said with a snicker. "No need to save on the fat with you, girl.

Slice it when it comes out, butter it, and then the butter just melts right into it." She nudged the honey pot toward Doreen. "If you haven't tried it with honey, you should."

"But it's great this way," Doreen argued.

"Sure it is," Nan said. "It's also great with honey."

"Maybe on a second piece," Doreen said. She lifted her tea, took a sip, and smiled.

Nan gave her a few moments, but it was obvious she was curious about the bag at Doreen's side. "What are those?"

Doreen smiled. "I just wondered if you were any good at reading bad handwriting."

"Of course I am." Nan sat up straight. "I have a knack for reading bad handwriting."

"These are handwritten names." She finished her piece of zucchini bread, moved her plate off to the side, and brought out the two ledgers. She flipped through the pages to the first entry she wanted Nan to see and then held it up and tapped the line she was looking at. "Do you know that name?"

Nan reached for the book, looked at it, and frowned. "Oh my, that's not so easy, is it?"

"No," Doreen said with a laugh. "I struggled with it myself. I think this is the same name," she said, pulling out the other book and flipping to the right page. There was a slight difference in the penmanship.

Nan looked at it and nodded. "Well, that makes it easier."

"It does?"

"Yes. That's *Ed*. Ed Burns," she said.

"You know Ed Burns? Millicent mentioned something about him earlier."

Nan held on to the ledgers, like she had no intention of

handing them back. "Maybe," she said, her eyes twinkling. "What's this all about?"

"Thaddeus here," Doreen began, pointing at the bird, and then Thaddeus squawked and ruffled his feathers at hearing his name, "found these little silver plates I showed you earlier, and he wanted to go back to that location. So we did," Doreen said. "And I found the tool that went with one of the tags. The ice pick—for ice fishing—was almost completely buried in the dirt and rocks and sand, plus completely tangled up in the ivy, but we found it."

"And you traced them back to the store where these ledgers were?" Nan asked in astonishment.

Doreen nodded. "I did." And then she told the story of the knife-sharpening place.

"Fifty dollars to sharpen the kitchen knives?" Nan said, as she swiveled her head to look in the direction where her small kitchen was. "That seems like not a bad deal, doesn't it?"

At that, Doreen had to laugh. Trust Nan to go off on a tangent when they were really talking about the ownership of these tools. "Exactly," she said. "I just haven't decided if that's what I'll do yet."

"What you mean is, you haven't decided if you should spend the fifty dollars yet," Nan said as she looked at Doreen. "And I understand where you're coming from. But there's nothing quite so frustrating as having dull knives in the kitchen."

"Well, we can get yours done," Doreen said. "I'm happy to drive you down there."

"Let me think about it," Nan said. She tapped the ledger. "Well, Ed Burns was an interesting character."

"Was?"

"Oh my, yes, he's been gone, maybe ten years by now."

Doreen's shoulders sagged. She realized that, after all her work to find the owner of the ice pick, she'd ended up with somebody who wasn't even living now. "Okay," she said encouragingly. "What can you tell me about him?"

"He was a great proponent of the local arts," Nan said. "When he passed away, his son inherited everything. And my, that was a stink."

"Why is that?"

"Because he had two daughters as well. But Ed himself left everything to his son."

"Why would he do that?" Doreen asked, affronted for the girls' sakes.

"That's the problem. You see? Nobody really understood anything about it, and the girls didn't appear to have a leg to stand on legally, so the brother ended up with everything."

"Including these tools. I wonder …"

"Maybe," Nan said. "The thing is, I can see Ed buying these tools and putting them on the wall somewhere. How they got from the wall to that Greenway path, I have no idea."

"Interesting, isn't it?"

"How close to a fence was it?"

"Right over the edge," Doreen said, "as if somebody stood on the side and dropped it over the fence, right out in the public area."

"But how many people walk there, really?" Nan asked, raising her eyebrows. "When you think about it, someone may have tried to throw them over the fence, thinking they were getting rid of them."

"Possibly, but I only found one," Doreen said. "That's half the mystery. I've got both of the metal pieces that go on them, and the numbers match the ledgers and designated both as ice picks. Just no sign of the other ice pick."

"Interesting," Nan said with a smile, closing the ledgers and handing them back. "I'm sure you will get to the bottom of this mystery in no time."

"Maybe," Doreen said. "At least Mack should be happier with me."

"Don't you worry about Mack. As soon as you discuss it with him, he'll get hooked on it too."

Doreen smiled because she knew Mack already was. Speaking of which, she needed to contact him and see if he'd found anything in his files.

She was about to say goodbye to Nan when she put another big slab of zucchini bread on top of Doreen's plate. "Oh, Nan," Doreen said. She really wanted it. "But ..."

"Have this one with honey," Nan said. "You'll be glad you did."

"Okay," Doreen said, giving in way too easily. She slathered on honey and cut it into four pieces, then took a bite. "Wow," she said. She picked up the honey jar, but she found no label on it.

"Oh, that's from a friend of mine," Nan said. "They have their own bees and harvest their own honey locally."

"Wow," Doreen said, "it's delicious."

"Take it home with you," Nan said. "I have another jar in the pantry." She hopped up, walked into the kitchen, and returned with a jar that had a fancy little label on the top. "Take that one home. I have this one here."

Delighted to follow those instructions, Doreen put the lid on the jar, wiped the outside free of any stickiness, and put it in her pocket. Just then, Nan came back out with almost a full loaf of zucchini bread wrapped in tinfoil and placed it beside Doreen. "Like I said, you won't have to make dinner now."

"It's hardly the most nutritious dinner," Doreen joked.

Nan waved her hand. "Don't worry about it. We're here to live, not just to live badly."

"It's hardly badly," Doreen said in protest.

"Sure, but come on. Let's be reasonable. If you can eat cake for dinner, eat cake and enjoy it and don't feel guilty about it."

Laughing at how incorrigible her grandmother was, Doreen polished off the honey-topped slice of zucchini bread, picked up the tinfoil-wrapped package, and grabbed her ledgers. She smiled and said, "Now I'll head home. I need to walk to wear off all those extra calories."

"If you do that," Nan said, "you'll need more for dinner just to add calories back onto your skinny frame."

"I'm not skinny," Doreen said. "I'm eating lots more."

"And that's a good thing," Nan said. "I can't stand to see you so scrawny."

"I'm fine." Doreen gave Nan a big kiss and said, "Particularly with you feeding me like this."

"How did you do with those veggies?" Nan asked.

"Mack cooked pork chops for me last night," Doreen said, "so the zucchini are all gone."

Nan hopped up yet once more and said, "Well then, hang on," and she raced inside. She came back out with a wicker basket full of vegetables. "This was delivered to me this morning. I can't even begin to eat it all." She quickly rummaged through it, split it into two piles, and then went back inside to get a plastic bag. She packed up baby carrots, a couple more tomatoes, a big bell pepper, some lettuce, and green beans, and she handed it to Doreen. "Most of that you can even eat raw. No cooking required."

At that, Doreen grinned. "What would I do without you?"

"I don't know," Nan said, "but hopefully you'd still eat."

Chapter 14

Friday Late Afternoon ...

S TILL CHUCKLING AT her grandmother, Doreen walked toward the creek with her goodies. "Good thing Nan is feeding us," she said. "Once I realized it could be months and months before I get any of that auction money from Nan's antiques, I hesitated to shop for groceries anymore."

As she walked back toward the property near the river's mouth—where the ice-fishing pick had been unearthed—she looked around and smiled. She could see the ivy on the other side of the privacy fence where she'd found the ice pick. She guessed that probably at least a ten-year growth took place to completely fill the fence. She stopped and wondered just who lived on the other side of the fence. She frowned as she tried to count the number of houses down from the lake itself so she could look on Google Maps and then potentially search BC Assessment and get a house address, but ultimately it would take Mack to figure out who lived here now, or back a decade or so ago. And, of course, just because somebody lived there at any time didn't mean they had anything to do with the ice pick found nearby.

As she walked back to her house and put her precious

food cargo on the kitchen table, her phone rang. She pulled it out and smiled. "Hi, Mack. I was just thinking about calling you."

"So, either you want something or you're in trouble," he said.

She frowned at her phone. "Or maybe I just wanted to offer you some more fresh veggies," she snapped.

"Maybe," he said, "but not likely. You need to be eating them yourself."

"I just came back from Nan's, and she sent me home with a pepper and a couple tomatoes, fresh green beans and more lettuce, so I can make a big salad for dinner if I'm hungry. I just finished some excellent zucchini bread," she said with a happy sigh.

"Darn," Mack said in an envious voice. "Now you've got my mouth salivating."

"Ha," she said, "then I won't tell you that Nan sent me home with the bulk of a whole loaf too."

"Now that's just cruel," he whined.

"Did you have a reason for calling me?" she said cheekily. "Maybe I'll put on the teakettle and sit down and have yet another slice."

"You're really being mean now," he said.

She laughed. "Maybe, but I did figure out who owned the ice pick."

First came silence on the other end, then Mack said, "You did?"

"I did," she said proudly. She proceeded to explain everything she'd found out so far.

"That's not bad for an afternoon's work," Mack said.

"Right now, of course, I'd like to figure out who lives in the house next to where I found the ice pick, which is something you could look up for me. And potentially I need to find Ed Burns's heir and see how that ice pick went from Ed's private collection to outside the fence of this particular property at the river's mouth."

"So, do you have a number on that second tin piece?" Mack asked. An odd note was in his voice.

"What do you mean? The metal piece I don't have a tool for?"

"Yes," he said. "What's the number on it?"

She ran it off for him.

"Interesting," he said. "It's mentioned in one of my cases."

"This actual tool?"

"No, somebody said something—but never mind. I might just stop by and have a slice of that zucchini bread," he said, "and take a picture of your ledgers."

Immediately her antennae went up. "So you do think I'm onto something?"

"Well, you're onto something," he said in a dismissive manner. "But, of course, it's probably nothing important."

"Now *that's* cruel," she complained. "I could be onto something really good."

He chuckled.

"Did you ever find out what happened to the parents?"

"The Darbunkles?" he said. "They were declared dead seven years after they were filed as missing persons."

"So they went missing after they moved back east?"

"Who told you that?"

"Wendy and Nan. Plus Millicent and the librarian. It's the popular rumor that the parents moved back east, probably with Henrietta," she said. "And did you also know Henrietta was adopted? And that her birth family lived in

Kelowna too, and then they moved south into the Penticton area after they gave her up at a very young age?"

Again Mack went silent on the other end before swearing lightly.

"You probably shouldn't swear," she corrected.

He chuckled. "Hey, I'm comfortable with the cuss words I use. And I hope I'm not making you feel uncomfortable when I say them. But you're the one figuring out if you could get these words out of your mouth," he said. "Have you been practicing?"

"Well, … you know I really don't like to even think about my former husband or my life with him. That's my past, and it's best for it to stay back there. But I did come to realize, about the time I was moving here, how my ex had me under such tight controls—as to what I wore, what I weighed, what I could eat, what I could say when allowed to speak. It's another form of abuse—verbal abuse, an abuse of my personal rights and freedoms.

"So, once I broke away from him, physically at first and then mentally, later, I did feel a certain very grand freedom in finding out who I was in reality, in being the real me, even able to say what I thought, with a curse word or two thrown in for added emphasis if needed. Granted I have my own self-imposed limits on that. I got as far as *fudge* and *fenster* and *fudgy winkles*," she said, "but I can't get that *F* word out."

At that, Mack laughed. "I really like *fudgy winkles*. The next time you get angry, upset, or under attack, I suggest you scream at the top of your lungs, 'Fudgy winkles.'"

Doreen glared into her phone. "Here you are making fun of me again, even though I would share my zucchini bread with you."

"I'll be there in ten," he said. "Don't eat it all." And he hung up on her.

Doreen smiled, looked down at the critter collection around her, and said, "Guess what, guys? Mack is coming."

Mugs woofed and woofed and turned around in circles at her feet. She smiled and walked into the garage, wondering if she could clean out some extra stuff before he got here. Just because she could park her vehicle in the garage didn't mean a ton of room had been cleared for it. She had a few more things to take down to Wendy's and some recycling that maybe should go directly to charity. She checked her watch but there wasn't enough time now. "Later," she promised herself. "I'll take more stuff to the charity later."

She had almost all the house cleaned up and clutter-free, except for the last bits in her bedroom, and that was such a good feeling. She'd cleaned up all this space on both floors of her house and had solved the latest cold case, creating a void in her life. How perfect that another mystery had dropped in to fill it right away. As far as she was concerned, that was perfect timing.

Then Mack called again. "Rain check," was all he said.

Chapter 15

Saturday Morning ...

DOREEN WOKE UP Saturday morning with a happy smile on her face and her phone buzzing beside her head. She rolled over, snagged it up, and hit Talk. "Mack, do you know what time it is?" she groaned.

Mack's silence came first on the other end, then he said, "Yeah, it's nine in the morning."

Doreen stared at her phone in shock. "Seriously?"

"Yeah," he said. "Are you still in bed?"

She rubbed her face and murmured, "I just woke up."

"Interesting," he said, his tone buoyantly cheerful.

"Why are you so happy?" she asked.

"I'll be there in fifteen for coffee," he said. "I'll tell you then." And he hung up.

She stared again at her phone, disgruntled. "And what if I didn't want to get out of bed?" she snapped in response. "What if I didn't want to get dressed today? What if I planned to have a pajama day and laze around the house just because I can?"

The trouble was, Mack wouldn't have called without a reason. And, for that alone, her curiosity got the better of her. She hopped out of bed, quickly showered, shampooed her hair, and washed the rest of her. By the time she was out, dried, and dressed, she could hear a vehicle pulling up.

She groaned. "We don't even have coffee on," she muttered. But Mugs was already ahead of her, barking joyously as he raced to the front door. "You're such a traitor," she muttered, as she dashed past him to measure the coffee. When Mack didn't knock right away, and she had time to put the coffee on and to feed her crew, she stopped and wondered if it was even him. She walked to the front door, opened it to find Mack's truck in her driveway, where he was unloading cement blocks. She stared at him in shock and then delight. "Are those for my deck?"

He tossed her a grin. "About time you got your sorry butt out of bed."

She snorted at that. "If you hadn't called me," she said, "I could have been in dreamland for at least another hour."

"You're a lazy slug," he said with a smirk. "Come and give me a hand."

She slipped on her sandals and walked down the porch steps. "How many are there?"

"This is all of them," Mack said. "I loaded mine, then stopped by my buddy's place this morning and picked them all up from him. And afterward went to my mom's and grabbed those."

Doreen grinned. "Wow, this is super." As she watched, Mack picked up two, put them in her wheelbarrow, put a third one in, and then rolled the wheelbarrow across the front lawn around to the side of the house. She stared at the deep indentations in the grass and groaned, but it wasn't the time to argue with his process. Free cement blocks for her new deck addition were free cement blocks. The grass would stand up again on another day.

By the time Mack had those unloaded, Doreen had carried a couple by herself, until he just laughed and took them from her hands. "Don't even bother." With them all lined up alongside her house where the new deck addition would be, Doreen felt mighty cheerful indeed. Then she followed Mack to his truck and saw something else in the bed. "What are those?" she asked, staring at the huge wooden beams traversing the back of the truck.

"The same buddy who had the leftover cement blocks had four of these posts. They're exactly what we need for the deck expansion, although I don't know if they're long enough."

He hefted one up, hoisted it onto his shoulder, and walked around to the side of her house. She raced behind him. "What did it cost you?"

"He was happy to get them hauled away," Mack said. "So now we've got four posts toward your deck addition."

"How many do we need?" She kept pestering him with more questions, not even waiting for him to answer. He was patient though, and finally he turned to her and said, "Remember your drawing? The list? Maybe go get it and take a look at your parts list."

She shook her head and said, "I don't know why I didn't think of that."

"Lack of caffeine?" he asked with a raised eyebrow.

She smiled and went inside the kitchen, where she grabbed her sketches and the parts list she'd typed up and printed off. "We still need at least six more of those, depending on what length they are."

"Yep," Mack said. "I did post a notice to the guys in the division to see if anybody had any spare parts we could use for the deck. A couple guys said they'd take a look this weekend and get back to me."

"Do you think they'd give the parts to us?" Doreen asked. "Because, wow, that would be huge."

"The beams are a big part of the remodeling cost, but decking boards and really the railing will kill you for most of the cost."

She nodded, thinking about it. "Do we need railings?"

"Depends on how high we go. To meet the approval of the city, if it's only two steps, nope, we don't, which is something we were looking at."

"And if we did steps all the way around?" she said. "Giving us all lots of places to sit …?"

"But that would up the cost too. Remember?"

Doreen looked back down at her papers and nodded. "It's easy to forget just how much some of this adds up to."

"Also, what will you do about weed control for under the deck? Have you got a way past that?"

"I'm not sure. I never really contemplated that. It seems a little foolish to think the landscape cloth would be enough."

"It probably would be if you got the heavy-duty stuff, and you might also want to consider buying a couple cheap tarps and putting rocks down underneath the deck. It would take a long time without sun exposure for the tarps to break down enough for weeds to pop through."

Doreen grinned. "I like that idea." And then she stopped and asked, "How cheap?"

Mack's booming laughter filled the backyard, and she could almost hear the neighbors closing doors and windows in disgust. Everybody here had no sense of appreciation for noise. But, then again, she'd caused more than a few disturbances since she'd arrived. In fact, Richard, that poor neighbor of hers—although he owed her a "thank you" for solving that pink-fuzzy-handcuffs problem that could have ended up backfiring on him—had so far stayed mum since that case. Those handcuffs weren't hers and were found in his garden. She'd found them, sure, but they were on his property. So, as far as she was concerned, they were *his*. She chuckled at that thought and returned to the deck project. "I guess another big cost is all the hardware?"

"Yep. That'll run you up quite a bit because you want it stable. So these beams are put into big brackets, and then we need the right decking screws to go on the top." He looked at her. "I don't suppose you want to pay for all-weather decking you never have to replace, do you?"

"I'd love to," Doreen said cautiously, "but somehow I suspect that's very expensive."

"Yep, it is, but just think. You never have to do any maintenance on it and never have to replace it."

"Is it slippery though?"

Mack looked at her in surprise. "That's a good question. I don't know."

"I wouldn't want anything slippery. I do like to have Nan around—and of course the animals and myself."

He nodded thoughtfully. "That's something to check into. And railings? Maybe with Nan coming over, at least add railings on one side?"

"I don't think she has any trouble with stairs."

"Not at the moment anyway. Something to consider for the future."

"Maybe even just a little railing somewhere."

"Yep, we can look at that too."

Doreen nodded, and then hesitatingly she said, "You

keep saying *we* ...”

He looked at her in surprise. “I said I’d give you a hand.”

“Yeah, but, so far, it sounds very much like you’ll be doing it all because I don’t know what I’m doing.”

He flashed that teasing grin at her. “Yeah, I probably will be. And it could take a few weeks, depending on the cases I’m working on,” he cautioned.

“I guess I just need to ask.” And then she let her voice trail off.

He glared at her. “You better not be asking anything that’ll piss me right off.”

She gave him a wide-eyed innocent look. “How will I know what’ll piss you right off if I don’t ask?”

He lifted a finger and shook it at her. “Do not—do not ask me about payment.”

Her smile when it dawned was as warm and as heart-warming as she could possibly have made it, and yet it came from the heart. “Thank you for that,” she said sincerely.

“But you will be responsible for keeping the coffee flowing.”

She rolled her eyes. “Ugh, that’s probably more expensive than paying you wages.”

He grinned. “Hey, at least I didn’t ask for beer, and I didn’t ask for meals.”

“Which is probably something we should consider because you certainly deserve a few meals out of this, and I imagine sitting down after working on the deck is almost perfect with a beer.”

Doreen walked inside and poured coffee, and, when she brought it out and handed it to him, she realized he was done, laying the last beam with her other decking materials in her backyard. "So we have to wait until Monday's email replies to figure out what else we might need, is that it?"

Mack accepted the coffee, gave his shirt a little shake from the wood he'd been carrying, and said, "With any luck, we can get some stuff. We won't likely get enough to do the whole job, but anything will help."

Doreen motioned at the big blocks of wood. "Particularly when it's stuff that's not terribly visible."

"Exactly. It's the deck and the stringers that are seen by all."

"What are stringers?" Doreen asked, before thinking how this set her up to be teased again. "And don't laugh at me."

Mack smiled, taking a moment to rein in his words. "The back plates to the steps themselves. The vertical pieces that join the horizontal deck to the horizontal risers." When she nodded, he added, "We could probably make stringers if you want steps all the way around. That's only expensive if we buy them. The wood itself can be ugly, but we'll see what we come up with by scrounging for leftovers with those Monday replies."

She smiled at that. "So, did you look up those cases on the missing parents? You did cancel on me yesterday."

He gave her a dry look. "I got a call and had to leave."

"I know you came here to drop all this off, and I am hugely thankful," she said, "but I'm also hoping you might have found a little information."

"You first," Mack said. She tried to give him an innocent look, but he laughed at her. "I know you've been up to no good. So tell me what you found."

Doreen sighed and sat down at the little table on her veranda. "Bits and pieces, that's all, and I've already told you what I know. I also really want to know who lived at the house where I found the ice pick."

"The house has changed hands four times in the last two decades, going back to the oldest dates in question regarding the Darbunkles—based on the oldest of those two tags you found," Mack said. "However, considering it probably didn't take twenty years for the weather and the ivy to have buried the ice pick—you said you had to dig up almost all of the tool—then the nearest house was probably owned by an old lady, Emma Bennett."

"Oh, interesting. Did she pass away?"

Mack shook his head, gave her a rueful look, and said, "She's in Rosemoor."

Doreen grinned wide. She pulled out her phone and texted Nan. **Do you know an Emma Bennett?**

Yes. Why?

She probably owned the property where the ice pick was found, at the estimated time of its disposal.

Several question marks crossed her screen initially, and then Nan added, **I'll go talk to her.**

Doreen laughed, tossed her phone on the veranda table, and said, "Nan's on it."

"You two are getting to be quite the pair."

"I know. Nan lives near a trove of interesting people with decades of Kelowna info at their fingertips."

"And sometimes those people don't always remember things correctly," Mack warned.

"Nope, they don't always. And sometimes they remember better than we expect. Particularly from decades ago. I don't understand how that works."

"I'm sure the neuroscientists have a heyday with it."

"So much money is being funneled into research on dementia," Doreen said, "and I can see why. It's very distressing when you have to deal with it. I'm a bit concerned about Nan at times."

"Yes, it's so hard on the other family members." Mack agreed, a soft smile on his face. "As far as the case of the missing Darbunkle parents, they did apparently disappear. First a lot of rumors swirled around, and, yes, some about them potentially going 'back east' are noted in our files, but the fact of the matter is, the brothers don't know what happened. The parents were last seen at some point, reported as missing, then declared dead seven years and four months later. The meager estate did pass down to the sons, which they shared equally."

"Meaning, the house basically, right?" she asked. "Because of the 'meager estate' that you just mentioned."

Mack nodded. "Correct."

"What about Henrietta?"

"That's where our file gets even thinner," he said, his tone dark. "She went missing, supposedly around the same time as her parents, so originally it was presumed she went back east with them. However, when the brothers filed for a declaration of death on their parents, they did so for Henrietta too. She was presumed dead along with the adults, but it remains a mystery what happened to them."

"Her disappearance is pretty sketchy," Doreen said, "and how very convenient that she wasn't part of the inheritance for the sons."

"She wouldn't likely have received it directly anyway—it would have gone into her long-term care. Maybe via a trust with an attorney or a banker overseeing it. However, the estate was meager, so maybe no money was there to fund Henrietta's future care."

"Same diff but still so sad for Henrietta. And what about her real parents?"

"I had to look that up separately," he said. "I didn't realize she was adopted. And technically it wasn't a formal adoption, but the two couples had a verbal agreement between themselves."

"Apparently the biological family moved away. The man's name was unique—Hilly."

"I've heard that a couple times now."

"It's still fascinating how this all works. But the thing is, I've got an ice pick, a couple little metal tags that indicate there should have been two picks, and I have a missing couple and a missing girl."

"Whoa, whoa, whoa," Mack said, holding up his hands, as if to break her train of thought. "You have absolutely no connection between those two events."

She stared at him in surprise. "Of course we do," she said. "A huge connection."

He stared at her. "And what's this *huge* connection?"

She gave him a beaming smile and said, "Me and Mugs and Goliath and Thaddeus."

Mack's shoulders sagged, and he looked so deflated that she had to burst out laughing. "I'm only half-joking, you know?"

"And I'm only half upset about it," he said, "because it *is* a connection. One I didn't really want to think about."

"I could help. ... Haven't you got enough work to do for a while?" she asked.

"How about *too much* to do?" he grumbled. "Steve is still hollering."

"His problem, not mine. He shouldn't have attacked me. For that matter, neither should have Mary or Penny or

Dean." The names rolled off her tongue of some of the people who had attacked her from her work on related cold cases.

"In your most recent cold case, we're dealing with a wife—who's besotted with Dean, her second husband—and she doesn't want to believe he killed her first husband or a *tramp* who used to work the streets."

"Manny deserves as much care and attention as anybody," Doreen said quietly. "Her circumstances weren't easy. She did the best she could."

Mack's smile was gentle as he said, "Believe me. I get where you're coming from. I totally agree with you. But my earlier statement? That was just recapping the killer's attitude. Or rather, the wife of the killer's attitude."

She nodded. "And such a wrong way to look at life, judging people like that."

"We have a lot of cases we're working on, and, of course, Crystal's case is ongoing too," he said. "It alone could take us years to get to the end of that, as we're still searching for more possible missing children. We've got districts all around the province looking into their missing kids too."

"And to think those brothers were just trying to save the children from abusive home environments."

"Which gives us hope that maybe some of them are still alive."

"As for Crystal, I don't think the brothers ever wanted to harm her. As long as they kept Crystal and maybe these other kids away from Crystal's very disturbed stepmom Mary and others like her, then there's a good chance those other missing children are all doing just fine."

He nodded, then muttered, "The captain is considering setting up a task force for you."

She stared at him. "For me?"

"For the cases you keep dumping in our lap. We have a lot of other pending cases too, you know?" Mack said in a wry tone. "We have all manner of break-ins, muggings, car thefts. It's just you seem to have this capacity to dive in for some of the deeper, darker, uglier ones. And the captain wondered about getting a task force together to handle your cases alone."

Something inside her warmed. "You know something? I really like that idea."

"I figured you would," he said. "At least you'd know we'd be giving those cases all the attention we could."

"But more than that," she said, "I'd have somebody to go to when I came up with more information." And she beamed at him.

"I don't think that's the way the captain meant it."

"But you know that's how I'll treat it. I get that you need to put a specialized team on this cold-case area because we've unearthed a lot of cases that have very far-reaching threads, each needing to be tracked down," she said in all seriousness. "But still, as you know, I'll always be working on a new case and needing more information." She smiled and pointed back to the front closet, holding all the journalist's investigative files. "Think of all of Solomon's cases that need further attention."

"You're still a civilian," Mack warned. "It's not like the captain can release information to you without getting himself into legal hot water."

Doreen thought about that and nodded. "So, as long as you guys keep telling me what I can legally have, we could work up a great partnership." She could feel her enthusiasm rising as she thought about it.

Mack shook his head and said, "I don't like that look on your face."

"That's okay," she beamed. "I think we have the start of a perfect friendship."

"I thought we were already friends," he said suspiciously.

"Start of a great partnership?"

"Pretty damn sure the captain isn't thinking you'll be any cop's partner," he said, laughing.

"Fine," she said. "How about an amicable working relationship? Mutual info-sharing?"

"I still think you're pushing it. We'll be handling the cases which you've brought to our attention with new evidence. If you go off and bring more cases to our attention, obviously we'll look at them too, but that doesn't mean we'll help you get into trouble."

"No," she said, "I appear to do that all by myself."

At that, he burst into a fit of laughter.

Chapter 16

Saturday Midmorning ...

DOREEN CHUCKLED. "I can't see them letting me into their echelons," she stated.

"Don't take it the wrong way," Mack said. "We are grateful that you find evidence and don't treat it like junk, which most of the public would probably do. So we really do appreciate you bringing all these cases to light."

"Well, some of you do," she said with a smile, "but I'm not doing it for you guys. I'm doing it for the families."

"And that's the true reason to do it," he said, "that and for justice in the name of the victims."

Her laughter waned. "So many victims," she said quietly. "Things that you don't even realize would ever lead to murder. People you didn't even know were dead and gone, yet labeled as missing."

He nodded. "The thing about police work is, you never know what you'll find, once you start turning over rocks. All kinds of nastiness crawls out from underneath."

Doreen nodded. "So, are we listing that Darbunkle couple as open cases now?"

"They're technically revived cold cases, yes. The declarations of death didn't resolve the missing persons' reports but neither did the assumption of death provide further evidence to support an investigation. Not that we were aware of."

"Not much of a foofaraw was made at the time, was there?"

Mack shook his head. "The parents were listed as missing—both here and back east, to cover their last known addresses—and a parallel investigation was done, but our guys found the couple's vehicle was at home, and it seemed just as if they walked away. Their bank accounts were never touched, neither were they working any longer. They just upped and disappeared. It didn't take long for all the leads to run out and for the case to go cold on our end. And the back east cops had no more luck than we did either."

"And, of course, with the brothers not doing much to bring the case to the media to keep it alive, it died a fairly quick and inevitable death, didn't it?"

"Yes, but, according to our file, the brothers were looked into pretty heavily. I only got a recap on the back east file, but it was light on facts."

Doreen nodded. "And what about Henrietta?"

"She was a completely different case. There was talk of her having gone to visit another family."

"Or her own birth family, and obviously she didn't go without permission. She was fourteen and had Down syndrome."

"Again the brothers were investigated. Frank's business too. No one found anything amiss or questionable," he reminded her.

"Right, and it's not necessarily been enough years yet for anybody to talk," she said, staring off into space. "Because I really do feel like most of these cases are being solved now as people realize the main event was just so long ago that it doesn't seem to make a difference to stir the pot now."

"And yet you and I both know it makes a hell of a difference. Especially if murder is involved. Canada has no statute of limitations on murder suspects."

"It seems like time loosens all tongues though."

"Very true," he said.

"I don't know if this is an official cold case or not, but it's definitely a mystery," Doreen said as she pointed to her notepad.

Mack looked at the notepad with all the deck measurements and said, "What are you talking about?"

She laughed, flipped over the page, and said, "These are my notes on the ice pick."

He said, "I do want to see that ledger."

Doreen hopped to her feet, walked inside, and brought out the clean bag with the ledgers and the papers she had clipped together. "This is what he gave me."

"You could charm the socks off a rattlesnake. You know that, right?"

"Do rattlesnakes have socks?" she asked with interest. "I know they have a rattle …"

Mack rolled his eyes at her, reached for the ledgers, and flipped through them. "These records are definitely sales," he said. "Prices are marked on the side."

"And yet Ed Burns is the one who bought the matching set of ice picks. They won awards for Frank."

Mack thought about that, brought up his phone, and made a couple notations. "Something was odd about Ed's death," he said.

Doreen brightened and leaned forward. "Really?"

He nodded. "But I'm having trouble accessing anything

on my phone. I'll have to wait until I get home again."

She nodded and sagged back, disappointed, but knowing there was no point in pushing the matter now. "And his son inherited the house, business, et cetera, and the sisters got nothing. So we have another case of brothers doing well and the sisters not."

"I said I'll look into it," Mack said with a warning. "You stay out of it."

"I'm not staying out of anything because there isn't anything to stay out of," Doreen announced triumphantly.

"Have you heard from Scott?"

It took her a moment to figure out who he was talking about. "Are you changing the subject?" she asked suspiciously.

He opened his eyes wider. "Hey, the man from Christie's will make you a ton of money. Of course I'm interested."

"He did say something about furniture repairs and pictures needed to be cleaned, and that was just the start, so I'm not sure how much money I'll end up getting—or when."

"I guess we didn't consider expenses like that, did we?"

"No, neither did he really, when we were talking. Likely he assumed I knew already. But it does mean any funds coming my way will be pushed back by several more months."

"Ah," he said, "which is why you're so worried about the cost of expanding your deck."

"If I can't afford it now, it'll have to wait." She wrinkled her nose. "But I'd really love to have the deck this year. This summer even."

"And again, let's wait until Monday," he said.

Chapter 17

Saturday Late Morning ...

MACK TOOK HIS leave soon afterward. Doreen watched him drive away, delighted he was collecting supplies for her deck. He was a really nice guy, inside and out. He hadn't said anything about the ledgers, aside from taking photos, but that was it. He probably thought it was all junk. To a certain extent, she agreed. But there was still the missing ice pick.

She turned around and headed out to her back garden to work on her own weeds. She kept looking around to see where the garden would stop and where the deck would start, and it was almost impossible to not feel the excitement surge through her. The fact they had come this far without a penny—and, no, it wasn't very far, she admitted that—but it was something. It was enough she could see it taking form.

She still clung to her hope that maybe, just maybe, it would become a reality. Soon. She wondered what the chances were of having a small barbecue at the end of it all. Maybe not this month, maybe in a few months. Of course, if she didn't know how to cook on a stove, how the heck would she learn to cook on a barbecue? But, of course, her

DALE MAYER

mind answered immediately that it would be Mack's job. She laughed.

She shoved her spade into the dirt one more time and picked it up, shook off a pile of weeds, and tossed them to the side into her growing weed pile. She would be delighted just finishing off this initial turnover in the garden as it was.

When she walked back into the house to get water a couple hours later, she saw a text from Mack, saying he forgot to leave her money. She laughed. **Yeah, and I could use it,** she replied. **I need groceries.**

I'm out running around, he said. **I'll stop by again and drop it off real quick.**

Good enough.

She leaned back, finished the glass of water, and then poured herself another one. Of course she couldn't get her mind off the Darbunkle brothers. She couldn't let the fact that she didn't like the gardener brother, Fred, sway her into thinking he was the guilty party, not his brother, Frank, but it was awfully convenient that both brothers inherited something from their parents. And both were still living in the house. So, what was the motive? The house? It didn't really make sense when the brothers had always seemed to live there, with their parents. With Henrietta.

Doreen hadn't seen anything to say the parents had been sick. Maybe the parents had just decided they didn't want to become any sicker. Wanted to leave what little they could to their children, not have it all eaten up by medical bills. Doreen would need to go a little deeper into their lives. She sat down at her laptop and searched everything under the parents' names individually and together. And thereafter searched both brothers.

Then she came across Fred's juvie record. Or at least

what she presumed was a juvie record. She sent Mack a text, asking about how that worked.

He called her to answer her text. "I can check when I get back to the office," he said. "But, if it's a juvie record, we can't look into it. They were sealed when he turned eighteen."

"So, once you turn a certain age, you're good to go?" She didn't understand that mentality.

"If he was in trouble as a young teen, yes, the records become sealed, and he gets a fresh start. But, if it's major, like he killed somebody, then he would have been tried as an adult, and his records wouldn't get expunged."

"What if he was even younger than a teenager?"

"Then it's hard to say. It depends on the case."

"Interesting," she said.

"Why?"

"Just getting an idea of who this family is," she said. "I'm interested if the brothers had something to do with their parents' disappearance or not. With Henrietta's subsequent disappearance too. The brothers' inheritance makes them look suspicious, although you don't seem to think their parents had much to pass on."

"Someone has to inherit, no matter how big or small," Mack pointed out.

"So, what else could the motivation be to get rid of Mr. and Mrs. Darbunkle, as well as Henrietta?"

"I don't know. That's the thing about this job. Sometimes you just don't get answers."

With that, Doreen could tell Mack's focus was off doing something else, and she was no longer at the top of his mind. He hung up shortly thereafter.

And the trouble was, it wasn't easy for her to let go of all this. She decided she'd had enough of hot and sweaty gardening work. She took a quick shower and changed into shorts and a tank top. Which reminded her that she still had more clothes to go through, so she went through the last of them. Well, she hoped it was the last of them. She probably needed to go through her own reserve too, but she already had a couple more bags for Wendy. She packed them up and took them downstairs in time to see Mack pull up.

He handed her the cash and said, "I'm not staying. I'm heading off to shop for groceries."

She nodded. "I might take these bags to Wendy and do some shopping too."

He turned to look at her, as he walked toward the truck. "What do you want to learn to make next?"

She followed along, then frowned, looked up at him, and said, "I don't know. Suggestions?"

"It's hard to say," he said. "Summertime is for barbecues, but you don't have one."

She nodded morosely. "I was just thinking about that earlier. Maybe once we have a deck, I can afford to put a little barbecue out there, and you could teach me how to use it."

"Maybe," he said. "You need some more basic recipes in your life."

"I'd love some, but I don't know what you call *basic*."

He replied, "The American dream. Burgers, hot dogs, and pizza."

She burst out laughing. "I like pizza well enough but not enough to learn to make it. That looks fussy."

"And it's cheap enough to buy," he said, "any time of year that you want it."

"But burgers?" she said with a smile. "Are they hard?"

Mack shook his head and laughed. "They're ground meat formed into a ball, flattened, and grilled. It doesn't get any easier." He studied her and said, "You've never made any, have you?"

"Nope," Doreen said. "I'm not really sure when I had one," she said thoughtfully.

He stopped. "Seriously?"

"Well, I'm pretty sure I've tried one," she said, "but I don't know what fast-food place it was."

"Nope, burgers should be barbecued," he said. "Anything less than that is sacrilege, but if we don't have a barbecue …" He tapped the door of his vehicle, contemplating it.

"If you can just fry them in a pan," she said, "would it be an easy enough thing for me to cook?"

"Like I said, it doesn't get any easier. What about hot dogs?"

She wrinkled her nose up at that. "I'm not sure what a good hot dog tastes like," she said cautiously, "but the ones I had didn't taste very good."

He nodded. "Well, you probably didn't have big Polish ones or brats."

"Brats?" she asked in confusion.

"Bratwurst in a bun, smothered in sauerkraut."

Her eyebrows shot up. "I like sauerkraut."

"Do you like pirogues?"

She stared at him. "I don't know what they are."

He groaned. "Okay, I'm going shopping," he said. "I'll pick up a couple meals' worth to show you how to cook them, and we'll do it one day next week, if you're okay with that—maybe a burger lesson too, thrown in there. And then maybe next weekend, we'll do pirogues or brats, something along that line."

"Sounds delicious," she said. "I'll pick up salad fixings."

"Aren't you eating more than salads these days?"

"Salad, sandwiches, and omelets," she said solemnly. "Some of the other stuff you showed me is too hard."

"You mean, the pasta?"

Yes," she said, "but I should try to cook just some plain pasta."

"Yes, you should," he said. "You pick up some, and we'll cook it tomorrow night. Well, I'm cooking burgers. You could cook your pasta tonight. The pasta can be cold in your fridge tomorrow, and you can warm it up in a pan or the microwave."

She beamed. "I like that idea."

"Good enough." And then he pulled out of the driveway.

Chapter 18

Saturday Noon …

DOREEN WALKED TO her car in the open garage, loaded it up, and looked around to see if anything else could be added to her trip. She found a bit more that needed to go to charity, and, by the time she was done, the car was full. Because she was also going grocery shopping, she had to leave the animals behind.

"Sorry, Mugs," she said, as she led him back into the house. Despondent, his tail down and his ears almost dragging the floor, he walked into the center of the living room and slumped onto the floor. She closed and locked the door, realizing she didn't really need to set the alarm, but it was a habit now.

Besides, the few belongings left were all she had, so, if somebody stole them, she wouldn't be impressed. She drove to Wendy's first and dropped off the bags of clothes. Wendy took them with a wave, tagged Doreen's bags with her name, and put them off to the side. Then Doreen headed up to the charity, dropped off the rest of the stuff, and went straight to the grocery store.

Grocery shopping was pretty easy when you didn't have

to buy much. She picked up enough for a couple salads, some sandwiches, and walked into the pasta section, where she was astonished at all the shapes available. She had a real favorite in spaghetti, but she was fascinated with every other kind, from pinwheels to weird shells to macaroni thingies to little shapes that looked like grains of rice. On impulse, she bought different kinds and put them in her cart. She needed a few other things, like oil and some fresh lemons, but she went quickly to add those things to her basket.

She walked to where the hot dogs were and studied them, not really understanding what made a good hot dog versus a bad hot dog. One package on sale looked interesting, but some ingredients in it she couldn't pronounce, so she figured maybe these hot dogs weren't real food. She hemmed and hawed until a familiar voice spoke to her.

"Those aren't the best."

She looked up to see Mack and smiled. "These things listed I wouldn't know how to say, so I figured it wasn't healthy."

He laughed. "You can knock off 90 percent of the packaged stuff in this store if you don't buy anything with names you can't pronounce. You'll be healthier by far."

She frowned. "But I was trying to eat healthy."

"And you can eat healthy," he said, "but maybe look at other packages of meat to compare."

She kept looking through a couple more packages, then he led her over to the fresh counter and found some nice-looking sausages.

"Those are bratwurst," he said, pointing to one row. "I was thinking of those next week."

"Oh, I like that idea. How many do we need?"

"They're fair-sized," he said, "so I'll need only two."

She nodded and ordered four, then studied them when they came wrapped in paper. "I really like the look of this."

"The paper or the sausages inside?" Mack asked in a dry tone.

Doreen shook her head. "Laugh at me all you want, but I've never bought meat from a butcher before. And rarely have I bought prepackaged meat, so this is a treat."

"I'm not sure you would call this from a true butcher," he said, "but, yes, it's definitely a fun way to buy meat."

She put the package in her cart and looked over at Mack's cart, stuffed full. "How can you eat so much?" she asked. She recognized potatoes and onions and lettuce, but some bigger vegetables she didn't know. "What's that yellow thing?"

"A yellow zucchini."

"They come in yellow?"

"Yep, they do."

"Okay," she said, "and can you make bread out of them too?"

"If you're talking about zucchini bread, yes." Then he stared at her in surprise. "How come you didn't bring out the zucchini bread today?"

"Because I forgot," she confessed.

"I was there twice. I could have had zucchini bread. You did that on purpose."

"No, I did not," she said. "I promise."

"Ha," he said.

She pulled her cart away and headed toward the cashier but felt someone staring at her. She turned to see Fred and nudged Mack. "That's the gardener from Rosemoor."

He looked over to see the portly older man raise his nose in the air before turning his back on the two of them. "The gardener from Nan's home?"

"Yes, you know? The brother to the one who made the ice pick that's missing half a set?"

"Interesting that you comment on the ice picks instead of the missing parents."

"Missing parents *and* a missing sister."

Just then a strange voice came up behind her. "You keep your nose out of our business."

She turned to look at a man who looked just enough like Fred to be Frank. "Hey, you must be the guy who made all those tools," she said with a winning smile. He looked at her, and she could see his anger warred with his delight at being recognized. She held out a hand and said, "I read about some of the awards you won. Congratulations."

He shook her hand and shuffled his feet. "Thanks."

"Do you still do that kind of woodworking?" she asked curiously.

He shook his head. "Not really. I tried to make a go of it as a business, but that didn't work out so well. No one wanted to pay for handmade quality."

"I'm sorry about that," she said. "I went to your old shop and found it was now a knife-sharpening place."

He gave a snort of disgust. "Yeah, not exactly what I had envisioned. But sometimes life just hits you sideways, and you can't keep it up."

"I'm sorry. It looked like the work you were doing was great stuff."

"Maybe," he said, but he sported a pleased smile.

"I found one of your pieces too," Doreen said thoughtfully. She could feel Mack behind her stiffening.

Frank looked at her and frowned. "What are you talking about?"

"Well, my bird found two little silver plates with names and numbers on them, and then I found an ice pick. One of the plates looks like it fits into the ice pick. But I didn't find a second tool for the other one."

"The ice picks?"

"Yeah," she said, "but honestly I didn't know whose they were. I just found them down at the mouth of the river."

He shuffled his feet again, almost like a little kid. "I made quite a few ice picks," he said with a frown.

"Like dozens?"

He shook his head. "No, not really. Maybe half a dozen. There was only one matched set. Don't suppose you remember the numbers, do you?"

She supplied both numbers off the top of her head; then she'd always been good with numbers.

His eyebrows shot up, and he swallowed hard. "That is the matched set," he said. "Ed Burns bought that off me."

"That's what I wondered," Doreen said. "It's an interesting thing, but I found it along the Mission Greenway at the mouth of the river."

"Weird, because you don't ice fish at the mouth of the river. As far as I know, he still had that set before he died."

"Well," she said, "I don't know how it ended up down there, and I have no idea where the second one is either."

"If you ever want to get rid of it, I'll take it back."

"For money?" she asked hopefully.

He shook his head. "No. Just so I can restore it. I imagine, if it's been lying out in the weather like that, it's probably in rough shape."

She looked up at Mack. "I'm thinking that's a good description. What do you think?"

Mack nodded. "The tool itself, the head is all rusted, and

149

the wood is dried out and looks like it's splitting."

Frank winced. "I'd definitely like to have it back then. It would be nice to keep it in decent shape. I put a lot of work into that handle."

"I understand that," she said. "I'll keep looking for the second piece of the set."

"They were both with Mr. Burns," Frank said, "so maybe talk to his son to see if he's still got the other piece."

"Great idea. I'll have to track him down."

"I saw him over at the gas station not five minutes ago. I would have stopped and asked him about it, if I had known."

"What kind of car does he drive?"

Frank's voice dropped into a sneer. "He's got a Porsche. You can't miss it. He drives like a crazy animal around town." And, with that, Frank carried on toward the checkout lanes.

Doreen looked at Mack. "Nothing suspicious or something suspicious?"

"Nothing suspicious," he said firmly. "I'm heading to the cashier. What about you?"

"Me too," she said and looked at her meager groceries. "Except I have to go to the bakery." She detoured across to the bakery, picked up a loaf of bread and a few fresh buns, and returned to the registers. As she studied the lines for the shortest, Frank caught her attention and pointed to somebody standing at the Express lane, holding a bag of coffee. Doreen raised her eyebrows and asked, "Burns?"

Frank nodded, and she changed course for the Express lane.

Burns looked at her cart and said, "Another person who can't count."

She stared at him. "Wow," she said, "I came to talk to you."

"Oh, great," he said, "another panhandler, looking for money."

Doreen knew Mack could hear their conversation because he was only one aisle over, and she also could see the anger radiating from his gaze and from the stern set of his shoulders. "Hardly," she said.

"Yeah. Sure," he said. "I heard about you. You had to sell everything out of the house in order to put food on the table." He sneered. "Talk about a loser. Get a job like everybody else."

"What's your job?" she asked with interest.

"I run several businesses," he said in a haughty tone.

"Ah," she said, "so the businesses your father built and you inherited, right?"

He narrowed his gaze.

"You're a Burns, Ed Burns's son. The only heir to his fortune. Even your two sisters didn't get anything."

"Why should they?" he said, stiffening. "They don't deserve anything."

"I wonder how they feel about that?"

"If they'd had any money, they could have hired lawyers to fight it," he said. "But, of course, they don't have any."

"No," she said, "because you're the only one who got any money from dear old dad. But I wonder if you rewrote the will so you'd get everything?"

By now, Doreen knew everybody nearby was listening to their conversation. But Kid Burns stiffened, glared at her in outrage, and said, "That is slander."

"Well, you're being pretty obnoxious yourself," she said calmly. "And, by the way, it's your turn. Go buy your little pack of coffee."

He glared at her, dropped the coffee at the cashier, paid for it, and, as he turned to walk out, he said, "Don't forget to do the dishes so you can pay for your groceries."

She smiled. "Even if I had to, it's honest work, instead of stealing from my father. Did you kill him too?"

Everybody around her gasped. But Kid Burns had a different reaction—the color drained from his skin, and he spun around and took off. She looked at Mack. "Now *that* was an interesting reaction."

Almost immediately the crowd around them tightened up. "You're Doreen, aren't you? Where are your animals? Is this a new case? Did he actually kill his father?"

Mack glared at her. "No," he said, to the crowd. "We don't have any information that leads us to believe he had anything to do with his father's death."

"Is it true he got everything and his sisters got nothing?"

Doreen nodded. "Apparently."

"That's not fair," one man said. "Those girls looked after their dad the whole time."

She smiled. "Seems to be the way of it."

"Well, you should fix it," said one older lady in outrage. "You need a new case anyway. You should take on the plight of the poor Burns sisters. They looked after their father and took care of that house. And, as soon as Old Man Burns was gone, the sisters moved out."

"The question is, *did* they move out?" Doreen asked. "Or did they *get* moved out?"

"If the bratty son inherited everything, you can bet he didn't let them stick around."

"No love lost there, huh?"

Everybody around them shook their heads.

The group of concerned citizens collected around Doreen and Mack. "We're surprised he got any of it. He hadn't been around for years but came back just in the last year before his father died."

"Not even a year," somebody called out. "It was just a few months."

"Interesting," Doreen said, but she didn't want to get into a big public discussion in the grocery store. This was already covering more than she had wanted to discuss. "I'll take a look into it," she promised.

At that, they started to cheer.

"Might not be easy," she warned. "I might not find anything."

"Nope," said one older lady with relish, "it definitely won't be. But we'd like to see him knocked down a step or two. Far too high and mighty, if you ask me."

"But, if he didn't do anything criminally wrong, then he doesn't get knocked down," Doreen said, not wanting everybody going crazy, but it was apparently too late.

"Do what you can do," said one old lady with badly dyed hair. "Those two sisters, they need help."

Doreen frowned. "Why?"

"Because they don't have any money. They're doing all they can to keep a roof over their heads. They're probably eating dog food."

Doreen stared at the old woman in horror. "I hope you're joking."

The woman shrugged. "I wouldn't be at all surprised," she said sadly. "Nobody gives a damn when we get older." She took her meager bag of groceries and walked outside.

Doreen, even though she was in the wrong aisle, was urged on through by the cashier and then quickly paid for her purchases. When she got outside, Mack joined her. She asked him, "She was joking about the dog food, wasn't she?"

"Hell," he said, "I'm still trying to get over the fact that the patrons in the entire grocery store want you to gang up against this guy."

"All I can think about are the two poor sisters." She worried on that for a moment. "Do you know where they live?"

Mack shook his head. "No, and just because everybody thinks they're in tough shape doesn't mean they're as bad as the gossip says."

"No," she said, "but sadly it could mean they're even worse off."

"True."

Doreen loaded her groceries and then got inside her vehicle and smiled up at Mack as he stood outside her door. "You know what? If you were to come by now, I would give you some zucchini bread this time."

He laughed. "I'm heading over to Mom's. Some of these groceries are for her. I'm sure she'll have something for me. You go ahead and eat it, even if just to make sure you don't end up like the sisters."

"Too late," she said. "Remember? I already did end up that way. Maybe that's why learning about them hurt so much."

"You can't fix everything," he warned.

"No," she said, "I can't. But maybe I can fix this, at least."

Chapter 19

Saturday Lunchtime ...

BACK HOME DOREEN unloaded the groceries, put on coffee, and led all the animals outside. She took her laptop with her, sat down on the grass, and leaned up against the post of the little set of existing steps, even though they were dirty. She had no lawn chairs—something she hoped to rectify soon.

She proceeded to look up Ed Burns's daughters. According to the articles she found, the Burnses were a religious family, and the girls had done their duty to their father well. But, somewhere along the line, he hadn't done his duty to them. Even though he was a multimillionaire, he had left them nothing. Everything had gone to his vagabond son. Immediately, of course, there had been an outcry from the townsfolk, but, with the girls not having any money to legally fight their brother in court, and the brother not being of a generous mind-set to help them out, he'd taken everything and had stepped into his father's role.

Doreen smiled at that. "You know something, you little egotistical sad excuse for a brother? We just might have to check into this. The fact that a set of special tools came from your father's collection makes me deeply suspicious about you and all that you may have been up to."

Her gaze caught on the corner of the ice pick. She walked over and took a look at it again. Then she texted Mack. **Any chance this ice pick has bloodstains on it, not just rust?**

She didn't get an answer right away but could see the pick was so coated and so rusted that she didn't know what the process would be to find blood on it. A lot of stains were evident here, but, whether that was just rust or other chemicals degrading over the years, she didn't know. When her phone rang, she picked it up. "Yes, Mack, it was just a question."

"You really think it's involved in something?"

"It's definitely dirty and covered in stains, but I have no idea what they are."

"Who are you thinking about?"

"I was thinking of Ed Burns," she said.

There was silence on the other end. "He's dead now. You remember that? He had a heart attack. He was old, and nothing suspicious was ever considered about his case."

She frowned as she studied the tool. "I'd still like the pick tested."

"Lab resources and all that cost money," Mack said. "I can't imagine it'll bear any fruit."

"My gut says it's involved in something," Doreen said. And that, at least, was the truth. But she'd need scientific evidence to make Mack happy.

"I'll think about it. I might do a couple quick tests to see if I find any human blood on it."

"That'd be a good place to start. Do you have a mobile test like that?"

He stayed quiet for a moment.

"You do?" she cried out happily.

"It doesn't take a whole lot," he said. "I'll talk to somebody and get back to you."

She put her phone down on the step beside her, then returned to her research on the Burns family. Ed Burns had made his money in orchards, and the girls had worked beside him the whole time. According to the articles, they'd been a very close family. One of the sisters had married and had a son, but he had died young, and her husband had died not too long afterward. "That's a terrible, grief-stricken life," she murmured.

Then to realize what happened to the sisters later—that made her very sad. Burns hadn't been dead for more than ten years. She thought about the ice pick being out there for that long and nodded. "It might not be connected to anything going on with Fred and Frank," she muttered out loud, "but it could be something important surrounding the death of Ed Burns."

About twenty minutes later she heard Mack's truck pull up outside her house. She bolted to her feet and went to the front door. "This is becoming quite the habit."

"You better have zucchini bread this time," he threatened as he hopped out of his truck with a small kit in his hand.

She looked at it with interest. "What's that?"

He motioned for her to go back inside, so she walked into the kitchen and waited for him to join her. She was curious about the small kit he'd brought, but he walked past her and headed out to the deck where the ice pick still lay. He opened his kit, took out a little spray bottle, and asked, "Coffee?"

She glared at him. "Do you get coffee anywhere else or just here?"

"I have to get something for making all these damn trips," he muttered.

She sighed and went back inside to put on coffee.

As she returned, he asked, "Zucchini bread?"

She crossed her arms over her chest and said, "Get on with it. You're not getting zucchini bread until the coffee's ready."

He nodded and sprayed part of the ice pick where the wood met metal and the sharp edges in two spots. There was also some inset wood piece too, which he sprayed as well. After a moment he took out three Q-tips and wiped off the residue at all three locations. He used a different Q-tip for each of the different places.

"I thought you were supposed to do it in reverse," she said.

He held up the Q-tips and waited. Sure enough, they turned color.

She gasped and stepped forward. "What does it mean?"

His tone grim, he said, "Human blood. On all three spots."

Chapter 20

Saturday Early Afternoon …

"Y OU'LL TAKE IT away from me now, won't you?" Doreen asked.

Mack nodded.

"I found it. It doesn't mean it was used in a murder. It also doesn't mean there was a criminal act."

"No, but I'll give it to forensics, and we'll see if we can match the blood."

"Oh," she said. Then she nodded. "That makes sense. It would be a horrible way to die."

"Yes, but, if this tool retained much blood, I highly doubt the person survived for long."

"Unless it was a foot or something," she muttered. She walked back inside, found her coffee cup, and pulled out a second one, placing them on the counter. When the coffee was done dripping, she poured it, but her mind was in turmoil. Something about seeing that test had cemented her gut feeling. As she brought the coffee out, she sat down beside Mack and said, "And, of course, we don't know who the victim could be, or do we?"

"No, we don't," he said. "And I may not have any DNA

in my database that we can match it to." He looked at the coffee and then over at her face and said, "It really upsets you, doesn't it? It means you're right though."

"Not quite," she said. "Like we just said, it doesn't mean it was a murder." She groaned. "But really, how do I find this stuff? Did Thaddeus know? I mean, I joke about the four of us a lot, but ..."

"I don't know," Mack said. "After this, you'll have to show me where you found it."

"If we have enough daylight," she said, looking up at the clouds. "I hadn't realized how late it was."

"It's not that late. Besides, if you're not eating dinner, you'd better be at least sharing the zucchini bread."

She went inside, pulled out the zucchini bread, grabbed a knife and a cutting board, and carried them outside. She then cut several slices. "Here you go," she said. She looked down at it, her appetite slowly returning.

"We still don't know what any of this means," Mack said. He looked at the ice pick and frowned. "I'd like to know where the matching piece is."

"Now you can go ask that snotty Burns kid," she said with a triumphant smile. "Rattle his cage a bit."

"I'm afraid you've rattled his cage enough," he said. "You know what you did back there?"

"I don't know that I've done anything," she said.

"He was pretty upset in the grocery store. The crowd didn't help."

"You saw the color drain from his face too, didn't you?"

"I did. He didn't like your implication."

"We'll just have to see how that pans out," Doreen said. She reached for a second piece of bread and motioned at him. "It's good, isn't it?"

He snagged up two more pieces and said, "Very good."

They enjoyed coffee and zucchini bread and silence. Finally she said, "It's really bad that he won't share with his sisters."

"People are people," Mack said. "Just because we want them to behave better doesn't mean they do."

"People should be nicer to each other."

Mack nodded. But then he added, "Even better is if they would be kind. We're running amok in a world full of lies and criminal behavior. People need to find a way to be kind to the person beside them."

"I guess there's a world of difference between nice and kind, isn't there?"

"There is, and I vote for kind."

She smiled at him. "That's because you're a nice person."

His eyebrows shot up. "I don't know what to do with this quiet reflective person who's being nice to me," he joked.

She frowned. "Am I always so mean?"

"Not always," he said.

Just then, Goliath hopped up into Mack's lap and batted him in the chin with his paw. "Ouch," Mack said, teasing, reaching up to rub his chin. "You pack quite a punch there, buddy." But he obligingly scratched Goliath's head.

At the same time, Mugs was determined not to be left alone, and he came over and jumped up so his front paws were on the chair where Doreen sat. She gently stroked his long ears. "You're doing just fine, Mugs. He's only getting a little bit of a cuddle."

"A cuddle. A cuddle." And Thaddeus hopped up on the café table. He gave her the eye and then turned his head and gave the other eye to Mack. "Thaddeus is here. Thaddeus is here."

"I can see that, big guy," Doreen said affectionately. As she went to pet him, he bent his head and snagged up a big piece of zucchini bread off her plate and backed up out of her reach.

"You could at least ask, you know?" she protested, but he was done with communicating because he was already eating the zucchini bread. He lifted his head, bobbed it a couple more times, and said, "A cuddle. A cuddle."

"No, this is bread," she said, "and it's got sugar in it. You really shouldn't eat it." She tried to pull a little bit off the side from the piece in her hand and give it to him, but, instead of going for the piece offered, he went after the bigger piece she still held in her hand. And he broke off a large portion of it and moved off to the side again. At that, a huge *woof* erupted beside her. She glared down at Mugs. "You shouldn't have zucchini bread either," she said, but Goliath was already batting Mack's hand for some too. She glanced over at Mack. "What is wrong with him?"

"Your nan didn't put anything funny in this, did she?" he asked suspiciously, inspecting the piece in his hand.

"What? Like catnip or something?" she asked, laughing.

"Just so long as there isn't any green stuff."

"There's zucchini. That's plenty green," she said and shrugged. "However, I know what you're saying. And I highly doubt Nan laced it with marijuana."

"It's hard to say now that it's legal in Canada, for both recreational use and medicinal. Everybody's getting into the act."

She couldn't imagine her grandmother doing that, but, hey, Doreen did remember some laced cookies that Nan had shared with Doreen, but someone else had specifically made them that way—so who knew? She just smiled and reached for another piece. "Whatever she did, it's very good."

And it must have been because Mack reached for a fourth piece.

When he was done with that, he gave a happy sigh. "Now I don't have to cook either."

"We're pathetic," she said. "We'd rather sit here and have zucchini bread now rather than a proper dinner later."

"I would have had some dinner later too," he said, "but I've been running around all day, so I forgot to take anything out to thaw."

"I can't eat any more now anyway," she said. "Plus my mind is focused on how to help the sisters."

"The sisters may not need your help," Mack warned. "Just because you see them in a sad, broken light doesn't mean that's who they are."

"True," Doreen said, "and, indeed, it would make me very happy if they weren't. I'd love to know they were running million-dollar businesses they started from the ground up themselves. That would be the best scenario because I think the best revenge is doing well."

"Just like you did with your ex-husband."

"Maybe," she said. "Although I'm hardly a success."

"You still haven't brought up talking to my brother."

"No," she said. "See? I keep pushing it off."

"Why would you do that?" he asked.

"Well, one, he's a lawyer," she countered with a smirk. "The other, I don't want to go back to that nightmare." She could feel her mood sinking. "I don't like to speak about my ex. That's part of my reticence in speaking with your brother about my biased divorce attorney."

"I understand," he said quietly. "But it might also help you get some resolution and some money to pay for your deck addition."

"That's a low blow. Even if I did get a little money, I wouldn't see it for months. Everybody's just dangling money out in the future that I don't ever get into my present-day bank account."

"Well, think about it," Mack said, "and we'll need to at least sit down and talk with my brother soon."

She nodded. "I get it, but give me a couple days, will you?"

"Only if you firm up a date," he said.

"Like next weekend?"

She glared at him when he shook his head. "No, I want a specific date."

"Fine," she said, "next weekend it is."

"Here?"

She sighed. "Okay, everybody else has come to this place, why not a lawyer too?"

He just laughed. "My brother's a good guy."

"I bet you didn't think so growing up," she said.

"Nope, I sure didn't. We were siblings. At moments we hated each other, but, underneath it all, we still loved each other."

"Then you were lucky. I didn't have any siblings, so I don't know what that relationship looks like."

"That's okay too," he said, "because you can still have relationships with people without them having to be siblings."

"I haven't really met any friends here," she said sadly. "You, of course, but no female friends, I mean."

"Well, that's because you keep jailing them," he said in a

joking manner.

"I was thinking that," she said, wrinkling her face up. "Why am I getting close to people who have behaved so badly?"

"I think we all basically project our inner thoughts onto others. So, where you are good-hearted, you see the world as filled with good-hearted people. Like that haughty Burns kid was calling you out for wanting money from him, where he's the money-grubbing one."

"I feel so stupid being taken in by these people."

"Don't," Mack said. "The alternative is to think everyone is out to get you."

"Maybe so," Doreen said.

"What about Crystal's mom? Could you ever be friends with her?"

She shook her head. "It would be really hard for me to be friends with somebody who abused a child."

"I understand."

He left soon afterward, getting a work call and grabbing her ice pick and leaving, this time for his last visit of the day.

Chapter 21

Sunday Morning...

WHEN DOREEN WOKE up Sunday morning, it was to peace and quiet—not a phone call, not an animal barking, no intruders. Peace and quiet. Perfect. She lay on the mattress on the floor and stared up at her ceiling.

"A bed frame would be nice," she announced. "If it'll have to wait until I get paid for the antiques, fine," she muttered to Mugs. His response was to roll onto his back and wave his stubby feet in the air, but she was pretty sure he was still asleep.

Maybe he was having a nightmare because he made an odd little woofing sound, and then his feet started to move. Being upside down, he was getting nowhere. She gently stroked the underside of his chin. He calmed down almost instantly, and then a heavy sigh worked its way up his chest and out.

She smiled at that. "You'll be just fine, buddy."

She hopped up, had a quick shower, got dressed, then decided it was time for laundry. Especially the linens. She stripped down the bed, disturbing poor Mugs in the process, and carried that and her week's worth of laundry downstairs to the washer and dryer. She put on the laundry, fed her animals, and then started some coffee for her. With that, she disarmed the alarm, unlocked the back door, propped it open, and stepped out into the early morning sunshine.

It was early, but not so early that the world wasn't awake with her. She checked her cell phone to see it was eight. But, on a Sunday, that was pretty early for this town. She sniffed the air because, although the sunlight competed with a few clouds out there, she felt almost an electricity, a sense of waiting, like a storm was about to blow through. And the smell of fresh rain on the grass reached her nose, moving into her area. She walked around her small deck, hating it even more but loving the area nonetheless. The thought of getting a big deck and some outdoor furniture—well, that was still looking more like a dream than anything.

With her first cup of coffee, she wandered to the creek, looking around at the area. That was one thing she hadn't done last night, shown Mack where the ice pick had come from. He'd taken it with him after a call had come through, and he'd bagged it up and rushed away. He was due to return tonight for sure, for another cooking lesson and to eat his creation. He might come by earlier today as well, so she could show him where she'd found the ice pick buried. Not wanting to be caught looking like a fool and maybe over-looking the second ice pick, she called the animals to her and headed downriver on the other side.

As soon as she came to the large ivy patch, she stopped to get her bearings. First things first. She took several photographs of the really nice houses in this area, as well as the path along the river toward the lake. Then she took several more of where she'd found the first ice pick. After that, she gave the area another good search because she didn't want to lead Mack down here and have him find something she hadn't. She wandered up and down but didn't see anything.

As she walked back, her phone rang. "Good morning, Mack. Did you forget I was supposed to take you down to where I found the ice pick?"

"I had to leave. Remember?" he grumbled. "I'm coming by now. Be there in five."

"What if I'm not there?" But there was no point in arguing. She meandered her way back and was on the bridge when she heard a shout. She looked out to see Mack walking through her rear kitchen door. She lifted a hand. He headed her way, and she noticed he had a coffee in his hand too.

"Where were you?"

"Down at the area where I found the ice pick," she said. "You didn't give me a chance to tell you that on the phone. And to thank you for fixing my little bridge." She smiled as she pointed to it.

"No problem." He shrugged, but his teasing smirk emerged. "I could smell the coffee from where I was."

She glared at him suspiciously. "There had better still be more left in the pot."

"Yep," he said, "but you can fill your cup up again when we get back. Show me where that tool was."

With the animals in tow and Thaddeus riding on Mack's shoulder, they crossed the little bridge. Doreen stopped on the other side and said, "You did such a good job repairing this. Thank you again for that."

He stared at it in resignation. "I had to, I guess. Otherwise you're likely to fall through again, aren't you?"

Doreen nodded. When they came to the big patch of ivy, she stopped and said, "It was in here."

"In where?"

She stepped forward and pointed as close as she could remember to where the ice pick had been.

"How far down in the ground was it?"

She shrugged. "Only part of the wooden handle was aboveground. So the rest of it was buried. Basically the whole length of it was hidden."

Mack looked at the area and said, "What in the world possessed you to dig into the ivy to find it?"

She groaned. "It wasn't me. It was the animals." She quickly explained how she came to be here. "I had to dig around in the rocks a bit to lift up the tool, but, once I got it loosened, it came right out."

Mack stepped forward, moved the ivy around, found the hollow, and said, "This is the spot all right, but it looks like it's been lying here for a long time."

"We do have somewhat of a date," Doreen said, "because it was only created about, what? Twenty years ago?"

"Interesting," he said.

"What kind of interesting?" she asked, stepping closer and peering down at what he was looking at.

"Nothing in particular." He looked over at the fence and took a lot of photographs.

"Do you see the second one? I did look," she said, "but I couldn't find it."

"No, I don't see it, but, depending on what forensics finds on that first ice pick, we may have to come back and look deeper."

"Right," she said, "that makes sense."

"Only to you," he said with a heavy sigh.

She chuckled. "You would have found it eventually."

"I never would have found it," he said. "I'm too busy

taking care of all the rest of the things needing to be taken care of."

"Me too," Doreen said. "Just think. I'm here, having an innocent little walk, and my animals go and find this ice pick. I wouldn't even know what it was if it wasn't for you. I also wouldn't have known what images to look up."

He looked at her in surprise. "You had to look up images?"

"Sure," she said. "I wouldn't just believe you blindly, would I?"

His jaw dropped. "I've never lied to you," he roared.

"Maybe, but you could have been delusional," she said with a big fat smile.

Mack rolled his eyes. "Come on. Let's get back. The first person there gets the rest of the coffee."

"That's not fair," Doreen said, as he raced ahead, his long strides eating up the path. She tried to brush past him, but he stepped into her way. She growled. "If you take all that coffee, I'll eat all the zucchini bread."

At that, he stopped and looked at her.

She nodded. "I will."

"The problem is," he said, "you will."

She chuckled. "Good to see that you know me so well."

He groaned, and they crossed the bridge single file. When they got to the other side, Doreen darted ahead to the house. She could see there wasn't much coffee left. She filled her cup and then turned triumphantly to look at Mack. "There was only a little bit left anyway."

He shrugged. "I'm good. I had a whole pot at home." She glared at him, and he burst out laughing. "But I got you," he said.

"Wow, that's just mean." She put down her cup. "Are

you leaving now then?"

"I am," he said, as he headed for the front door.

She checked her watch. It was almost nine. "I guess it's really quiet around town at this hour because of church, right?"

"Sometimes, but, the minute you expect that, it becomes something different, and you'll end up in the middle of traffic."

Just then, an old rattletrap of a car puttered around the corner. It slowed as it came into the cul-de-sac and stopped to look at various houses. Mack walked down to his truck, checking out the rattletrap. He shook his head, hopped into his truck, and slowly reversed down the driveway. As he did so, this little rattletrap of a car pulled into Doreen's driveway and parked. Mack frowned and looked at Doreen. She shrugged.

Two ladies—both fairly small in stature, maybe five-two, five-three—hopped out. They moved quickly and with lots of energy, but they appeared to be in their mid-fifties, so she wasn't sure just what their real ages were. As they came closer, Doreen was afraid it would be religious-pamphlet time.

There was a honk of a horn from Mack in his truck. Doreen lifted a hand and waved goodbye. He was basically checking to see if it was okay for him to leave. With that, he did. She smiled at the two ladies. "What can I do for you?"

One said, "You can help us."

And the other chimed in, "At least, we're hoping you can help us."

It wasn't long before Doreen realized one would start a sentence, and the other would finish it. And, when she asked them what this was all about, they just smiled and said,

"You're the one who talked to our brother in the grocery store."

"Are you the Burns sisters?"

Both nodded.

"Oh, dear," she said. "I understand you didn't get any of your father's inheritance."

They shook their heads. "No, we didn't, and he promised us we were in the will, and we would be taken care of," said the one on the left. She wore an almost identical outfit to her sister, but she had some turquoise trim around her blouse whereas the other one had lavender trim.

"Did you ever see the will?" Doreen asked.

Both ladies shook their heads.

"Was your father a fair person? Was he a man of his word? Could you trust him?"

"Absolutely, that's who he was."

Doreen thought to herself. "Okay," she said, "but I don't understand what you think I can do about it."

The two sisters looked at each other, back at her, and said, "We don't have much money, but we're hoping you can advise us."

"What possible advice could I give you?"

"We don't know how to get some of our inheritance," the first one said.

In her head, Doreen thought maybe she should just call them Turquoise and Lavender.

"Our dad swore to us we were taken care of. We spent all our lives working on the farm with him, and we were never paid. He made a lot of money, and he continued to earn more money as we looked after the orchards while he was in the offices."

"Did you see the ice pick set he bought?"

The two sisters stopped talking, looked at her, and frowned.

Doreen smiled and shook her head. "Sorry, I didn't mean to go off tangent like that, but it does relate."

Slowly, as if not sure of what she was saying, Lavender said, "We were there when he bought it."

"I know Frank was delighted," Turquoise said.

"I'm sure," Doreen said. "Do you know where your father kept them?"

"Dad hung them on the wall," Turquoise said. "He had a little art display, and he put them up on the wall with special lights on them."

"Oh, wow," Doreen said. "He must have really liked them."

The two sisters exchanged worried glances, then looked back at her.

"He loved them. But maybe not for the reason you're thinking. He used to laugh at them and diss Frank's work as cheap and homemade looking. Frank was delighted initially, until my father used his pieces as a talking point, and not in a nice way."

"Interesting," Doreen said, "any idea what happened to them?"

The two sisters looked at her in confusion.

"They aren't still hanging in that spot in the house," Doreen added.

"I think they are. Or rather they were when we were last in the house—then again that was around the time our father died. Jude kicked us out soon afterward, and we haven't been back since. He's our blood, but ..." Lavender said faintly. "There's fifteen years between us, and he's in the prime of his life and on top of the world. We've worked hard, physically hard. Both of us are having some health issues, and it's hard for us to get jobs. We're in our fifties, and nobody wants to hire us, and we don't have any education."

"Except as orchardists?"

"True," they said. "Well, we haven't been able to get anybody to give us a job."

"Have you asked anyone in that particular field for a job? Surely you're well-known for your work?"

"No. Our father was credited for our success, so he had the name and the expertise, not us." They turned to each other and frowned. "She's right though, you know? I wonder if we could get hired in that capacity."

"I don't know," Lavender said, her voice quiet. "I feel like we have been unjustly treated. We worked all that time. If we'd at least pocketed our wages, we would have something in our bank accounts."

Doreen frowned. "I know you're saying he's a good man, but *that* is not the sign of a good man."

The two sisters hesitated. "It's come to our attention," Lavender said, "that maybe he did take advantage of us."

"I don't think there's any *maybe* in this," Doreen said. "He definitely took advantage of you. How dare he not pay you wages when he was making that kind of money. The fact that he is gone and that he hasn't left you money in his will is another big issue."

"The thing is, we're pretty sure he did," Turquoise said excitedly.

"How do you figure?"

"Because the lawyer said so."

"Which lawyer is that?" Doreen asked. "I'm a little hesitant to trust any lawyer."

"I know," Lavender said. "My father's old lawyer said we would be fine. But the other lawyer, the new lawyer, says we don't get anything."

"Wow," Doreen said, remembering her own marriage and what she didn't get from her years building up her husband's business because her own divorce lawyer ended up being her husband's mistress. "Lawyers are slippery," she said, trying for a neutral tone of voice.

"The old lawyer though, he was almost like family to us, and he said we were being taken care of. The new lawyer just laughed and said nothing was in the will, and we could contest it, but we won't win."

"Right. What happened to the old lawyer?"

"He died," Turquoise said.

"And who inherited his practice?"

"This new lawyer."

Doreen tapped her arms with her fingers and said, "What is it you want me to do?"

"We need to figure out if that will is legitimate," Lavender said quietly.

She seemed to be the more talkative of the two sisters, the more earnest, although they both looked a little worn out and broken down. "How am I supposed to help with that?" Doreen asked curiously.

These two sisters looked at her, and she could see the blank looks in their eyes.

"You have no idea, right?"

They both shook their heads. "No, we don't have a clue."

"Look. I can ask around and see if anything pops up. By the way, how did your father die?"

"He had a heart attack," Turquoise said. "And he was

gone very quickly."

"Who was with him at the time?"

"He was alone when he had the heart attack. We came home from work and found him collapsed in his office."

"Where was your brother?"

"He said he was out and about, doing whatever he does," Turquoise said with a note of disdain.

"How's the relationship between you guys?"

"He kicked us out onto the streets," Turquoise said, "so how do you imagine it is?"

"But have you done anything to aggravate issues or in any way to harm him?"

Both sisters shook their heads. "No, that's something we couldn't do."

"Did your father have any other children?"

The two sisters shook their heads. Lavender said, "If he did, we don't know about it."

"What happened to your mother?"

"She died giving birth to our brother," Lavender said.

"So did you raise him?"

"Nannies did," Turquoise said. "He was, of course, the apple of our father's eye because, in our family, we still believe strongly in the male heir."

"So work the women to the bone and give everything to the man who did nothing?"

Both women winced. "He wasn't supposed to get everything. We were supposed to get enough to live on."

"Which would be normal," Doreen said. "What do you have for me to go on?"

"Not much," Lavender admitted. "Just our father's and the old lawyer's words."

"Do you have any investments or any money?"

Lavender shook her head. "No, we handled the household accounts, and, as we needed individual money for our own personal needs, we took it and marked it down as part of the accounts. But, once Father died, we didn't even have access to that."

"Where are you staying now?"

"We share a room at a friend's house. And we do work around the house and look after their child. They were the only ones to offer us a place after Jude said we had to leave. So we've stayed with them ever since."

"And you get paid for that, right?"

Both women just looked at her mutely.

"Oh, boy," she said, "we're so going to have a talk with this *supposed* friend of yours."

"But they have given us a home, where nobody else has."

"We're all entitled to a day's pay for honest labor," Doreen said. "To even consider working for years like this without pay is not acceptable." She pulled out her cell phone. "Who is it you are staying with and working for?"

"I can't have you ruining our lives," Lavender said in alarm. "Don't you understand we have no place to go?"

"I hear you, but this isn't a friend of yours. They're taking just as much advantage of you as your father did."

"We know that," Turquoise said quietly, "which is another reason why we're trying to get money from the estate."

"And, if you got money, what would you do?"

"We'd leave," she said.

"I still need to know who is doing this," Doreen said, "because that's very much against the law."

The two women started to fret, shuffling their feet, their hands clenching and unclenching as they looked at each other.

"Look. I won't rock the boat until I can figure out what's happening with your brother and the estate, but that family owes you big-time."

"Something about us people take advantage of."

"For one," Doreen said, "you need to grow a spine. Like I had to."

Both women looked at her in horror.

She nodded. "And I know I'm hardly one to talk, but, since I've been on my own, you can bet I'm not the same person. I was the one who was taken advantage of. Once you start being taken advantage of, you almost think you deserve it and think that's all you're worth. And that's not true. You ran your father's businesses for decades. And, yes, you're both in this house, and I presume they don't need both of you to look after the one child and to look after the house. But they owe you wages regardless."

"But they said then they'd have to take away expenses for the other person, so, therefore, we were back to zero."

Doreen just muttered, "People will be people." She remembered everything Mack had told her recently about people. "Let me check into this," she said and was about to enter their contact information into her phone. "I presume you have a phone."

They both shook their heads.

"Jesus, what do you have? Nothing? Anyway, whose vehicle is that?"

"It's ours," Lavender said. "It's the only thing we were allowed from the estate."

"Do you get any cash to put gas into it?"

She nodded. "Fifty a month is our allowance."

"For what?"

"Everything," she said. "They can't pay us more."

"Like I believe that," Doreen said. "They better be driving beaters themselves and not live in a gorgeous home and not both have good jobs before I listen to anybody saying that!"

But she understood all too well how the women had slid into this abusive situation. In this mental state, well, they didn't think they were entitled to more. Of course they were desperate and thinking maybe they could get more, but they didn't have the attitude that said they deserved more and that the world needed to watch out because they were getting some backbone.

As the women drove away, Doreen stared after them. What the heck was she supposed to do with this? She went back into the house and walked out to the kitchen deck. Her phone rang.

"Who was that?" Mack asked.

"You won't believe it," Doreen groaned. "It was Jude's sisters. Ed Burns's daughters. And you really won't believe what they told me."

Chapter 22

Sunday Late Afternoon ...

BY THE TIME Doreen finished explaining it all to Mack, he was livid. "You can't just get involved in every sob story in town."

"I know that, but are you seriously upset about the sisters' arrangement?"

"I'm seriously upset about this. That is highly illegal. They are deserving of full wages."

"What about the fact they're having to pay for the expenses of each other. That between them, they only do the work of one, so they need to cover the cost of the second one?" She smiled, knowing he was hurt by what was happening to the sisters.

"That's an excuse," he said. "I'll have a talk with this family."

"I didn't get a name. I just have their phone number, and it's not even a cell phone."

He snorted at that. "Which means the sisters probably don't have any privacy to talk. But I'll trace that number and have my own private conversation with that couple taking advantage of the sisters. And I'll make sure they don't fire them on the spot."

"Does that fifty a month even cover car insurance, not to mention medical care?"

"No," he said. "This is basically part of the domestic slave trade, and that is an issue. We need to check into this asshole of a brother too. It's possible the courts would take another look at the will."

"The sisters obviously don't have any money for a lawyer," Doreen protested.

"Sometimes, in a case like this, they don't need one," he said. "Again, I'll have to look into it. And I have to cancel our cooking lesson tonight."

When he hung up, she had more questions than answers, but at least she felt a sense of somebody helping Lavender and Turquoise.

She created a sandwich for her dinner and then sat outside, mulling over the sisters' problem. Doreen had come a long way, and solving these mysteries had given her a purpose and a sense of identity that she hadn't had before. It gave her a sense of self. And that was what both sisters were missing. It was painful to look at the sisters and see parts of herself in there. She had heard the phrase that the people in front of you were mirrors, and, although she understood it in theory, she didn't like it one bit. Again, she remembered that whole thing about projection, like Mack had told her just the other day.

But it wasn't her job to help the sisters find out what they wanted from this life. It was more a case of making sure that, from here on out, they were at least independent and looking after themselves as much as they could.

Sitting down, Doreen looked up the name of the old lawyer. Everything she read held him in good standing.

"Look at that. A lawyer you could trust," she said sarcastically. And then she read his business had been taken over by this younger attorney, and people weren't happy. She found the Google reviews and a review sheet on the law firm. As she read it, she found no more comments were allowed.

"Of course not." There was a cached page though, that said he had seven reviews, and they were all one stars. She studied that for a long moment. "What are the chances he's a good buddy of the Jude guy who inherited all the Burns's money?" she muttered. "How much did this new lawyer get paid to create a false will?"

But she couldn't make assumptions. If the former lawyer died, what age had he been? It took a bit to figure it out, and she discovered he was only sixty-eight. Would Nan know him? She picked up her phone and texted Nan. Instead of texting back, Nan called her.

"My, what are you asking about Ranford?"

"Was he a good lawyer?"

"The very best," Nan said.

"I'm sorry he's gone then," Doreen said. "I'd like to have met an honest lawyer."

At that Nan laughed.

"Do you know Ed Burns's daughters?"

"I'm sure I've seen them around," Nan said. "They are wallflowers though, aren't they?"

"Yes, but, then again, they've not had an easy time."

"Maybe not. They have to make changes. Otherwise they'll keep making the same mistakes."

"I'm pretty sure," Doreen said, "they already are." And she explained about their current living situation.

"That's terrible," Nan cried out. "I wonder what family that is," she said thoughtfully.

"I don't know, but Mack vowed to have a talk with them. Still, this whole thing puts me very much on edge."

"Time for a bath to relax," Nan said. "You don't have to solve everybody else's problems, you know? Some people will have to solve them for themselves."

"And some people can't," Doreen said sadly. "Not everybody has somebody like you, who was thinking of her granddaughter."

"No, but you might be surprised. The sisters have each other, and, for that, they should be grateful."

"I think they are," Doreen said, "but it's still hard."

"If I do hear anything, I'll let you know."

"What about the other people I mentioned?"

"Well, Ed Burns, he was a bit of a cheapskate," Nan said. "The lawyer Ranford was lovely. But I'm not sure there's anything suspicious about his death. They both had heart attacks, I think."

"That's interesting. I wish I knew where the will came from and how to find the original."

"It would have been filed with the BC government," Nan said, "but another will could be around. As long as it's signed properly, it would be legal."

"Well, that's the problem with legal wills, right? Who declared it legal?"

Nan went on. "Oh, now I remember something about that."

"What about it?"

"The old lawyer was still on the case when Ed Burns died. I remember some kerfuffle in the news about it."

"About everything going to the son, you mean?"

"Yes, about there being a different will, as the one that was final was not the one the original lawyer had dealt with."

"Wouldn't he have been forced to do an investigation?"

"I think he died pretty soon after that," Nan said thoughtfully.

"And that's just way too convenient," Doreen said.

"Sometimes things are just as they are," Nan said. "You can't necessarily pin a crime on everyone."

"Maybe not, but maybe I'll check with the lawyer's family and see if they have any information on it."

"You do that," Nan said. "His wife, Sarah, is a lovely lady."

"I just have to track her down," Doreen said.

"That's easy. She owns the little flower shop down at the corner of Pandosy and KLO Road."

"Oh, well, maybe I need to walk in and take a look."

"You should go buy yourself some flowers," Nan said, chuckling.

"No, I don't have any money for that."

"I'm sure you'll come up with an excuse." And, with that, Nan hung up.

Doreen checked her timing, but it was a Sunday, which meant not a good day to talk to anybody about the lawyer. As it was, she ended up taking Nan's advice and had a long, soaking bath. As she read her favorite murder mystery while soaking, it was hard to keep her mind on the page because now she had so much else going on. Again, she wasn't sure of the connections yet between the Burns family and the Darbunkles, but something was there, and she knew it. She just didn't know how she knew it.

And she didn't know how she'd prove it. She had to have evidence worthy of Mack's regard.

She wanted Jude Burns, that bum of a brother, to pay his sisters back. Even better, she wanted him to lose everything, and it all to go to his sisters. She'd even be happy if they just had enough to live off of. Talk about greed. But it still didn't mean Jude did anything criminal. Unfortunately being greedy wasn't a crime. And what did the ice picks have to do with anything? And then she still had the issue of the missing-but-declared-dead Darbunkle parents and sister. She shook her head. "Mack, Mack, too many pieces are here. You're the one who's good with puzzles. You'll have to help me sort this all out."

But, of course, he didn't answer her. In fact, if she told him right now what she had just posed to the empty air, he'd laugh and say, "You're the puzzle master. You figure it out." And, as she lay in the hot water with the animals seated around her in the bathroom, keeping her company, she realized he was right, and this one definitely needed solving.

Chapter 23

Monday Morning ...

BRIGHT AND EARLY Monday morning Doreen took Mugs with her and headed to the Pandosy area. The flower shop was located on the corner of Pandosy and KLO, just like Nan said. Doreen parked and walked into the small shop and asked, "Hi, are you Sarah?"

The young woman in front looked up. "No, Sarah is my mom."

"Is it possible to speak with her?"

"Maybe." The woman turned into the back and called out, "Mom, you there?"

An older lady came in with some flowers and an arrangement in her hands. She looked up at Doreen, frowned, and said, "Hi, were you looking for something special?"

Doreen didn't know any other way to start but straightforward, so she nodded and said, "Yes, I was looking for some help on one of your husband's cases."

"I don't know anything about that," Sarah said. "He's been dead and gone many years now."

"I know," Doreen said, "but unfortunately a case just landed on my plate, so I have to take a look into it."

As the woman brushed her hands on her apron, she asked, "What's this all about?"

"Ed Burns," Doreen said.

Immediately both the mother and daughter scrunched up their faces and went, "*Eeewww.*"

"Wow," Doreen said, "that's not the reaction I was expecting."

"Well, the son is very much an *eww*," Sarah said. "And the father wasn't much better."

"And I understand the sisters didn't get anything out of the will."

"They were supposed to," Sarah said. "Both were supposed to have enough to live off of for the rest of their lives."

"So, what happened?"

"The son produced another will. It was dated and signed, official in every way. And, as a newer will, it preempted the older will. There was nothing Ranford could do."

"What if it was forged?"

"That was the problem, and my husband was trying to figure out how to handle the problem when he died. I figured it was the stress of that case that killed him because he was so upset that Ed Burns would do this to his daughters."

"Not only are they not fine but now they're in another equally bad situation," Doreen said, and she explained a little bit about their current living conditions.

The daughter stared at her. "Oh my," she said, "that's like white slavery."

"Maybe," Doreen said. "I'm not sure what they're doing is anywhere near legal."

"No, of course not," Sarah said. "So often these cases

aren't. When a lot of money is involved, people get greedy."

"Was there nothing to go to the sisters? Nothing in their names?"

Sarah raised both hands in frustration. "My husband used to come home every night and talk about it. He was so upset and kept trying to find an answer."

"Did he ever come up with one?"

"He told them the only thing they could do was try to overturn the will."

"And yet they didn't do that?"

"He wasn't sure what the process was, whether they needed their own lawyer or not, but he was willing to find out. Except he died, and the sisters came to me. But I couldn't tell them any more than I can tell you now. I don't know anything."

"The practice was passed off to somebody else. Is that correct?"

"He had a partner, and then, when Ranford was gone, a lot of those clients stayed with the other partner."

"I guess you don't happen to have his files or anything, right?"

Suddenly the young woman said, "I know who you are."

Doreen tossed a quick glance her way. She didn't want anything to be a distraction at this moment.

But Sarah was looking at her daughter. "What are you talking about?"

"She's the bone lady," the daughter said excitedly. "Oh my." She looked around for the animals, saw Mugs, and grinned. "That's him. That's him."

She came out from behind the counter, squatted beside Mugs, and petted him. Mugs, the complete sucker that he was, lay down and gave her his belly and licked her hand.

The daughter fell in love with him, oohing and aahing about what a beautiful dog he was. After a bit, she looked up at Doreen and said, "Do you have the other two with you?"

Doreen shook her head. "No, not at the moment. They're both at home."

"Wow, I got to meet you."

Doreen could see from Sarah's face that she didn't have a clue what her daughter was talking about.

Her daughter straightened up and said, "Remember? I told you about the case with the little boy—Pauly Shore—who was washed away in the river with the handyman, Henry Huberts?"

The confusion on the woman's face cleared. "Yes, of course." She turned to Doreen. "You're the one who figured out where they were, aren't you?"

Doreen shrugged and said, "Yes, I guess so."

"And she figured out about those poor women buried on that sneaky guy's property and a whole pile of others. You're really famous."

Doreen stared at the daughter in horror. "I hope not," she said. "That's the last thing I want to be."

The young woman smiled and said, "Fame is good. It'll make you rich."

"Well, I'm not rich," Doreen said. "And, right now, I'd like to see the Burns sisters get some justice."

"What about the old guy?" the young girl said. "Was he murdered?"

"Not that we can see at the moment," Doreen said. She turned toward the mother, who was staring at her daughter in fascination. Doreen pivoted, but she kept both women in her sights, while addressing the daughter. "Did your father leave any files or information on the sisters' case?"

Sarah's face tried to shut down, but the daughter wasn't having anything to do with that. "Mom, you know you do. If anybody can help, it'll be Doreen."

"I don't know," Sarah said. "I don't think your father would appreciate me handing off files to a complete stranger."

"She's not a stranger," the daughter said. "She's famous. She'll fix this."

"Well, I wouldn't go that far," Doreen said cautiously. "I'm looking into it to see what's going on, and I certainly can't promise to solve anything, but I need information in order to figure out what I can do for the sisters."

"Come on, Mom, please, please," the daughter said. "It'd be so cool. I could tell all my friends."

"I really wish you wouldn't until I get to the bottom of this," Doreen said quietly. "It would mess things up if you say I'm looking into it."

"Of course, of course, I'll wait," she said, and she laughed. "Mom, come on. You've been hanging on to that bloody envelope since forever."

"Sure," Sarah said. "I didn't know what to do with it."

"What is in it?"

"My husband's notes on the case. As I said, it really bothered him."

"If you have any information whatsoever about the Burns case," Doreen said, "I could really use it."

The daughter laughed. "Come on, Mom."

"Fine," she said, "but I don't have it."

"What do you mean, you don't have it?" Doreen asked.

"I don't have it right here," she said. "It's at home."

"Right," the daughter said. "I'll run home and get it."

Sarah looked on helplessly as her daughter dashed out

the front door and disappeared. "She's such a trial and such a joy. A late arrival after we'd resigned ourselves to being childless. Then I did marry a man who was twelve years older than I was." She shook her head as if confounded at the way life turned out and smiled at Doreen. "She won't be but a moment or two."

"Do you live that close?" Doreen asked.

"Sometimes it's too close," Sarah said sadly. "It's been a very tough decade without him. He was well-loved, and he was a great father."

"All I can tell you is," Doreen said, "I'm doing this for the right reasons. Those two women were shafted. And that young man who took everything even now refuses to make sure his sisters are okay, but he's wallowing in millions and millions of dollars that he's not sharing."

"That young man isn't alone," Sarah said. "So many people are selfish."

"Not all of them though," Doreen said. "So let's hope this one, when he's given proof of his father's intentions, will do something to help them."

"We'll see," Sarah said. "I'll give you the information. But I want to know if you ever find anything or if anything comes out of this."

"I promise," Doreen said.

Chapter 24

Monday Late Morning ...

WITH THE 9X12 envelope in hand, Doreen walked back to her vehicle. She put Mugs inside and then drove straight home. She had a bunch of other stops she could make, but now she didn't want to do anything except go home and read what was in the envelope. So that's what she did. She'd made a promise to let Sarah and her daughter know if anything came out of Doreen's work, and Doreen would keep that promise. She really, desperately wanted to know if she could do anything to help those sisters.

And, of course, she couldn't forget the fact that the ice pick had blood on it, nor the fact that Fred and Frank were more than slightly suspicious concerning what happened to their parents and little sister. Doreen would love to find Henrietta alive and well but highly doubted that was possible. Still, Doreen had pulled off a couple minor miracles already. Maybe she could tap yet another one.

Back home again, she unloaded Mugs and headed inside. She put on a cup of tea this time and headed out to her little table on the veranda—next to her small nondescript deck that she couldn't wait to turn into a proper deck—and sat down with the lawyer's notes. As far as an envelope went, it was pretty substantial.

She pulled out papers to find copies of everything and a sticky note to Doreen. "Smart daughter," Doreen murmured to herself as she read it. *Kept the originals. You can come and get them later if you need them for a court case.*

She perused through them and found the will giving the daughters half of everything and the son half. She frowned at that. "He's still a lazy lug and about to have half of *millions*. But that's incredibly greedy, to be unsatisfied with half." As she read through the list of holdings, her eyebrows shot up.

"This could be my ex-husband's portfolio," she murmured. "A lot of money is here." And, for that, the son just dropped down yet another rung. "Talk about greedy and selfish," she muttered. Then she found notes from a private detective. That brought her eyebrows right back up again. As she went farther through the notes, the detective made a point of going through the son's recent history but said there was no proof he'd had anything to do with the father's death.

Doreen sat back and wondered about that. The only two people who would know would be the new lawyer and the son. Somebody had to have made up that new will—the new lawyer obviously—and somebody had to have made it legal. Like filing it with the court or whatever. Again the new lawyer could have done that too.

She didn't understand the complete process, but, as soon as a will was declared the new and active one, then the old one ceased to be. What she had here was *one* will dated a good ten years ago. When was the supposed new will signed and dated? Maybe this one trumped that one. And who signed it? They would need witnesses. Could she find out who those people were? Not without a copy of the new will.

She couldn't text the sisters because of their strange living situation. That bothered Doreen as well. She wondered if Mack could find out who the witnesses were on the new will. Or would that mean requiring a warrant to get into the lawyer's office? Surely wills were filed in public, weren't they? She texted Mack, asking him. He responded with a question mark. She groaned and texted him back. **Can you see who the witnesses are on Burns's *new* will?** She decided to put "new" in italics, of course.

You can ask.

I can?

Yes, he typed, and **you'll get the same answer I will, which is, it's none of our business.**

Unless something's fishy about it?

Correct. Do you really think there is?

Yes, the old lawyer even hired a private detective to look into the son.

At that, her phone rang. Mack asked, "How do you know that?"

She explained about her morning's jaunt and the fact she'd been given an envelope with the lawyer's notes. And then she amended that. "They're photocopies," she said.

He groaned. "Send them to me."

"I just—"

She stared down at the phone as he hung up. She snapped, "Sure, no problem, don't mind helping you out."

But she did get up and took the entire stack of paperwork and walked over to her scanner. It wasn't a bad idea to have a digital copy, given everything else she currently had. With a digital copy scanned through, she emailed it to Mack, then sent it to herself, so she could save it on her laptop in her case files. She had collected a huge amount of information on people. Even she was getting confused. She went back to the folders Bridgeman Solomon had gifted her and searched in his boxes for a file on Ed Burns. Solomon had gathered a little, nothing too bad, except Ed Burns had a few dicey business practices. "And a few dicey fatherly practices too apparently," she muttered.

She could only do so much research online. Sometimes she had to do her research among the living. She walked back to the paperwork, took a look at the private detective's name, researched his name and office info, and picked up her phone.

He answered, "Corey Junior Agency, how can I help you?"

"I'm looking into Ed Burns's will," Doreen said clearly. "I understand you were hired by his lawyer to look into Burns's son, Jude."

There was a hesitation on the other end.

"Unless it is something that you're being paid to keep quiet about now that Ranford is dead?"

Corey snorted at that. "Like that'll happen," he said, "but how the hell do you know I was hired by the lawyer? And what do you know about Jude Burns?"

"I spoke with Sarah this morning, and she and her daughter gave me copies of Ranford's notes. And I know nothing about Jude. That's why I'm calling you."

"And who are you?"

Now she hesitated. "I'm Doreen."

"*Doreen*," he said suspiciously. "Doreen who?"

"Doreen Montgomery, but I doubt you know me."

He laughed. "Are you kidding? I think everybody in town knows who you are by now."

She frowned at the phone. "All good things I hope." But she knew it wouldn't be.

"If I could have the advertising you've managed to get yourself," he said, "I'd be doing really well businesswise. I mean, I do okay, but it's not as if the town knows who I am, the way they know who you are."

"I didn't go after the notoriety," she said glumly. "It seems to have found me instead."

At that, he laughed again. "I'm not upset because, if you can do something to right this wrong, I'd be a happy camper. I dug and dug, and that little weasel is just really slimy. He's never worked a day in his life. Women supported him in his adult life until his dear old dad kicked the bucket, and then he inherited everything. He'll run it all into the ground in no time, and he'll be back looking for some rich woman to support him again."

"Multiple millions are shown here. Surely he can't be that bad."

"The estate might survive him," the private detective admitted, "but I wouldn't count on it. I don't think he has a head for business. Now, the sisters, on the other hand, they're solid people. They worked their butts off, and they've been really good at pulling forward and doing what they need to do."

"Right," she said. "I talked to them too. But I'm not sure you understand how dire their situation is. What's been done to them is a travesty."

He nodded. "I've got a few additional notes for you," he said. "I didn't hand over everything. The things Sarah has are just my rough stuff. But you'll have to come to my office."

"Fine," Doreen agreed. "I'll be at your office in fifteen." And she hung up. She left the two animals at home, taking only Mugs, and dashed to her car and down to his office. It was in the Pandosy area too. One of the small offices on a side street.

When she walked into his office, she saw a madcap mid-forties man with a mop of hair hanging long past his ears and a baseball cap turned sideways on his head. "I'm Doreen," she announced.

He looked at her in surprise, then his face split into a big grin that only widened as he spied Mugs at her feet. He shook her hand and said, "I'm Corey. Nice to meet you."

"And now that we have that over with …"

He walked over to his filing cabinet, pulled out a file, and said, "I've been paid once. I don't want any money for it. If there's anything I can do to help nail this little runt, I'll be happy to do it."

Doreen was delighted with his attitude. "That guy's making friends all over the place, isn't he?"

"He's so not," Corey said with a big, beaming smile. He took his files and said, "Let me take a quick look. If it's of any value I'll scan it for you."

"Thanks," she said. "I'll read it and add it to my notes. I would love a chance to get this guy. Did you happen to get a copy of the death certificate?"

He replied, "I got the death certificate. I spoke to the coroner. There didn't appear to be anything odd about Ranford's heart attack."

"Any unexplained deaths in Jude's other relationships?" she asked, watching as Corey fed things through the scanner. At that, he stopped, turned, and looked at her. "You really do have a dark turn of mind, don't you?"

She smiled. "Is that a yes or a no?"

"It's a yes," he said, "and I tried to nail that on him too, but I never got that far."

"Nail what?"

"His ex-girlfriend. She was older with a heart condition already, and she had a heart attack that killed her."

"Oh, interesting. I don't like that."

"Why is that?"

"That's three heart attacks, *bang, bang, bang.* Burns, Burns's lawyer, now Jude's girlfriend. Way too convenient. Did he inherit anything from the girlfriend?"

"She was supposed to write him into her will, but whether she never got around to it or just told him that to keep him on the string, I don't know, but he never did get anything from her."

She snickered. "Good," she said. "However, did the girl-friend die first? Then Jude's dad?"

"Yeah," Corey said, a frown on his face.

"Because, depending on when she died in relation to when his father died, my concern is the fact that, *maybe* his own father died because of her not leaving Jude something. That, since he was left with nothing, he found another way to get what he needed."

Corey stared out the window as he fed paper through the scanner. "Meaning that, if she had left him enough to live on comfortably, he might not have been too bothered about killing his own father?"

"That's what I'm wondering because she died of a heart attack, his father died of a heart attack. and his father's lawyer died of a heart attack. All in that order. Doesn't that sound like too many related heart attacks?"

"Yes," he admitted. "It's not like we have any proof though."

"Nope," she said. "We don't, but, if it's there, you can bet I'll do my best to find it."

He gave her a big grin. "I like your attitude, and I gather

because of who you are that people tend to give you things that maybe I don't have access to."

"I don't know about that, but it does seem like people have been very helpful." She nodded at his files. "Case in point."

"A journalist was on Ed's case for a while."

"Bridgeman Solomon," Doreen said triumphantly.

Corey stared at her in astonishment. "For someone who just arrived in town a couple months ago, you seem to know a lot."

"Bridgeman is a friend of my grandmother's. He's in hospice care."

"Wow," he said. "That's too bad. That guy is great. He's been a huge icon in town."

"That's what I figured."

"Don't suppose he gave you any insight into it, did he?"

Doreen nodded. "I have a copy of his file too."

He stopped feeding the scanner and asked, "Anything valuable?"

She shook her head. "Nothing concrete, nothing I can take to the police, nothing that can get any warrants or injunctions. Nothing."

"Damn." He shot her a sideways look and a bit of a sly smile. "I hear you have an *in* at the police department too?"

She gave him a bland stare. "You mean, besides the fact that I keep pissing them off and making them work over-time?"

He chuckled at that. "I imagine they're doing a lot of overtime. You've brought a ton of cases to light."

"And solved a large portion of them," she said. "I think I've found more evidence on six or seven cold cases. Maybe more. I don't know."

"You should keep track of it," he said. "Build yourself a little file and put checkmarks beside them, so you know which ones you've solved. If nothing else, when you have a bad day, you can take those out and see where you are doing something with your life."

His tone made her take a closer look. He was in his early to mid-forties. Well, he could even be a well-preserved fifty. What did she know? But a note of sadness was heavily present in his voice.

"I've already been through some of the most depressing times in my life," she said, "and so what you just said is not a bad idea. If nothing else, maybe set up some cue cards with notes of how people have reacted and the thank-yous I've gotten."

"I like that idea too. It's hard to get kudos, and, when we do get them, we need to remember them."

"True."

"You're not thinking about going into the business permanently, are you?"

She was grateful to hear no edgy tone to his voice, as if maybe he was worried about competition. Something was in there, but she didn't quite understand it. She shook her head. "No. I'm just a happy camper with a hobby."

He nodded. "Well, if I can help you with this case, I don't have a problem with that."

"Thank you. I appreciate it," she said. "I'm doing it for the sisters more than anything."

"Right," he said. He smiled, put everything into a big envelope for her, and handed it over. "Remember where you got it from. If you ever need to hire a private detective ..." And he let his voice trail off.

It struck her that maybe his company wasn't doing well.

Kelowna wasn't a huge town, and did anybody really need a private detective in this place? But, right now, as she thought about the murderers and thieves and whatnots she'd come across, she realized there definitely was a need.

She smiled, thanked him, and said, "And if I can help you with any other cases, I'm more than happy to."

He smiled at that. "An unholy alliance," he said.

"I think Mack would think that was what he and I have," she said cheerfully. "The good thing is, because I'm not constrained by police procedures, I get to do what I want."

"And that is huge," the private detective said with a smile. He walked her to the door. "And if you get too much business, send it my way."

"Happy to." Doreen turned and asked, "You have any cards?"

He dashed back to his desk, pulled off a good inch-thick slab of cards, and handed them to her.

She smiled. "You never know, now that people are finding me. I'm trying to figure out what I'm doing with my life," she said. "Not too sure I want to be bothered about fixing up everybody else's lives."

"I hear you. In this business, you do see a lot of the terrible sides to people."

"And that's downright depressing." They shared a commiserating look, and then she led Mugs back out of the office.

At the doorway he called out, "Do the animals really help in your investigation?"

She looked up, smiled, and said, "Not only do they help, they've saved my life many times by now."

His eyebrows shot up at that, and she nodded. "You

have no idea. I've been attacked multiple times, usually by people trying to avoid jail time for their crimes, and my animals have saved me each and every time."

Corey looked down at Mugs and said, "You know that he doesn't look like anything fierce, right?"

She said in a dry tone, "You know he's a pedigree show dog, right?"

He laughed at that. "But I bet he prefers digging in the garden."

"Not only that," she said, "so do I."

"Are you saying you were a pedigree show bitch too?" His grin was infectious, so no insult had been intended.

"I was," she said, "when I was married. But now, like the dog, I much prefer the garden."

And both of them laughed. She walked out and took Mugs back to her vehicle. "Now that was a very interesting visit."

Chapter 25

Monday Late Morning ...

BACK HOME, DOREEN found and scanned in the information herself. "I should have asked him to send me a digital copy, but whatever." She forwarded it to Mack as well.

When he called a little later, he asked, "What are you doing now?"

"I visited the private detective the lawyer Ranford had hired to look into Jude Burns."

Silence. "What did he have to say?"

"Pretty much the same as everybody, that he'd like to do anything he could to help nail this little guy."

Mack snorted at that. "Just love helpful citizens," he said.

"I got the impression his PI business wasn't all that great and that some of the cases were pretty depressing and that he was taking another look at his life and maybe not seeing anything he enjoyed the view of."

Doreen heard a frown in Mack's voice when he asked, "So who is this guy?"

"The owner of Corey Junior Agency," she said. "He's

Corey, according to his cards." She pulled one from her pocket.

"I've heard of him," Mack said, "but I've never met the guy."

"Well, he knew a lot about me," she said, "maybe a little too much."

"What do you mean by that?"

"Just that he knew my name and about the cases I had worked on. Also the fact that I knew you—he called it an 'in' with the police. Of course I told him it was more like an unholy alliance."

At that, Mack laughed. "That's the problem with solving all these cases," he said, "you've become famous."

"Notorious," she said. "Please, *famous* is for the Hollywood jet set. That's not me."

"That's where you came from," he said in all seriousness.

"The glittery outside costume does not match the free spirit inside," she said. "I get that it has taken me a long time to figure that out, but I'm slowly working my way into it."

"Fascinating," he said. "You really are a very interesting woman."

"I'm just me," she said simply. "And the thing is, for the first time, I'm figuring out what *just me* is."

"A very generous, kind-hearted, hardworking woman in transition. Don't expect yourself to be anything yet. How about you just be you for now."

She laughed. "You know what? That's a pretty darn good way to be. I sent you a copy of the PI's file."

"I see that," he said. "So, now I've got all these emails about a case we don't have a case for."

"A copy of the death certificate is there too," she said.

"Right. Ed Burns died of a heart attack."

"Yes," she said, "but do you realize Jude's previous girl-friend also died of a heart attack?"

Silence.

She grinned triumphantly. "I get this was never a case for you guys, so you never investigated. Why would you? It wasn't something brought to your attention. But I am now bringing it to your attention."

"Thank you," he said in a dry tone. "It's not like I don't have a million files sitting here already which you've brought to my attention."

"You're welcome," she said cheerily. "The thing is, three heart attacks makes me suspicious."

"Maybe Jude likes to date the geriatrics set," he said in a low voice.

"Plus, as a gardener, I happen to know that digitalis in our gardens can bring on a heart attack or can help soothe a heart in distress. Just saying ..."

"And you remember what I always say about assumptions."

"Remember that thing called proof and evidence?" she countered. "Because the thing is, if you don't look at the PI's file, we can't possibly know if there is any further evidence or not."

He groaned. "Fine, but I doubt I'll find anything." And he hung up.

She chuckled, and then she realized she hadn't asked him about the forensics on the ice pick. She picked up her phone again and texted him. **What about the ice pick?**

His response was **What about it?**

Human blood?

We said so.

Any matches?

Not yet.

She groaned. "Why does science move so slow?" But, of course, there was no answer. Part of the problem was time, energy, effort, money, probably a myriad of other reasons. Like a bunch of other cases being on Mack's desk. She decided she needed food now. She'd run through enough of her energy, and here she was missing the most basic sustenance of life.

It was Monday, almost afternoon now, and she didn't even remember what they were supposed to do for their next cooking-lesson meal. Technically they had missed their last cooking class, supposedly to be last night, due to Mack's crazy work schedule. She thought they had decided on the upcoming weekend for the next one, but what was it they were eating? She frowned as she made herself a sandwich. As she stared at it, she murmured, "It's a good thing I still love you."

At that, Thaddeus hopped up and tried to steal a piece of lettuce from her sandwich. Goliath jumped up onto the chair next to hers and then on his back legs, his front paws on the tabletop. His nose was almost against her cheese. Doreen shuffled her plate over and said, "Oh, no you don't. Guys, this is mine."

She went to the cupboard—carrying her plate with her—and got out a few treats for each of them, which she placed in front of them. Instantly they gobbled them up, and, just as fast, they were right back to staring at her sandwich.

She shook her head and tried to mumble around a mouthful of food, but they ignored her, staring with their soulful eyes on her sandwich and then glancing up at her and then back at the sandwich. She rolled her eyes at them, and, from her last bite, she carefully separated a piece of cheese, a piece of lettuce, and a little bit of ham—one for each of her critters—and then popped the very last bite of bread into her mouth.

The pieces disappeared.

She grinned. "You're welcome," she said. She got up and put away the food, but she was restless. There was just so much more she wanted to see and to do and to solve. She figured another confrontation with that idiot of a son would be necessary, but she didn't want to get herself into trouble with the police.

And, if Jude started to feel threatened by her, he was just as likely to say she was causing trouble and get an injunction against her. Not that that would be fair, but she couldn't exactly see him going any other way because being an obnoxious and overbearing bully was just who he was. She had looked up where Ed Burns's big house had been and found it easily enough—a huge famous old house on Abbott Street. Just that location alone meant the price tag on the taxes went up by triple what Doreen's were, but the property value itself was easily ten times what her property would sell for.

It was a perfect time to take the animals for a walk. The Burns estate was a good ten-minute drive away, but that was okay. She planned to drive there and then to walk the neighborhood. Monday afternoon found a few cars driving on the streets, and it was a beautiful avenue for walking. She loved the huge trees that overlooked the sidewalks on both sides, plus it led to a walkway under the main bridge into the downtown core.

So, with all three of her animals in her vehicle, she piled in, took her notepad, just in case she had observations to put down, and she had her app to record on her phone now too. It was a gorgeous day—not too hot, not too cold, sitting around the twenty-seven-Celsius degree mark—with the sun, blue sky, and enough clouds to take down the heat of the sun beating on her back by a couple notches.

With Mugs on a leash, Goliath loose, and Thaddeus on her shoulder, she walked toward the address she had on her phone. It couldn't be too far away.

She walked down the sidewalk, smiling at others walking with animals, most remarking at her odd trio. So many people were on bikes and Rollerblades and out enjoying life. The foot traffic was surprisingly heavy for a Monday. She thought for sure people would be at work. Maybe that was the difference here in this residential neighborhood. These people may have retired or may be working from home. The street traffic itself wasn't terribly busy, as it meandered more than going on a straight thoroughfare.

The houses were fascinating. Some had massive gardens. She stopped in front of one in awe. A woman was bent down in the middle of a huge echinacea patch. She lifted her head and smiled, and Doreen exclaimed, "Wow, this is gorgeous."

A flush of pleasure washed over the other woman's face, but Doreen meant it. She appreciated the selection and just the vibrancy. "This is truly beautiful."

The woman smiled and said, "Thank you so much. I have to tell you. It was chosen to be on one of the garden tours."

"I am not surprised," Doreen said. "It's stupendous." After a few more minutes of talking, she wandered on, beaming a big smile at her critters. "You guys were so good back there, letting me talk without causing a fuss. Thank you, guys."

The next interesting place, about three houses down, had a mossy front lawn, but it was done in such a way that the lime-green moss and the dark-green moss were almost like a patchwork around a flagstone sidewalk. It was also fascinating—completely no maintenance, and that had stopped Doreen in her tracks. She stared at it for a long moment and shook her head. "Wow, I never even considered something like this."

A couple walking behind her smiled and said, "Isn't it great? We love walking this street to see so many beautiful gardens."

"Never thought I'd see anything quite like this," Doreen said. She waved at the moss. "And talk about no maintenance."

"Exactly," the husband said. "We've been talking about turning our front lawn into something similar."

"I presume some local business can get these kinds of mosses, and I can't imagine how many years it would take to have them grow into each other like this."

"I think it took two or three years," the woman said. "We've been walking past it for at least five, and I remember it used to be a green grassy lawn but always involved all the irrigation and mowing. Then they took it all out, scraped it flat, came back with topsoil, and planted all the mosses. It was a little sketchy at the beginning. Brown spots were showing up," she said with a smile. "But now it's just stunning."

Doreen was amazed. "Do you think they'd mind if I took a picture of it?"

"Not from here," she said with a laugh. "People come just to take pictures of these properties all the time."

"I didn't even know this area existed," Doreen said,

looking around.

"If you're not a multimillionaire, you wouldn't be living here, so you'd have to find it another way."

"I don't fit that rich category," Doreen said with a smile, "but I could certainly do something like this at home."

"If you have a lawn that's costing you water bills, and you need to do something that'll take back the maintenance, this is a great idea." They gave her animals each a quick pet and said a happy "Have a good day," and walked away.

Doreen pulled out her phone and took several photographs of the lawn and then walked back to the woman in her echinacea garden and asked, "Would you mind if I took some photos of your beautiful garden?"

The woman beamed. "Of course not. Have a go at it. I've been working on this garden for twenty-plus years."

"And it shows," Doreen said with joy. "Some of these plants have to be at least that old."

"Lots of them are, yes," she said.

Doreen smiled to see huge hollyhocks along the corner of the house against the neighbor's. "I haven't seen hollyhocks in a long time."

"My grandmother planted those," she said. "They do ramble over time though."

"I don't mind a little ramble," Doreen said. "It adds that natural touch to a garden, so it's not quite so cultivated looking."

"I agree. Some people place their flagstones at perfect right angles to each other and cut their grass exactly one inch above," she said with a shake of her head. "Not me. I enjoy my garden. I don't want it to be something I have to be militant about."

"Good point," Doreen said, and, for the second time, she waved goodbye and walked on.

Chapter 26

Monday Noon ...

DOREEN AND HER crew still hadn't reached the house she'd been looking for. Several houses later she came to one with a huge imposing brick wall and a massive steel gate in front. Of course this was the Burns house she was looking for. She stopped in front, her trio sitting right beside her feet, while she stared at the old brick that gave the house an estate-looking appeal.

She loved it.

The mammoth wrought iron gates connecting in the center had a big intercom on the side. "Top of the line for everything, isn't it?"

She wondered if the sisters had lived here right up until their father's death. She thought so. It did appear a secondary house was on the property as well, and no reason Jude couldn't let his sisters have that place. She shook her head at that and studied the big imposing place in front of her. It was seriously stunning. But it was also old, with ivy crawling all over it, giving it a bit of a creepy vibe. Just brightening up the windows would help a lot.

She walked to the edge of the property, guiding her animals over with her, where big cedars were lined up, giving the yard and house complete privacy. The old man had been a bit of a loner and had kept to himself and probably kept the girls to themselves too.

Of course the orchards were not here on this property. They were farther south in East Kelowna. And from everything she'd seen about orchards in general, they usually came with a caretaker's house on them too. So why couldn't the girls have had that?

As she and her trio stood here off to the side, admiring the estate, the gates opened, and a Porsche sports car backed out of the driveway. It was him—Jude Burns.

The gates themselves closed automatically. She timed it in her head, trying to figure out if she should go in and take a look around. That would be trespassing though, and a No Trespassing sign was right in front of her. She continued walking to the corner and saw these big properties had alleyways. Delighted, she walked along the back until she came up behind the one she was interested in. The garbage cans were outside, and she already knew from Mack that anything in the garbage was free and clear to be picked through. Not her favorite pastime, but curiosity had her heading toward the recycling bin.

Pizza boxes, pizza boxes, pizza boxes. She stared at them. "Are you serious? You can't even cook yourself a meal in that fancy kitchen you must have in this fancy estate?" Then she stopped, and she pulled herself upright. "At least make a sandwich?" Because, of course, she wasn't doing any cooking either—not that she had this gorgeous house and its matching gorgeous kitchen. But Jude could have hired a cook for that matter.

Amid the pizza boxes was also a stack of papers jammed

down on the side. After snapping a photo with her phone, she reached for them, pulled them out of the recycling bin, tucked them under her arm, and kept going, calling her animals to keep up. She walked all the way around to the front, until she came back to where her car was. Mugs and Thaddeus appeared to be completely content to stick by Doreen's side. Goliath, on the other hand, stalked every bird and squirrel as he came to them. She groaned and—for the umpteenth time—called to Goliath, "Come on, buddy. Let's go."

He just glared at her. She shrugged and said, "We do need to go home." It had been about fifteen minutes since Jude's vehicle had left, and, just as she got Mugs into the front seat and Goliath into the back, the Porsche returned.

It went past her, stopped, and his driver's side window rolled down. She'd already put her purse and the paperwork inside by the time Jude asked, "What are you doing here?"

She looked at him in astonishment. "What do you mean?"

"You don't live here."

"No, I don't," she said, "but I love walking down here. It's beautiful."

He sniffed. "Lazy no-good riffraff," he said, "that's all you are."

"A murdering, lying cheat is all you are too," she said cheerfully, throwing the insults right back at him.

He glared at her. "You are not allowed to say things like that to me. I'll get my lawyers after you."

"Oh, yeah? The same one who put in the fake will for you?"

At that, his eyes turned beady dark, and his face blanched white.

She smiled and nodded. "Oh, yeah, we know," she said. "You can expect some visits from law enforcement any day."

"You're bluffing," he said, glaring at her.

"Yeah, and what about your ex-girlfriend? Did you kill her too, expecting to be part of that inheritance? Too bad you didn't get a chance to change her will for you to inherit that estate as well, huh?"

He hit the gas and tore into his property. She shouldn't have let him get to her, but just seeing that smug, supercilious look on his face had her own ire rising. She knew she would have to confess to Mack—but not right now. Besides, he didn't need to know if it was not important. As far as she was concerned, this guy was not important.

She hopped inside her car and drove home. By the time she got there, Mack and his truck both were in her driveway. He leaned against the side of his vehicle, his arms crossed over his chest, as he glared at her.

She groaned. "What did I do wrong now?"

"Apparently you threatened our little son?"

"He was basically telling me that I wasn't allowed to walk on the streets down there because I was … He did say something about being lazy no-good riffraff or something like that."

At that, Mack's eyebrows shot up. "Seriously?"

She nodded, and then she remembered her phone. She brought it up and hit Replay, and the conversation followed. She was getting good at turning it on without anyone noticing. Good thing this time.

He stared at her. "You can't leave well enough alone, can you?"

"Maybe not, but he killed three people," she snapped, although she had moved closer to Mack to keep her voice down. "Doesn't that count for something?"

"First off, you don't know that he killed anybody. We're back to that assumptions-versus-evidence thing."

"Maybe not yet," she said, "but what if he did?"

"If he did," Mack snapped back, "there's a damn good chance he'll go to extremes in order to not get caught because he has a lot to lose. And, if he's already killed three, he won't give a damn about killing a fourth time."

"I won't be quite so easy to kill by heart attack now," she snapped again.

"And that's why I'm here," Mack said, looking around to see if any nosy neighbors were eavesdropping. "I talked to the captain about Ed's death certificate, and I eventually went down and talked to the coroner. He stands by his report, but, because it was transferred to another area, another autopsy was done, and the case was moved over to the Kamloops District, so our coroner said it never came to any of our attention."

"And why was that?" Doreen dropped her voice like Mack had his.

"The coroner is not at all happy with the heart attack determination. He said Ed did die of a heart attack, but there was no reason for it. There was no heart disease. There were no high cholesterol counts. Ed Burns had a very clean, almost suspiciously clean health record."

"What do you mean by *suspiciously clean?*"

Mack shrugged. "Just the fact that he didn't have anything wrong with him. He should have lived a lot longer. But he didn't."

"And can't sudden heart attacks like that come along normally, without any outside help?"

"Sure, with extreme stress or for all kinds of reasons. But

the second coroner did a drug analysis and didn't come up with anything."

"So Jude found a perfect murder weapon."

"Because that first coroner put *suspicious* on his finding and refused to put down a heart attack as a cause of death, Jude Burns requested and paid for another autopsy, where that doctor flat-out said it was due to a heart attack and did not give a damn about why."

"Money does allow people to say all kinds of things."

"I phoned the second coroner, and he said Jude Burns was pretty strict about making sure the report said just a heart attack caused Ed's death, and Jude didn't want to bother his sisters with worry over trying to find solutions to a problem they couldn't solve. The second coroner said it was obvious it was a heart attack, so that's all he put down—a heart attack."

"And the coroner here?"

"He said he wasn't at all surprised because Ed *did* have a heart attack. Our coroner was just hoping somebody would take a closer look as to why because he didn't have an answer."

"Interesting. How can we figure it out?"

"We can't," Mack said. "If Ed was given something, it was something untraceable."

"I would love for Jude to be responsible here. But let me come at this differently. I'll play devil's advocate for a moment. Is it possible that an untraceable drug brought on the heart attack?"

"Yes."

"But any sudden stress could have brought it on too, right?"

"Yes."

"Not to mention people drop dead for no reason all the time."

Mack nodded slowly. "I did ask our coroner all that, and he said, 'Absolutely.' And he named a couple things I haven't had a chance to research."

"So, it's possible Ed did have a heart attack, and it could have been brought on by something given to him."

"It's possible."

"Did you look into the death of the lawyer?"

Mack just glared at her.

"I know," she said, raising her hands, palms up. "You know how to do your job."

"I do know how to do my job," he said, "and I did talk to the coroner who looked into the lawyer's death. She said it was a heart attack, clean and simple."

"Did Ranford have a history of heart problems?"

He shook his head. "No."

"That's what Sarah said."

"Sarah?"

"Yes," she said. "The lawyer Ranford's wife. He had a few health issues, but it had never been his ticker. Apparently it was clean."

"So you're thinking the lawyer wouldn't accept this new will as valid, and so he had to die?"

"If you've got a will, and it's a new one, and the lawyer won't listen to you, you need to get a new lawyer," Doreen said. "And, if the old lawyer finds anything suspicious about that, then, of course, he'll send up alarms, won't he?"

"Yes," Mack said. "We did look into the girlfriend too."

Doreen beamed at him. "I love it when you're so thorough."

He gave her an eye roll. "You love getting information."

"Yes," she said. "So, what about the girlfriend?"

"Heart attack," he said. "And, yes, she did have a heart murmur, but that was about it."

She stopped and said, "What? A murmur?"

He nodded.

"I'll have to double-check with Corey," she said slowly, "because his report said she had a history of heart issues."

"I just wonder who and what gave him that impression?"

"Right," she said. "Come on. I want to take a look at the file and confirm that."

They walked inside, the animals more than happy to get inside instead of lying around outside. He looked at the critters and said, "You took them all with you?"

She nodded. "Some beautiful gardens are down there, Mack. I took a bunch of photos, but wow. Like seriously. Wow."

"I know," he said, "that area is fairly well-known for it. It's a majorly upscale neighborhood, and the residents have money for gardeners and landscapers and maintenance crews."

"Obviously," she said, "and some of them are stunning."

He just smiled.

Doreen picked up the envelope she had from the investigator, pulled out its contents, and reread his notes. "He says there's a history of a heart condition."

"Sure, but a heart murmur only, that's it."

She read farther. "From birth."

He nodded. "She had a hole in her heart when she was born. But not an issue."

She thrummed her fingers on the table and then pulled out the investigator's card and called him. "Corey, its Doreen."

"Hi, Doreen," he said. "Questions already?"

"You've got a history of heart conditions, so the heart attack wasn't unexpected, right?"

"Whoa, who are we talking about?"

"Oh, sorry," she said. "The ex-girlfriend."

"Yes," he said.

"Where did you get that information from?"

"From the autopsy report, for one. And her sister, I believe."

Doreen flipped through the paperwork and saw the notation there. "Right, the sister. Who inherited?"

"The sister did," he said, then stopped, and went on. "You're thinking it wasn't a heart attack?"

"Oh, it was a heart attack," she said. "I'm sure of that. I was just trying to figure out why the coroner thought it was not unexpected."

"Because of the heart conditions everybody was talking about."

"It was just a murmur," she said. "From all my various research—yes, of validated scientific studies—I've read that, with a murmur, no one should have any reason to expect a heart attack would have taken her. She was pretty young."

"Forty-two," he said, "but unfortunately a lot of people are having heart attacks earlier and earlier."

"Quite true there," she said. "Anyway, thank you."

Before he could ask anything else, she hung up.

Chapter 27

Monday Early Afternoon ...

MACK WAS ALREADY looking at the file in Doreen's hand when she put down her phone. "So now you're thinking Jude might have had something to do with the girlfriend's heart attack?"

"Well, the girlfriend's sister is the one who apparently convinced Corey that her sister did have a heart condition, and, of course, the autopsy report confirmed she did die of a heart attack. But I'd like to see his cause and effect there. What caused her to have her heart attack?" Doreen asked. "I also wonder if Jude really believed his girlfriend had changed her will to include him. Maybe the girlfriend wanted her sister and Jude to share her inheritance. And we all know how Jude feels about sharing. So, before she had a chance to change it, he killed her, only to find out the sister is the one who inherited it all."

"So, now what will you do?" he asked, crossing his arms over his chest again.

"I'm not forgetting about it," she said, "but I was thinking that maybe I would give the sister a call."

"Interesting," he said.

"Why?"

"That's what I would do too."

"Good," she said. "I just have to come up with contact information." She looked through Corey's notes and smiled. "I do like somebody who is thorough," she repeated.

"So, this Corey guy is thorough too?"

"So thorough," she said, "because here's the sister's number." She dialed and realized it was long distance and had to redial. "Of course it'll cost me," she grumbled, but she didn't hang up either. One day she could afford a better cell phone plan. But for the moment it was the cheapest she could find.

"You've got money coming," he said.

"I do but not exactly quickly."

"Hello?" said the voice at the other end.

"Hi, my name is Doreen Montgomery, and I'm calling from Kelowna. It's regarding your ex-boyfriend, Jude Burns," she said.

"No," the sister said with a snap to her tone. "He was my sister's ex-boyfriend. Goodness, who would say such a thing?"

"Oops," Doreen said, "you're right. I'm sorry. I have my notes here, but I got confused for a moment." She rolled her eyes at Mack. "I just wondered what you could tell me about him?"

"He's a sleaze and a gigolo, looking for an opportunity to move up in life."

"Wow, okay, that's fairly succinct," Doreen said. "So, trustworthy, not trustworthy?"

"Not on your life. My sister was looking to break up with him. She was getting a little afraid of being around him."

Doreen had the phone on Speaker, and she asked, "Any idea why?"

"The last few months before her death, she said it felt like he was always watching her."

"But isn't that normal in a relationship?"

"No," she said, "not the same way, in a creepy way. It's hard to explain. But she got really nervous. Plus she told him that she was changing her will to include him, and then it seemed like, after that, their relationship changed."

"*Did* she change her will?"

"No. I talked her out of it," the sister said. "And I didn't know I would be the one she gave everything to, but it makes sense because there are only the two of us, and she was the recipient of everything in my will too."

"How did you feel about her saying she would leave him something in her will?"

"He was one of many," she said snidely. "Why he should think he was that special, I don't know."

"Was there anything suspicious about your sister's death?" she asked.

"I thought about it for a long time," she said, "but honestly the answer is no. I don't believe so."

"Okay," Doreen said. "I just wondered."

"As much as I would like to think that little bugger had something to do with it, I don't think he did."

"He wasn't around? He wasn't there when she died?"

"No, not really. He was there the day before and that evening. But I was with her the next morning, or rather I found her the next morning. He had already gone off to do whatever."

"So, he could have been there during the night?"

"She was still alive when I found her," she said. "We

rushed her to the hospital, and she died a short time later."

"And her boyfriend?"

"Well, security showed him leaving the house at around midnight."

"So you think maybe the heart attack was brought on by an argument? Maybe her breaking up with him?"

"That is exactly what I thought," the sister said. "Back then, you know, I didn't really have any reason to think anything different. She was hung up on him, but, like a lot of her relationships, it was a one-sided situation."

"I'm sorry," Doreen said.

"Me too. Is there anything else you want to know?"

"I just was checking on him," she said. "Did you know his father died, leaving him a massive fortune?"

The woman sucked in her breath and then said, "So typical of a guy like him to end up smelling like roses. He's a user. Every woman on this planet should stay away from him."

"Well, this user just ended up in the roses," Doreen said. "So potentially, very potentially, he doesn't have to prey on women now."

"That kind doesn't change ever," the sister said. "A leopard doesn't change spots, and that little gigolo doesn't change either. He's only out for one person, and that's himself. Now, if you don't mind, I'll hang up and go puke in the toilet," she said caustically. And she hung up with a *click*.

Chapter 28

Monday Afternoon ...

DOREEN LOOKED OVER at Mack. "Wow," she said, "that was interesting."

He shook his head. "You keep pulling on threads."

"The threads are there," she said quietly, "but I don't know what it'll take to prove a will is fake."

"I don't know either," he said, staring off into space. "I'll have to talk to the captain about it."

"Meaning?"

"Meaning, there has to be a reason to go down this path," he said quietly. "Police resources are not to be used willy-nilly."

"And, without any evidence pointing that Jude's done something wrong, we're at a dead end?"

"Exactly," he said. "Just because you want him to be a criminal doesn't mean he is."

"I probably prodded the cat this morning," she said defiantly.

"Let's just hope he doesn't put in a formal police complaint."

"How did you know I was there?"

"He called in, asking what his rights were."

"And?"

"He was given the same notification as everybody—you didn't attack him, you just accused him of something. Our guy says you have to watch that."

"I didn't *actually* accuse him of anything," she said.

"Jude has lawyers, and that could make life difficult for you."

She grumbled as she thought about it and nodded. "Fine," she said, then she smiled, remembering the stack of papers still under her arms. "You did say anything in the garbage was free and clear for other people to sort through."

"If you mean, it's not an invasion of privacy. and you don't need a warrant for it," he corrected, "then, yes."

She dropped the stack of papers on the table and said, "Well, these came from his recycling bin."

She could feel his glare all the way across the kitchen. She turned and looked at him. "Hey, I heeded the No Trespassing sign, even when I wanted to dash inside the security gates and have a look around. What else could I do that at least was legal?"

"Fine," he said. "What is it?"

"For all I know it's just pizza flyers because that's the only thing in his recycling bin. A million pizza boxes."

"Really? With all that money?"

"Right? That's what I thought," she said. "He could have a private chef, but who knows?" At that, Doreen picked up the stack, divided it in half and handed him half. "Take a look to see if anything's there."

They went through the papers and found receipts and bills.

She whistled at the amount on the electric bill. "Seriously? People pay this much for lights?"

"For big houses like that, yes," he said.

She had a bunch of other bills. "His phone bill is here."

Mack looked up at that comment. "Does it have a listing of calls made?"

She nodded and handed over the top couple pages. "Why would he print off this stuff?"

"Maybe he prefers paper bills over digital." He looked at them and frowned. "These are older."

"These are newer," she said. "This is last year anyway."

"What number did you just call? For the sister?"

She read it off to him.

He nodded. "We've got lots of calls from that area code but not to the same number."

"So, probably somebody else."

"Maybe." He pulled out his phone and dialed one of the numbers. "I'm so fishing this time."

Doreen looked at him in delight. She loved it when he took the initiative. Often it was to the case's advantage.

"Yes," he said, "Jude Burns recommended you to me. I understand you might help me with a problem."

At that, Doreen's jaw dropped, and she sank back against her chair and watched the pro at work.

"Yes, I understand there's a price," he said. "Can we meet?" He turned his gaze to Doreen. But she didn't understand his expression.

"No, I'm not in the same province," he said. "That's part of the problem."

Doreen *so* wanted to hear what the guy was saying on the other end.

"Right, of course, you only work by reference." His eyebrows shot up, as he listened further. "I guess I'm wondering what the fee is." He nodded at whatever was said on the other end. "For the same deal as Jude, yes."

Doreen held her breath.

"It's hard to say. Right now there is a heart condition." Mack stared at Doreen, his eyes going wide. "Right, so we're talking ten thousand if there's already a heart condition. But it'll be what, two to three times that if we don't have a heart condition?" He nodded. "Right. Okay, I can see that. And I guess you don't have a website or an email or anything like that?" He stared at Doreen. "Of course not. Just a phone number."

Another moment of silence passed.

"Okay, let me know how I'll get back to you." He hung up. "Jesus Christ."

"Did you just contact a murderer-for-hire?"

He raised his gaze to hers and said, "Yes. Not only that, basically I said Jude referred me to this guy, and that's the only way he works—by word of mouth. And to get the same deal as Jude was literally to have somebody declared dead by a heart attack if they already had a heart condition."

"For ten thousand dollars?"

"Ten thousand dollars with a heart condition, three times that if not."

"What do they do if not?"

"Let's just say it's a whole lot more complicated," Mack snapped.

"But ..." she said, staring at him. "It looks to me like you have a killer out there charging fees, and Jude might have paid him."

"Based on what I just heard," he said, "Jude definitely paid him. I don't know if it was for his ex-girlfriend, his father, or the lawyer."

"Well, if I get to add my opinion in the matter," she said stoutly, "it'll be all three."

Mack looked at her and nodded. "I'm afraid you're right. I need to talk to the captain."

And, like that, he booked it.

Chapter 29

Tuesday Morning ...

DOREEN WAITED FOR the rest of the evening to hear back from Mack—but nothing. Tuesday morning, she woke up a little groggy. Just something about the ultimate lack of humanity in a person who makes a phone call that orders the death of somebody for ten grand could do that to a person. At least to a good person. The fact of the matter was, she and Mack now had that phone number and had contacted the person on the other end of the line.

But she was the one who had taken the material from the recycling bin. She also worried she would have to go to court over a lot of this stuff, which was definitely not what she wanted to do. A roomful of lawyers did not make her feel warm and fuzzy. She frowned as she thought about all the issues going forward and then just shrugged. "It will be what it will be."

To keep her mind otherwise occupied, she opted to dig in her garden in the backyard. Nothing was quite as good as pulling weeds on a mild sunny day to keep a person happy. And sane.

She looked down at the animals sprawled out on the

grass around her. She was still working her way back from the creek toward the house, taking out weeds, fixing the beds. The compost bins were well past full, so she was just making a big separate pile for when the compost bin got picked up and emptied. Then she'd refill the bins. She could do only so much every week because she was filling them so fast.

She could ask Mack to do a dump run or pay for somebody to come and get it, but that wasn't what she wanted to spend her money on. Money wasn't that fluid for her. In fact, it was a whole lot less than fluid.

When she needed to take a break from digging, she made a huge pitcher of lemon water and sat outside drinking it. She kept studying the area of her future deck, wondering if anybody from Mack's department had said anything to Mack regarding extra building supplies they might have. She also needed to clean the house. Just because her house was mostly empty didn't stop the dust from collecting.

Determined to at least accomplish something else today—and it all stopped her from worrying too much—she turned on the vacuum and swept the living room and then wiped down the inside of the big windows here. As she stood in front of them, watching the weekday traffic, another vehicle drove slowly into the cul-de-sac and around. Jude's Porsche. She stared at him, her hands on her hips, wondering if he knew she lived here. But, when he parked right in front of her house and just sat there, she figured he must know. She pulled out her phone, stepped out onto her front porch, and took a picture of him. Immediately the Porsche engine roared to life, and he took off.

She smiled. "Yeah, run away, you little coward." She went back to doing her windows.

When she was almost done, another vehicle pulled up, an old rattletrap truck, and backed into her driveway. She frowned, stepped out onto the porch, and thought she recognized the guy. Sure enough, it was old Arnold, the grizzled cop she'd met her first day here. She smiled at him. "Hey, what's up?"

He just gave a "*Hmmph.*" He walked to the back of his truck and put down his tailgate, allowing her to see a whole pile of beams.

"Oh," she said in delight, "are those for my deck?"

"I guess," he said. "They've been sitting in my yard for at least six months. No sense in them sitting there any longer."

She thought back six months and figured it was before Christmas. "What were you building?"

"We did an extra set of railings and widened a small deck. I don't need these three. Mack said you could use them." He lifted one over his shoulder and said, "Where do you want it?"

She raced around to the side of the house, saying, "Over here, please. Over here."

He made three trips, and she saw they were the same length as the others. She clapped her hands. "Thank you," she said. "I really appreciate it."

He just looked at her, scratched his head, and said, "Well, you'll need a whole lot more yet."

"I know, but every penny I don't have to spend on a piece of wood somebody else doesn't need can pay another bill," she admitted.

"I'll check around," he said. "I don't know if you need two-by-fours. I got some of them hanging around that I don't want either."

She remembered two-by-fours were also on her supply

list. "Hang on a sec. Let me get my list." She raced back into the house, grabbed her diagram and her list, and came out with both.

Arnold took a look. "So, wow, that would be good. Would give you a lot more entertaining space in the backyard, wouldn't it?"

Doreen nodded. "I'd like a decent deck to enjoy. We're looking for ..." and she named off the list of things she needed.

"I got the twelve two-by-fours," Arnold said, tapping one of the lines. "I'll go get those and bring them over in the next day or two."

She put Arnold's name beside that entry. "That would be perfect," she said, beaming.

"I might also have extras. It's always good to have a few spares, in case they split."

She didn't know how many that meant, but she figured a few spares would be helpful. "Thanks so much."

He hopped into the battered old truck, honked at her, and disappeared. She was beside herself with happiness. She had to walk around to the side of her house to look at the big stack of beams once more. She was a little confused about how they were all supposed to go in and stand in place, but, hey, she was happy with what she had so far. She sent Mack a text and a photo of them, saying, **The pile is growing.**

Then she sent him the other photo.

He called her. "Was that from Arnold?"

"It was," she said, laughing. "And guess who came to visit just before him?"

"I saw that too. What did he want?"

"He didn't get out of his Porsche. I stepped out in front and took his picture, but he took off then."

236

"You let me know if he comes back," Mack said in alarm.

"Why?" she asked.

"Because it's possible his killer-for-hire called to confirm he'd given us a reference."

"But how would he know it was me?"

"He wouldn't," Mack said, "unless he saw you in his backyard."

"I don't think so," Doreen said. "He knew I was around the neighborhood, but he couldn't have known I was in his alley. It's impossible to see from the house. Besides, he drove away and only came back when I was leaving with the papers I took from his recycling bin."

"Maybe, but he might have realized what he'd thrown out, gone looking for it, saw it was gone, and thought it had to be you because who else would take it?"

"And meanwhile, I'll be sure not to eat or drink anything he offers me in case it induces a heart attack," Doreen said jokingly. However, she would take Mack's warning seriously. She locked the front door, and she reset the security.

"I'm not joking," he warned.

"No," she said, the fatigue hitting her again. "I'm not taking this lightly."

"Good," he said. "We're on it on this end."

"Good," she said. "Just get on it a little faster."

No sooner had she hung up her phone rang.

"Hello," she said as she walked back into the kitchen.

"Bitch, I'll get you," snapped the angry man on the other end.

"Oh, hey, Jude. How you doing?" Doreen said in a totally bored tone of voice. "You got nothing better to do than rag on another woman? What's the matter? You can't get your girlfriends to talk to you? Oh, yeah, right, they're dead." She hung up on him.

"Probably not a good idea to poke the bear," she said to Mugs. He sat on the floor at her feet, looking at her, a real hangdog look on his face. She crouched in front of him, and he woofed. "I know. I'll be careful."

He shook his head, his big ears flipping and flopping in all directions. She scratched him. "Let's go for a walk," she said. "Someplace to cheer us up."

Mugs raced for his leash, bringing it back, the red handle flying in the air as he dashed toward her.

Doreen laughed. "Okay, but, if we just go down to the creek or something, you don't need a leash."

"*Woof, woof,*" he barked.

She looked over to find Goliath sitting in front of the rear kitchen door, with Thaddeus hopping back and forth on the table, flapping his wings. "So, you all want to go out?"

"Go to Nan's. Go to Nan's," Thaddeus repeated.

She looked at him in surprise. That was a new phrase. "Wow. Thaddeus, you are full of surprises. You know what? That's not a bad idea. We haven't seen her today. Not sure if we saw her yesterday either." Doreen pulled out her phone and sent Nan a text. **Up for a visit?**

Absolutely.
Ten minutes?
Perfect.

"Okay, guys. We're off to Nan's."

Chapter 30

Tuesday Late Afternoon ...

IT WAS LATE afternoon, heading toward dinnertime, but, if Doreen visited with Nan for a bit, she could eat when she got back. With the animals in tow, she walked down to the creek and stopped, amazed as it was even higher yet again. It wasn't dangerously high; it was just amazing to see the water rush by at a terrific rate. The sun shone and twinkled as it danced across the moving surface.

Mugs got a little too close to the creek's edge for her comfort, and she tugged him back in fear. Goliath, on the other hand, was on the other side of the creek a long way away from the bank. Thaddeus squawked and rushed toward her, trying to jump onto her shoulder. She gave him a palm, and he hopped up to her arm, then to her shoulder and to safety. Obviously he didn't like the rush of water either.

"Thaddeus is here," he crooned. "Thaddeus is here."

Doreen rubbed her head gently against his and said, "I'm so glad to have you here."

Together, the four trooped down toward Nan's place. Doreen wondered how long they could walk the path before the high water levels forced them to go another route. That would be sad, indeed. If there was one thing she adored, other than Nan and her animals, it was walking along the water. Something was so freeing and so special about it.

As she walked, she remembered her conversation with Jude and wondered how bad this would get. Should she tell Mack? Then she decided she probably should. She took out her phone and called him.

"Now what?" he growled into the phone.

"Hi, Mack. How are you?" she asked in a sarcastic voice. "Are you home yet?"

"Yes," he said. "Where are you?

"I'm on the way to Nan's."

"Good. What's up?"

"After I talked to you, he called me." Doreen relayed the call as they came up around the turn on the creek, after the last of the residential fencing.

"Interesting," Mack said. "So he seems to have a vendetta against you, which is probably what you can expect after you attacked him publicly."

"Whatever. Just checking in to let you know. I'm coming up to Nan's, so I'll talk to you later." She pocketed her phone again and smiled as Nan stood there, a teapot in her hand. She put the teapot down and bent over as Mugs tried to get away from Doreen so he could go see Nan. Doreen let go of the leash, and he raced across the flagstones and hopped into her little patio. Nan laughed. Fred stood on the other side of the lawn, glaring at Doreen and her animals. Doreen smiled and gave him a nice wave.

"I saw some of your brother's work online," she said. "He seems like a really nice guy who does lovely woodwork." And then she turned away and sat down at the little patio. She loved Nan's bistro set. It was perfect for the two of them;

it was a small table and a little crowded sometimes when Nan brought out a lot of things, but it was cozy.

Nan greeted the rest of the animals, and Thaddeus, not to be outdone, hopped onto the table and walked over to Nan. "Thaddeus is here. Thaddeus is here."

Nan chuckled and gently stroked the bird. "I'm so happy to see you, Mr. Thaddeus." His head bobbed up and down and up and down, as if to say, *Of course you are, of course you are.*

Doreen laughed. "I have to admit it. The animals keep me on my toes."

"They're quite a handful, aren't they?" Nan said.

"Very much so," Doreen said. "But all very worth it."

Nan poured the tea and asked, "So, what kind of trouble are you in now?"

"The usual. I don't really have any evidence. I don't have much except lots of supposition, so I pushed a button on that nasty little son, and he's been pushing back."

"Oh, really? How badly?" Nan's eyes lit up. "Tell me," she said. "Let me see if I can help."

Doreen told her about going to Abbott Street to see the Burns estate and getting sidetracked once or twice with garden talk and then told her about collecting Jude's recycling.

At that, Nan stared at her. "You dug in his garbage?"

Doreen shook her head. "No, no, not his garbage. The recycling bin. It was all pizza boxes, but I also found this stack of paper. Mack is not happy with me."

"Of course not," Nan said. "So, what was in the paperwork?"

Doreen hesitated.

Nan's gaze narrowed.

"You can't tell anyone," Doreen said.

Nan huffed.

"You have to promise," Doreen said quietly. "No betting pools, no going off and talking to your neighbors, *nothing.*"

Nan raised her hands in surrender. "Fine," she said, "but life was never so interesting before you arrived. Then now, with all this hoopla, you're such a stickler for not letting me share. You sound like Mack. I could have such fun with these tidbits."

"It could get me killed," Doreen worried.

Immediately Nan sobered. "Right," she said, "let's stick to what's important."

At that, Doreen explained about what Mack had done, fishing on the phone.

Nan's jaw dropped. She lowered her voice into a hoarse whisper, "He talked to the killer?"

Doreen nodded. "We think so, yes. But now Mack's gone to the captain because Mack didn't pick up the recycling. I did it. They want to confirm they can use it for evidence."

"I never thought of that," Nan said thoughtfully. She nodded. "Very, very important."

"But it still doesn't help us with Fred and Frank," Doreen said, lowering her voice as she looked around.

"I don't know if we can do anything about them," Nan said. "Their parents just went missing."

"And Henrietta too. Remember?" Doreen added.

"And Henrietta." Nan nodded. "Everybody here thought they went back east."

"Except for the fact the parents and Henrietta were legally declared dead seven years after they went *missing*, so they didn't *just go back east.* They might have originally gone back

ICE PICK IN THE IVY

east, but then they went missing, never to be found again."

"Right." Nan nodded in a wise manner.

Doreen just chuckled. "See? Instead of just the one Darbunkle mystery, we now have the Burns mystery, so two mysteries at once."

"But it doesn't really mean it's a mystery," Nan said. "For all you know, one of the Darbunkle parents ended up with a crippling disease, and they decided to self-terminate."

"Self-terminate?" Doreen rolled that term around in her head. "That sounds a little dodgy, doesn't it?"

"Call it murder-suicide if you want. It's all dodgy," Nan said with a chuckle. She looked down at her tea. "Too bad I don't have any more zucchini bread."

"I still have some at home," Doreen said, "although not much because Mack had several slices."

"I ended up sharing another loaf around here too," Nan said. "I saved myself one piece, and I had that this morning."

"I'm fine without it," Doreen said.

"Do you need any more veggies? We keep getting baskets of it here." Nan hopped up, returning a few minutes later with more of the same fresh vegetables. They divvied up some for Doreen to take back.

"I'll make a big salad for dinner," Doreen said, "maybe add a can of tuna or something."

"You do that," Nan said. "I have a couple people here I could talk to. Let me get back to you on those mysteries of yours."

"Are we talking about Ed Burns or are we talking about the Darbunkle parents?"

"Both," Nan said thoughtfully. "You never know who here might know something."

"True," Doreen said, "but we have to keep it on the

down-low."

"Will do."

As soon as they finished their tea, Doreen picked up her fresh veggies, gathered her crew, and headed back up the creek. She took her time—the sun was beautiful. As she got closer to her house, she thought she saw somebody in her backyard, and she raced around the corner, but no one was there. Instinctively she headed to the front of the house, only to see a Porsche heading down around the cul-de-sac. "So he's getting bolder," she said. "Just how bold will he get?"

At her door, she found the security lock was still on. Grateful she'd set it, she opened the door, disarmed the security, and let everybody back into the house. She reset it afterward. It was past dinnertime, so she made a big healthy green salad with lots of raw veggies and a can of tuna and then sat back outside, while she thought about all the happenings so far.

She didn't know about a lot of the connections here. The big one was, who was this killer-for-hire, and how would Mack and the local cops go after him? After all, he seemed to live in another province—not exactly Mack's territory. And what would the cops do about Jude Burns, the little piss-ant of a greedy murdering son? While she ate her salad, her phone rang. It was Nan. Doreen put it on Speaker. "Hello, Nan. I'm having a salad right now, with all your fresh veggies. Thanks again. What are you up to?"

"I talked to Sylvia," she said. "She was Ed Burns's cleaning lady."

"Oh," Doreen said. "I never thought about that angle. Is she in Rosemoor with you?"

"She is. She's one of the younger residents. I know she's always worried about not having enough money to make it through. Ed was supposed to leave her money too, but he didn't."

"Wow, nice guy."

"No, everybody thought it was all settled, but then Jude arrived with this new will that the new lawyer said was perfectly legal, and they took everything away from everybody."

"Right, that's what I'm trying to fix," Doreen said.

"She said there was another will because she was a witness to it."

"Another one?"

"Yes," Nan said, "and it's in Ed's home office somewhere. But, if Jude found it, she figures he destroyed it."

"Would that will supersede the one Jude produced?"

"Yes. Not to mention you can't legally get into his house or that home office," Nan said.

"No, it might take Mack to do that. I wonder though, can you find out where in the office it would be? Because, if it was just in his desk, Jude would have definitely gotten rid of it. But if it had been hidden—"

"His desk had a secret drawer," Nan said, "kind of like our furniture. It was an antique desk, and it was in there."

"Do you know when he signed it?"

"It was just a few days before he died. He was feeling angry with his son. Jude had only wanted to come back if something was in it for him to come back for. And he had no intention of waiting until his father died. His father was angry about the whole thing and called his lawyer to come over to his house and to draft a new will."

"But wouldn't the lawyer have had a copy?"

"There was some discussion about it, and he was supposed to do something with it, but then, as far as I understand, he died."

"The lawyer did pass away, but he didn't pass away until after Ed Burns did. Although it was soon afterward." After hanging up with Nan, Doreen sent Mack a text. **Dingbat was here in the backyard.**

Her phone rang immediately. "Are you serious?"

"I saw somebody come around the corner of the house, as I came back from Nan's, so I went out front and saw the Porsche disappearing."

There was silence on Mack's end of the call, but Doreen could hear his anger thrumming through the lines. "He didn't do anything," she said gently.

"But he's getting bolder," Mack snapped.

"Yeah, he is. Also," she said, "Nan had an interesting tidbit," and she told him about the cleaning lady.

"I'll have a talk with her myself tonight," Mack said. "If she confirms this, I need to open an investigation."

"Good," Doreen said. "You need to make it official. I wish I could go to Ed Burns's home office and take a look. I did learn a lot about antiques and their secret drawers."

Mack hesitated.

"I can come with you."

"No," he said. "We can't do that without a warrant, and I need cause in order to have a warrant."

"I hear you there," she said, "but ..."

"No," he said firmly. "I'll talk with the cleaning lady, and I might stop in and talk with Jude too."

"Good," she said. "I'd like to see him pee in his pants. I really don't like being threatened by him."

"Maybe you could just stay out of trouble for once," Mack said in exasperation.

"Maybe," Doreen said cheerfully. "But maybe not." And she hung up.

Chapter 31

Tuesday Late Afternoon ...

DOREEN WALKED BACK to her computer and studied as many different angles on these cases as she could, but everything she did drew a blank. She needed Jude to either break or do something stupid, like attack her, so they had a reason to go into his house, particularly Ed's home office to search the desk for that later will.

"Which would be perfect," she said out loud. Or she needed to find a way to get in there without anybody knowing. She hemmed and hawed over the possibilities, but, no matter what she thought of, it would put her in the wrong light. And that, she didn't want to do.

She walked out front and sat on the porch steps, and it didn't take long for the Porsche to come around again. As soon as it came up to her driveway, it stopped. She watched as he got out, apparently not seeing her. She crouched down on the front step so she peered around the bushes through the railing. She sent Mack a text. **He's here again.**

And, indeed, he snuck up around the back of her driveway. As soon as he was out of sight, she snuck back into the house and raced to the kitchen door, which was propped open for the animals sprawled out in the backyard, enjoying the warm evening air. As she watched, he came around the side, crept up to the door and into the house. She was hiding in her kitchen area by her printer, and she started videotaping his entrance into her home. He swept through the kitchen and all of downstairs and then she heard him go upstairs.

She wondered what he was looking for, then she knew. He was after the papers she had taken from his recycling bin. She frowned and saw them under her laptop. Did she dare move them? She grabbed them and shoved them into her scanner. As it started working, Jude came back down the stairs and confronted her.

She cried out in false alarm. "What are you doing in my house?" This guy had a lot of nerve ...

"You stupid bitch," he said, "you don't know what you're dealing with."

"What are you talking about?" she said, advancing on him. "How dare you come into my house?"

"I'll go wherever the hell I want," he said. "You stole from me."

That stopped her in her tracks. "What are you talking about? I didn't steal anything." Mugs, hearing her raised voice, was suddenly in the doorway. And darn if Thaddeus wasn't riding on his back. Of Goliath, there was no sign. ... And that made her even more suspicious.

Jude paused for a moment. "You stole from my recycling bin."

She laughed. "Seriously?"

"I accidentally threw something away," he said, "and you're the only one who would have found and taken it."

"What was it?" she asked.

Just then, he looked behind her to see the last page on the scanner. He snatched the papers from the machine and held them up. "These," he said. "I'll have my lawyer after you for this."

"You could," she said, "but I'm pretty sure the lawyer will be covering his own butt. Besides, I didn't steal those. Anything you throw into the garbage and into your trash bins off your property is for anybody to collect. It's not theft. You threw it away. I have full rights to take it."

Jude stopped.

She gave a crisp, clean nod. "You should learn the law before you start accusing people of breaking it. If you hadn't hired that jerk to kill your father and your girlfriend and your previous lawyer, you wouldn't be facing three murder charges."

He stared at her, his jaw working.

"Oh, yeah, I know," she said. "I also know there's another will. But I won't tell you where it is." She smiled sweetly. "So, I highly suggest you come up with a decent story to get yourself off the hook on that one."

"You interfering no-good ... witch." He stepped toward her.

But Mugs jumped behind him, barking ferociously, momentarily diverting his attention.

Doreen sidestepped him and ran outside into the backyard. She still had her camera on and was recording.

As he charged toward her, she said, "I'm taping this. Go ahead and hit me. We'll add assault and battery to your charges."

"I didn't touch you," he said, stopping in his tracks.

Surprisingly, Doreen's grouchy neighbor Richard popped up over the top of the fence. "Doreen, are you okay?"

"No," she said, "Jude Burns has threatened me, entered my home without my permission, and has now taken something of mine from my house."

Jude stared at her in astonishment. "These papers are mine."

"Which you threw away," she said. "Now you've come into my house illegally, and you've taken them away from me." She turned to Richard and said, "Call Mack."

As quickly as he arrived, Richard's head disappeared around the corner.

"I thought nobody liked you. Why would your neighbor help you?"

"Because I helped him," she said. "But what do you know about helping people? You are just a taker."

He glared at her. "I'm not going to jail," he said. "There is no way."

"Of course not," she said. "You didn't actually kill them, did you? I mean, it was your killer-for-hire who you paid to do it. I wonder where you got the ten grand to pay for each of their murders though. That's a lot of money. Of course, maybe your girlfriend kept that loose change around, and you took advantage by searching her place while she lay dying."

Jude's face worked, and Doreen nodded. "Yeah, you think I don't know how this works?" she said. "I wonder if you have something to do with that ice pick though."

"I don't have a clue what you're talking about. This is all so long ago. Why are you dredging any of it up?"

"I know it was a long time ago," she said, "but some things never change. Your sisters are living terrible lives."

"Why do they deserve anything better?" he asked.

"They're no different from me. Why should they get all the money, and I get nothing?"

"Why didn't you share with them?" she asked.

"Why should I? He left the money to me," Jude said and tapped his chest. "My dad left the money to me."

"Did he though?" she said with a snarky smile. "Funny how your father's lawyer died around the same time. The police are opening an investigation into your will," she lied. She hoped Mack would, but it was premature at this point.

Jude paled at that.

"You think I didn't know about that? I've got all the lawyer's notes, and I turned it all over to the police."

When she said that, something came over him. It was almost like a coldness, a chill. "Then I have nothing to lose." He advanced on her.

She realized she was in imminent danger now and took several hurried steps backward. "What will you do?"

"Well, according to you, I've already killed three people," he said, "so what difference does a fourth make?" His words echoed Mack's earlier words.

"I guess the question is whether you killed anybody else too. Somebody killed by an ice pick."

He stared at her, puzzled. "What are you talking about?"

"I'm missing an ice pick," she announced. "I'm expecting to find out it was used to kill somebody."

"Just who are you?" he asked, puzzled.

"Doreen," she said with a wave of her hand. "Somebody with a hobby of solving cold cases."

"My life was never *a case*. Get your nose out of my business!" He glared at her. "Why do you care?"

"Because it's wrong. And, if I get a chance to cheer on the underdog and right some wrongs, I will do so. If you had anything to do with your father's death, your girlfriend's death, or your father's lawyer's death, then you need to pay for it. And stealing all that money from your sisters is just nasty."

He shook his head. "What does any of that have to do with an ice pick?"

"I'm missing one," she said. She looked at him hopefully. "It was a set your father had on display."

He stared at her, then scratched the back of his head.

"Good Lord," she said, "you know what happened to it."

He looked at her and groaned. "I do know what happened to the ice pick, but it didn't murder anybody."

"I'm glad to hear that," she said, "because the maker would like it back."

"I gave the set to the maker's brother."

"Fred? You gave the set to Fred? Why would you do that?"

"He wanted them badly, so I gave the set to him. Something about my father having ruined his brother's reputation or some such thing. I don't know anything more about that."

"You don't look like the giving type."

Frustrated, he snapped, "Because he saw something, and the set was payment for his silence."

"What did he see?"

Jude frowned. "It doesn't matter."

She nodded. "What were you doing that Fred saw?"

"None of your business," he said. "I'll call my lawyer about this." He pulled out his phone.

"Go ahead," she said. "Contact the one cheesy illegal lawyer you've got. I'm sure that'll make for great courtroom drama." She stopped and said, "It wasn't Frank you gave it to. It was Fred."

"I know that. I just said I gave it to the maker's brother. Don't you listen?" he asked, dialing his phone again and then stopping, hesitating as if not sure what to do.

"You gave them back to Fred because Fred did the landscaping for Ed Burns," she said. "I'm slow, but I do finally get there. He saw you kill your father."

"I didn't kill my father." He tried for outrage but failed miserably.

"Fred saw something," she said, letting a smirk show. Anything to rattle Jude more. "Something ugly. Although I'm surprised that's all he wanted because they don't have much."

"Maybe," Jude said. "But that's all I'll say on the matter."

"No, it's not. The only reason you'd buckle to that type of pressure is if Fred saw something really good. Although maybe Fred was too scared to ask for more. What did he see? He saw you kill your father?" She was fishing and taking a chance on pissing off yet another potential killer, but something had to get him to talk. At least he seemed to have forgotten that she was recording this conversation.

A pale sickly look washed over his face.

"Aha. I was right. Why you weaselly greedy lazy ..." Words failed her then. "Why couldn't you have found another way. You didn't have to kill him."

"I'm not talking to you anymore. If you want information, I want a deal." He stiffened his back and stuck his nose in the air.

Like she hadn't seen the best of the snobs do that. He couldn't even begin to pull off that maneuver. "I can't give you a deal, and I doubt even the cops will give it to you.

Why should they? You're just another no-good greedy killer who couldn't be bothered to get a real job." She gave him a big fat smile. "That's okay. I think prison will give you a job, so you can finally work for a living."

"I'll give you the other killer," he cried out desperately. "Then I can walk free."

"You just admitted to killing all these people." She shook her head. "Why would you go free?"

"I didn't admit to anything. I had nothing to do with any of this, but I know someone who's way worse than I am," he blustered. "Why the hell couldn't you just go away and leave me alone?"

"Why couldn't you have looked after your sisters?" she countered, hating that it was all about money.

"Is money what this is all about?" he asked, relaxing, as if seeing a way out of his corner. "Fine, I'll give them some money."

"You realize they're both working as nannies. Unpaid but for their room and board. They can't even have a cell phone of their own, and they get only fifty dollars for gas. That's it."

He stared at her. "Is that even legal?" he asked in amusement. "I knew they were losers but to end up there …" He just shook his head, pissing her off more.

"All you had to do was treat them like people, and they would have been happy. You even have that spare house on the property."

"They used to live there," he admitted.

"Why did you kick them out?"

"I was afraid they'd find out, figure it out," he snapped. "If they are anything like me, they'd have stuck their nose into my business and found out what I was up to. I couldn't have that. I risked too much for this."

"And you'd throw another killer under the bus to keep it?"

"Absolutely. Deal?" he asked, looking at her hopefully. "It's about Fred and Frank. They are the killers."

"Bingo," she whispered under her breath.

Chapter 32

Tuesday Evening ...

"BUT THEN, *LIKE you said*, you can't make that kind of a deal." Jude nodded, but he glanced about in the growing gloom as the sun sank around them, as if his mind spun with options.

"Maybe the cops will make you a deal though. Fred and Frank, huh?"

But he clammed up and shrugged his shoulders, an insolent look shifting across his features. Not liking Jude's assessing gaze, Doreen could only hope Richard had contacted Mack. As she studied Jude, she said, "Did you have to kill your girlfriend?"

"She was breaking up with me," he said absentmindedly. "At the time I wasn't thinking of my father. But, once it worked so well with her, and my father being old, I knew it would work well with him."

"So you killed her, then realized you wouldn't get her money, so you came home to make sure you got something. But instead of being happy with half of it, you had to change the will so you got all of it."

"What can I say?" he said. "I got greedy."

"You're no happier," she said quietly. "In fact, I can't see that you're happy at all. You've got nobody who cares about you, nobody who wants to be with you. You don't seem to have any friends."

"That's a problem," he said. "When you don't have money, you collect friends who do have money, so you hopefully don't have to pay for everything, and so you can get something from them. But, when you do have money, you know that's what other people are like, so you stay away from people because all they're after is your money."

"Wow. What a horrid way to look at money, friends, life, all the while living your life that way." Then Doreen laughed. "It's almost like karma got you. And you've got to watch it because, when she comes around, she bites you in the butt."

"What does this have to do with Frank or Fred anyway?"

"Oh, I have a pretty good idea," she said, "but it'll take a little more to figure this out."

He groaned. "What's this got to do with you? What's your price? How much to make you go away? Or to have you at least disappear long enough for me to sell up and move?"

"You're talking to the wrong person," she said, as she watched Mack come around the side of her house. "Because really, when you kill people, you can't walk away free and clear."

"I didn't kill anybody," he protested.

"Paying ten grand a head to get medication to induce a heart attack *is* killing," she said. "I'm sorry you seem to be so disassociated from the reality of your actions."

"You called my contact, didn't you?" He glared at her in disbelief. "What a bleeding nosy busybody you are."

Doreen shrugged. "We had to confirm the price. I mean, everybody's got somebody they'd like to get rid of for ten thousand dollars. It's just most people don't actually do it. They have more morals than to kill somebody for that paltry amount of money."

"It's the only money I had, and he was the cheapest I could find," he snapped. "Like you said, everybody has somebody they'd like to get rid of."

"And, of course, a fake will helped too, didn't it?"

"That was my lawyer's idea, something to add to the pot. He didn't see why I should only get half."

"And this is, of course, your new lawyer."

"Yeah, he knows my hitman too. The thing is, you either take the money I'm offering you, or I end up paying another ten grand," he said with a wave of his hand. "With the money I've got, I can wipe out this town."

"And you think nobody will notice?" Doreen said with a smile because, of course, Mack was now listening with two cops behind him.

"I don't give a shit," he said. "Ten thousand to get rid of anybody you don't like—that's cheap."

"Well, it's thirty if they don't have a heart condition," she said, "and you can bet I don't have a heart condition."

"I'll pay thirty grand to get rid of you anytime," he sneered.

"Too bad," she said, "because you can't do that now."

"Oh, yes, I can." He turned but still stared at her.

"I wouldn't sleep at night if I were you. I'll just arrange one time to make sure you never wake up. You won't know *when*, so you will spend your life looking over your shoulder."

"Maybe you should look over your shoulder now?"

Mack asked, his arms across his chest, the two cops at his side.

Jude spun around to see the cops, then looked back at Doreen.

All three men watched Jude, and Mack said, "By the way, you're under arrest."

Doreen shrugged. "You know what? You really have a big mouth. All you had to do was be a nice guy, share the money with your sisters, and you could have kept your half."

"You," he snapped, "will pay for this."

"Maybe," she said with a sunny smile. "But it won't be because of you."

"I get a phone call," he said.

"Yeah, you do, but I'm pretty sure the cops can take care of your ten-thousand-dollar-a-deal killer too."

He sneered. "You have to catch him first."

"We already accomplished that," Mack said. "Our officers picked him up about twenty minutes ago. When he found out you gave him up, he was pretty livid. So you might want to watch what you drink when you're in jail because he has better connections than you do."

"You lied! I didn't give him up. Then you have to protect me," Jude cried out. "You don't know how many people that guy has killed."

"No," Mack said, "but we'll enjoy hearing about it."

Jude turned to look at her. "Remember? I said I want immunity."

At that, Mack's eyebrows shot up. "She doesn't have the authority to give you immunity."

"I did tell him that," Doreen said with a smile at Mack. "But he's talking about information on Frank and Fred."

At that, all three of the men looked at her in astonishment.

"What?" Mack asked.

"He gave Fred the matching ice picks," she said.

Mack nodded, but he was still staring at her in disbelief.

"Fred was doing the landscaping when I was going through the desk, looking for the will," Jude snapped. "My father was already dying, and I didn't do anything to help him. Why would I help him?" he sneered. "I'm the one who gave him the pills in his drink so he would die. I heard my sisters coming home and hid. Thankfully their intervention didn't save my father."

Doreen held up her phone, so Mack would see she was still recording.

He nodded. "So you gave Fred the ice picks to keep him quiet?"

"That and some money," he added for the first time.

Doreen perked up at that. She didn't think Fred would pass up an opportunity like that.

"Fred said he needed to make some people disappear a little better."

"Interesting," Mack said. "Any idea who it was?"

"Of course," he said. "Same as me, his parents."

"Disappear where?"

He shrugged. "How would I know?" he said.

Mack just looked at Doreen.

She shrugged and said, "I highly suspect we need to check their property. You'll find a missing ice pick buried somewhere. So maybe use a metal detector or at least the cadaver dogs. They're getting quite a workout here lately."

Mack groaned. "We need a little more than that. We can't just go digging up people's properties."

"I don't think Frank had anything to do with it. He's

the one who had his parents declared missing. If you check the paperwork, I bet Fred didn't say anything."

"You think Fred killed them?"

She nodded. "Or paid to have them killed. I just don't know why, and neither do I know where Henrietta is."

"What? There's something you don't know?" one of the cops beside her asked as he flicked a hand through his hair. "Amazing. I guess if we give you another ten minutes or maybe an hour, you'll figure this all out?"

She glared at him. "You guys didn't even know Jude had three people killed," she said, "or the fact that Fred might have killed his parents. Now, I don't know what happened to Henrietta. And that does concern me, but I'm pretty sure, if you talk to both brothers now, you'll figure it out."

At that moment, Jude bolted toward the creek.

Doreen groaned. "Seriously?"

The two cops ran after him, but *they* didn't get him. However, Mugs was already waiting for him. As soon as Jude got close, Mugs jumped him. Jude tried to avoid the dog, but Mugs grabbed him by the ankle and gave a hard shake.

Doreen had to admit Mugs might not look like much of an attack dog, but he was solid and hefty. Jude went down, and Goliath jumped onto the back of his head with his claws. Jude screamed, trying to come up onto his hands and knees, but Thaddeus was crawling up and down his arms and shoulders, digging in his claws with every step. "Thaddeus is here. Thaddeus is here."

Finally Jude roared, "I give up. I give up."

Doreen looked at Mack and shrugged. "You should be happy," she said with a smile. "This suspect didn't attack me this time."

He rolled his eyes at her. "Maybe not," he said, "but it's

still a big mess."

"But a big Burns mess with a couple killers caught," she said. "And two or three more murders we have to look into the Darbunkle family about."

"I get it," he said, in a gentle voice. "And now I get what this is all about. The sisters. All three of them."

"Somebody's got to look after the women because, way too often, they just get taken advantage of."

He gave her a soft smile. "And since you were taken advantage of, you're trying to help those who can't help themselves?"

"To a certain extent. I think in Henrietta's case, it's already way too late."

He gave a sober nod. "I'm afraid you may be right."

Chapter 33

Wednesday Morning...

O N WEDNESDAY MORNING, Doreen woke up bright and early, feeling mighty cheerful. She got up to answer Nan's call.

"Wow, they came and picked up Fred," she said. "Mack, Darren, Richie—everybody was all over him."

"And?"

"Well," she said, "he bolted. They're still looking for him."

"Great," Doreen said. "With my luck, he's coming here."

"Why would he do that?" Nan asked.

"Because I might have sicced Mack on him."

Nan gasped.

"Look. I'll get up, get dressed, and put on coffee," Doreen said. "When I have some caffeine in my system, I'll call you back." She hung up, quickly dressed, and went downstairs. While she was piling her hair up into a clip, she looked outside. The bright morning sun was shining in, and it looked like a gorgeous day—except it felt off. Ugly in a way she couldn't describe. She popped open the back door after disarming the security and then put on coffee. When she turned around to face the door and look outside, there was Fred.

She sighed. "Sorry, Fred," she said, "but, when you do something like that, it comes back to bite you in the butt."

He shook his head. "I didn't mean to."

"Maybe not," she said gently. She reached for her phone, putting it on video again, and setting it on the counter so he didn't think she was still looking at it. "I know you didn't mean to kill them," she said, "but, when bad things happen, you know that, while you like to think you can keep it all hidden, eventually it comes out."

"It was self-defense," he said sadly. "Me hitting my dad."

She raised her eyebrows at that. "In that case, you should have gone to the cops."

"I figured they wouldn't believe me," he said, his tone low, "because it involved Henrietta."

"What about Henrietta?"

"My father beat her," he said, "and killed her. I don't think he meant to, but they were at the top of the stairs, and he hit her really hard, so she fell down, and she died. And he couldn't turn himself in because the blow to Henrietta's head would have shown up. Dad committed murder. We were all shocked and didn't know what to do."

"What did you do with Henrietta's body?"

"She's buried on the property," he said, shoving his hands into his pockets. "Frank knows about it too."

"And your parents?"

"It was pretty sad. My mom was inconsolable, and she wanted to die too. She'd just sit outside in the yard, bawling over the spot where Henrietta was. Finally Mom pleaded with my dad to please kill her so she could be with Henriet-

ICE PICK IN THE IVY

ta. Mom said Henrietta shouldn't be alone, that somebody needed to be with her. Finally she grabbed my dad's gun and shot herself."

"Oh, dear," Doreen said, "and now you'd lost two family members."

"Honestly, I got so mad at my dad that we got into a fight. I ended up hitting him hard in the nose, and it's like he stood there for a moment, and then he just keeled over dead." He paused, such sadness in his eyes. "I think that punch sent a bone straight through his brain."

"Oh, no," she said, reaching up a hand to rub her temple. "I'm so sorry. I'm sure that still would have been the time to contact the cops."

"We've always kept it to ourselves," Fred said. "It wasn't any different then. I know I'll have to face charges, but I don't want my brother involved. We started the rumors that they'd left to cover their disappearance but we had to keep the house somehow, it's all we had. So well after seven years we applied to have them declared dead." He shrugged. "There didn't seem to be much else to do."

"So what was the deal with the ice picks?"

He groaned. "The only reason Ed Burns bought them was so he could put them up on the wall and show everybody what a lousy town it was and how poor the craftsmen were. He didn't buy them because he was proud of Frank and his work. Ed bought them because he wanted to jeer at Frank. Ed made him the laughingstock of the town. Frank had a hard time. He lost the business because he couldn't do anything anymore, and he was just so heartbroken. And every time he talked to Ed, Frank asked to get the set back, and it was always the same thing. Ed said, no way. He would keep it as a reminder of how shitty Frank's work was. So when I saw that little weasel son in his father's office, with his dad dying beside him, he gave the set of ice picks back to me and fifty thousand, so we could get ahead. I took it. I shouldn't have, but I did. I wanted that set back for my brother."

"And yet your brother didn't hang on to them?"

He shook his head. "No, he didn't. He tossed them."

"But one is covered in human blood," Doreen said with a gentle smile. "So somebody found it."

"Maybe," he said. "I don't know about that."

"Yeah, you do," she said, crossing her arms. "Who did you kill with that ice pick?"

He glared at her.

She shrugged. "I'm not done yet," she said. "Whose blood is on that ice pick?"

He groaned. "You never quit digging, do you?"

"No, I don't. Whose blood is it?"

"It's mine," he said. "That's why I limp. My brother and I had a fight, when he found out I'd blackmailed Jude to retrieve my brother's ice picks. I thought he would want them back. I thought he would think about his award. But, at the time, keeping the family secrets for five years had taken their toll. Ed's shaming of Frank had taken its toll. To see the tools again, Frank was reminded of all that bad stuff that he didn't want to remember, yet he could never stop thinking about it all. Or at least I can't stop thinking about it. Anyway Frank reacted immediately, striking out at me with one of the ice picks. So, the blood is mine," he said sadly.

"After I got hurt, he took the picks out ice fishing and chucked them. He should have chucked them into the lake. Instead, he tossed them both into the mess of ivy on the far side of the trail. He didn't even think about it after that, at least not for a while. He came home. I got my leg treated, and we moved on. He did go look for them later but only found one. Still, you don't get over death and loss fast. You don't get over anything that devastating in any way that is fast enough. We haven't been the same since."

"Did Frank have anything to do with your sister's or your father's deaths?"

He shook his head. "No, but he helped me clean up everything because we didn't know what else to do. Frank was always good with his hands. No matter what Mr. Burns thought of him, Frank made beautiful tools. But, like you, he wanted me to go to the police. And I wouldn't do it. I thought Jude's money was a good solution when I got enough from him to build the big greenhouse on top of Mom and Dad and Henrietta, so they'd be even more hidden, but Jude was bound to get caught too. I was always afraid of the damage he could do to me and my brother over that blackmail, making us accessories to Jude's dad's murder. I figured I could get Jude into more trouble at the time, but his money has allowed him to skate through so much." He shoved his fists even deeper into his pockets.

"I get that, and, at this point," Doreen said, "the best thing you can do is turn yourself in."

"I know," he said. "I heard the rumors that you got a hold of that weasel Jude Burns. Is that correct? I sure hope it is. I hope you throw him in jail and toss away the key."

"It'll take a while to prove everything, but it looks like he had three people killed, including his father, and forged a will in order to steal everything from his sisters."

"People are just greedy," Fred said, "and my dad? Well, he had a horrible temper."

"I'm so sorry."

He nodded and headed out the back door again. "I'm heading down to the police station right now."

She walked with him to the door. "Please do," she said. "I'm not sure how to make it any easier on you."

"It doesn't matter," he said. "I'm ready to face whatever it is they want to throw at me." He looked at her and said, "I knew that, once you were on the case, you would never let it go. So I might as well confess and make it easier on myself."

With that, he headed out around her house to the driveway. Doreen raced to the front door to see him get into his car and drive away. She phoned Mack immediately and told him what was happening.

"Good," he said, "that should tie up another one."

"Maybe," she said. "Where are you?"

"I'm down at Jude's place with a warrant. We're looking for the will that was supposedly in this desk. I talked to the cleaning lady too, and she says it's here, but I can't get the damn drawers open."

"Can I come?" Doreen cried out. "Please, please, please."

"Fine," Mack said, "but you look at the desk to see if you can find the secret drawers, and that's it."

"I'm on my way." Doreen loaded up her menagerie and headed to the beautiful house on Abbott. The gates were open, and cops were all over the place. She walked up to the front steps, and the guard cop looked at her, groaned, and said, "Really? Your animals too?"

She shrugged. "They're part of my think tank." And she walked into the home office, looked at the desk, and smiled. "You know something? I think I *do* know this one."

"How would you know that?" Mack asked.

"Just one of my many talks with Scott," she said, "but I

better see first." She sat down at the desk, studied it for a long moment, and felt along the side where she thought the secret drawer might be. But instead, she found a tiny indent along the back. She pressed that, and a drawer popped out.

Mack dove for it and pulled out the will. He unrolled it while everyone crowded around him. "It's dated two days before his death, all signed, nice and legal." He looked at it and laughed. "He changed it and left everything to his daughters."

Doreen looked up at Mack and smiled. "Justice is served."

Epilogue

Friday Morning ...

IT HAD BEEN two days since Doreen had been at Ed Burns's house. She'd kept her head low and had stayed out of sight since then. It was Friday morning, and she was back at Millicent's place. Millicent hadn't stopped talking since Doreen had arrived to weed, but that was okay. Doreen was more than happy to listen while Millicent reminisced about the Jude and Ed Burns family drama and then about Frank and Fred Darbunkle.

"Who knew Fred would have gone down like that and talked to the cops? I know they let him go back to his home to say goodbye to his brother," Millicent said. "And, for that, I'm happy. But it makes you wonder just what kind of charges he'll face."

"I don't know," Doreen said. "I'm sure they'll exhume all three bodies to corroborate his accounting of his family's deaths. After that I don't know."

"You, my dear, are an absolute marvel," Millicent said.

"Not at all," Doreen said. "Who knew I would find out all this just from finding one ice pick in the ivy?"

Millicent chuckled. "Did I ever tell you about the jewels

I found?"

Doreen sat back on her haunches. "Jewels? Where?"

"They were in the juniper," Millicent said. "It was years and years ago. I never did find out who they belonged to."

"Did you ask Mack to find out?"

"Mack wasn't even an officer back then. Not sure I have mentioned them to him since he joined law enforcement, now that I think about it." She frowned. "You know what? I'll see if I can find them."

"Especially if you want to find who they belong to," Doreen said. "It might take time to find the owners."

Millicent looked at Doreen and smiled. "Not with you, my dear. You are so darn fast. I'll go take a look now because I want you to have the jewels, and I want you to find out who they belong to."

"Oh, but …" Doreen started.

However, it was too late. Millicent was gone.

Doreen laughed. Apparently she now had a new cold case.

This concludes Book 9 of Lovely Lethal Gardens:
Ice Pick in the Ivy.
Read about Jewels in the Juniper:
Lovely Lethal Gardens, Book 10

Lovely Lethal Gardens: Jewels in the Juniper (Book #10)

A new cozy mystery series from *USA Today* best-selling author Dale Mayer. Follow gardener and amateur sleuth Doreen Montgomery—and her amusing and mostly lovable cat, dog, and parrot—as they catch murderers and solve crimes in lovely Kelowna, British Columbia.

Riches to rags. ... Chaos is still present. ... Memories are fading, ... but not for everyone!

The problem with notoriety is unfair expectations. When Mack's mother, Millicent Moreau, requests Doreen's help with a small problem she's kept hidden for decades, Doreen feels obligated to help. And what harm could it do, after all? Worst-case scenario? It'll annoy Mack, but that's something she does on a regular basis anyway.

But when Millicent's "small problem" turns out to involve a failed marriage, a bag of jewels from a jewelry store that mysteriously burned down decades ago, possible insurance fraud, and maybe even a case of murder, ... Doreen will admit that she's in way over her head.

With her trusty trio of furry and feathered cohorts, she brings an old case into the present—and finds it's more current than ever ...

To find out more visit Dale Mayer's website.

https://geni.us/DMJuniperUniversal

Get Your Free Book Now!

Have you met Charmin Marvin?

If you're ready for a new world to explore, and love ill-mannered cats, I have a series that might be your next binge read. It's called Broken Protocols, and it's a series that takes you through time-travel, mysteries, romance… and a talking cat named Charmin Marvin.

Go here and tell me where to send it!
https://dl.bookfunnel.com/s3ds5a0w8n

Author's Note

Thank you for reading Ice Pick in the Ivy: Lovely Lethal Gardens, Book 9! If you enjoyed the book, please take a moment and leave a short review.

Dear reader,

I love to hear from readers, and you can contact me at my website: www.dalemayer.com or at my Facebook author page. To be informed of new releases and special offers, sign up for my newsletter or follow me on BookBub. And if you are interested in joining Dale Mayer's Reader Group, here is the Facebook sign up page.
http://geni.us/DaleMayerFBGroup

Cheers,
Dale Mayer

About the Author

Dale Mayer is a *USA Today* best-selling author, best known for her SEALs military romances, her Psychic Visions series, and her Lovely Lethal Garden cozy series. Her contemporary romances are raw and full of passion and emotion (Broken But … Mending, Hathaway House series). Her thrillers will keep you guessing (Kate Morgan, By Death series), and her romantic comedies will keep you giggling (*It's a Dog's Life*, a stand-alone novella; and the Broken Protocols series, starring Charming Marvin, the cat).

Dale honors the stories that come to her—and some of them are crazy, break all the rules and cross multiple genres!

To go with her fiction, she also writes nonfiction in many different fields, with books available on résumé writing, companion gardening, and the US mortgage system. All her books are available in print and ebook format.

Connect with Dale Mayer Online

Dale's Website – www.dalemayer.com
Twitter – @DaleMayer
Facebook Page – geni.us/DaleMayerFBFanPage
Facebook Group – geni.us/DaleMayerFBGroup
BookBub – geni.us/DaleMayerBookbub
Instagram – geni.us/DaleMayerInstagram
Goodreads – geni.us/DaleMayerGoodreads
Newsletter – geni.us/DaleNews

Also by Dale Mayer

Published Adult Books:

Hathaway House
Aaron, Book 1
Brock, Book 2
Cole, Book 3
Denton, Book 4
Elliot, Book 5
Finn, Book 6
Gregory, Book 7
Heath, Book 8
Iain, Book 9
Jaden, Book 10
Keith, Book 11

The K9 Files
Ethan, Book 1
Pierce, Book 2
Zane, Book 3
Blaze, Book 4
Lucas, Book 5
Parker, Book 6
Carter, Book 7
Weston, Book 8

Lovely Lethal Gardens

Arsenic in the Azaleas, Book 1

Bones in the Begonias, Book 2

Corpse in the Carnations, Book 3

Daggers in the Dahlias, Book 4

Evidence in the Echinacea, Book 5

Footprints in the Ferns, Book 6

Gun in the Gardenias, Book 7

Handcuffs in the Heather, Book 8

Ice Pick in the Ivy, Book 9

Jewels in the Juniper, Book 10

Psychic Vision Series

Tuesday's Child

Hide 'n Go Seek

Maddy's Floor

Garden of Sorrow

Knock Knock...

Rare Find

Eyes to the Soul

Now You See Her

Shattered

Into the Abyss

Seeds of Malice

Eye of the Falcon

Itsy-Bitsy Spider

Unmasked

Deep Beneath

From the Ashes

Stroke of Death

Psychic Visions Books 1–3

Psychic Visions Books 4–6

Psychic Visions Books 7–9

By Death Series
Touched by Death
Haunted by Death
Chilled by Death
By Death Books 1–3

Broken Protocols – Romantic Comedy Series
Cat's Meow
Cat's Pajamas
Cat's Cradle
Cat's Claus
Broken Protocols 1-4

Broken and... Mending
Skin
Scars
Scales (of Justice)
Broken but… Mending 1-3

Glory
Genesis
Tori
Celeste
Glory Trilogy

Biker Blues
Morgan: Biker Blues, Volume 1
Cash: Biker Blues, Volume 2

SEALs of Honor
Mason: SEALs of Honor, Book 1

Heroes for Hire

SEALs of Steel

Laszlo: SEALs of Steel, Book 5
Geir: SEALs of Steel, Book 6
Jager: SEALs of Steel, Book 7
The Final Reveal: SEALs of Steel, Book 8
SEALs of Steel, Books 1–4
SEALs of Steel, Books 5–8
SEALs of Steel, Books 1–8

The Mavericks
Kerrick, Book 1
Griffin, Book 2
Jax, Book 3
Beau, Book 4
Asher, Book 5
Ryker, Book 6
Miles, Book 7
Nico, Book 8
Keane, Book 9
Lennox, Book 10
Gavin, Book 11
Shane, Book 12

Bullard's Battle Series
Ryland's Reach, Book 1
Cain's Cross, Book 2
Eton's Escape, Book 3
Garret's Gambit, Book 4
Kano's Keep, Book 5
Fallon's Flaw, Book 6
Quinn's Quest, Book 7
Bullard's Beauty, Book 8

Collections
Dare to Be You…
Dare to Love…
Dare to be Strong…
RomanceX3

Standalone Novellas
It's a Dog's Life
Riana's Revenge
Second Chances

Published Young Adult Books:

Family Blood Ties Series
Vampire in Denial
Vampire in Distress
Vampire in Design
Vampire in Deceit
Vampire in Defiance
Vampire in Conflict
Vampire in Chaos
Vampire in Crisis
Vampire in Control
Vampire in Charge
Family Blood Ties Set 1–3
Family Blood Ties Set 1–5
Family Blood Ties Set 4–6
Family Blood Ties Set 7–9
Sian's Solution, A Family Blood Ties Series Prequel
    Novelette

Design series
Dangerous Designs
Deadly Designs
Darkest Designs
Design Series Trilogy

Standalone
In Cassie's Corner
Gem Stone (a Gemma Stone Mystery)
Time Thieves

Published Non-Fiction Books:

Career Essentials
Career Essentials: The Résumé
Career Essentials: The Cover Letter
Career Essentials: The Interview
Career Essentials: 3 in 1

Made in the USA
Las Vegas, NV
07 April 2023

70332155R00164